## TORONTO STORIES

# Streets of Attitude

TORONTO STORIES

# Streets of Attitude

Edited by Cary Fagan and
Robert MacDonald

Yonge & Bloor

PUBLISHING
Toronto Canada

"Christmas Lunch" is from *Digging Up the Mountains* by Neil Bissoondath © 1985. Reprinted by permission of Macmillan of Canada, a Division of Canada Publishing Corporation. "At the Lisbon Plate" is from *Sans Souci and Other Stories* by Dionne Brand © 1988. Reprinted by permission of Dionne Brand and Williams-Wallace Publishers. "The Black Queen" is reprinted by permission of Barry Callaghan. "The Sins of Tomas Benares" is from *Café Le Dog* by Matt Cohen. Used by permission of the Canadian Publishers, McClelland and Stewart, Toronto. "Maybe Later It Will Come Back to My Mind" is reprinted by permission of Shirley Faessler. "Figuring Her Commission" is reprinted by permission of Cary Fagan. "A Gift of Mercy" is reprinted by permission of Timothy Findley. "Beatrice" is reprinted by permission of Cynthia Flood. "Brunswick Avenue" is from *Fables of Brunswick Avenue* by Katherine Govier. Copyright © Katherine Govier, 1985. Reprinted by permission of Penguin Books Canada Ltd. "The Neilson Chocolate Factory" is reprinted by permission of Irena Friedman Karafilly. "Because of the War" is reprinted by permission of Norman Levine. "House of the Whale" is reprinted by permission of the Estate of Gwendolyn MacEwen. "Swimming Lessons" is from *Tales of Firozsha Baag* by Rohinton Mistry. Copyright © Rohinton Mistry, 1987. Reprinted by permission of Penguin Books Canada Ltd. "Designer Death" is reprinted by permission of Jay Scott.

### Canadian Cataloguing in Publication Data
Main entry under title:
Streets of attitude : Toronto Stories
ISBN 1-895204-02-X
1. Short stories, Canadian (English) – Ontario – Toronto.*
2. Canadian fiction (English) – Ontario – Toronto.*
3. Canadian fiction (English) – 20th century.*
4. Toronto (Ont.) – Literary collections.
I. Fagan, Cary. II. MacDonald, Robert, 1947–    .
PS8323.T67S86 1990    C813'.5408    C90–094950–3
PR9197.35.T67S86 1990

Cover illustration: *Titanicar*, Charles Pachter, 1976.
Silkscreen collage, unique. Collection: Bruno Gerussi.
Design: Robert MacDonald, MediaClones Inc.,
Toronto, Ontario and Banff, Alberta
Printed in Canada by Gagné Printing, Louisville Quebec.

### Yonge & Bloor Publishing Inc.
2 Sultan Street, Suite 505
Toronto Ontario Canada M5S 1L7

# TABLE OF CONTENTS

# INTRODUCTION

# Streets of Attitude

I imagine myself standing at the main entrances and exits of Toronto: Yonge Street, the 401, the QEW, Union Station, the Dundas bus terminal, Pearson Airport. And to every man and woman who passes by, to every person entering the city with a hopeful heart or fleeing it with a curse, I hand a copy of this book. What effect will it have on them? Will it make some about to leave suddenly decide to stay? And will it make others just arriving turn around and go back again?

To those who know Toronto, its street names are like poetry: Queen Street, Kensington Avenue, Harbord, Foxley. To find them in fiction makes them both more real and greater than real. We are amazed to discover that stories happen here and we realize that this place may be more than it seems.

But mere documentation of the physical city does not make a story of Toronto. The city is not just old brick and new glass, it is a swarm of humans whose personal histories have brought each of them to this city on a lake. If Toronto has never really shaken off its Victorian cloak, waves of new immigrants have stitched that cloak through with a multitude of colours. They have brought new memories, desires, grievances, complexities.

There are other new colours, for Toronto is a late-twentieth century city. It has become both richer and poorer, faster and shinier, a place of exhibitionism and dark secrets. It has become a thrilling city and a disturbing one.

A writer separates the threads and then weaves them into something new: a fiction. There is no such thing as the definitive Toronto story, or even the definitive Toronto immigrant or old money or whatever story. This should not disappoint us, but make us glad of the infinite possibilities of fiction. Yet somehow, Toronto has been slow to find its storytellers, an indication of its earlier modesty, uprightness and hunger for conformity. The recent blossoming of talent – writers who were born here, or arrived here, or passed through here – is as profound a proof of the city's change as any.

Most of the stories in this collection were written in the last ten years, and many in the last five. Although four writers also appeared in *Toronto Short Stories* of 1977 (edited by Morris Wolfe and Douglas Daymond), only two are represented by the same stories. Back then (and yet what a short time ago that was) several of the writers in *Streets of Attitude* had not yet made their first appearances in print.

My co-editor, Robert MacDonald, and I have made our choices based on our personal responses and feelings for this city. Editors of anthologies like this one often feel compelled to state that they have chosen stories first and foremost because they are worth reading, and only secondarily because they reflect the anthology's subject. We have chosen these fourteen stories because they affect us and also because they reveal something about Toronto. In these two needs of ours there is no contradiction.

**Cary Fagan**
Toronto, June 1990

# JAY SCOTT

# Designer Death

Well, darling, Darla's fabulous, I mean, her hairdo, it's fabulous, I mean, we trade petite quipettes at Vidal Sassoon's and we pretend at Hazelton Lanes to be attracted to each other's persons but what we're really after is not anything so low as the unfashionably physical, I mean, ish, getting physical destroys the LOOK, which is a no-no, you know, and you never know just what you're going to get if you so much as suck a straw after someone else, do you?

So at Sassoon's Darla sits in her chair, Sean does her, always, and Sean's got great teeth and a great earring and a great LOOK that just looks different every week, Sean's LOOK is Giorgio Armani Uomo Vogue today and Ralph Lauren Coors Beer tomorrow, but tasteful, toujours tasteful, and Liz does me and Liz has got a great LOOK too, I mean of course she does, she has a nose jewel, oh darling, she was just in pain over it for so long, but it was worth it of course, and she always thinks so, except maybe when she has a cold, and she has punkadoodle hair, she calls it that, it just changes colours more often than anything and she's very spiritual, she's like been to Nepal, she got a horrible virus there, they told her at Toronto General when she got back that it was toxic-shock syndrome and she said, "So why did my 75-year-old guru in the Himalayas have it too?" but even when she's bad, and she can be mucho bad, she's still very spiritual, I mean she knows about herb teas and things.

So one day Liz was like trimming my tresses, she says that to me, she says, "Time to trim those tresses, sweetheart," and I asked her why she wore so much skin, like lizard skin and leopard skin and I don't know what, and she said, "That's because in a past life, I was a snake," and well, I just didn't know WHAT to say, I was just so taken aback, I mean I just sat there, like a veg brain, imagine being able to know that! and so I said, "Liz, these tresses are HONOURED to be trimmed by hands that were once a snake's," and I started to wonder about my past lives and Liz promised to introduce me to somebody who would read the reincarnation beads for me, at least some of them, and I can't wait, and she said, "You wear a lot of denim and wool, sweetheart, you're a designer-jean sweater queen, you were probably, oh, I don't know, a cotton gin, or maybe a cocksucking sheepherder."

Liz can be wicked, I mean, she knows all my sweaters are mohair.

So by the time Darla and I left Sassoon's, we were in love with our shells, I mean we were hot over our styling gels, her hair was modified Mohawk, très present, brown and bossy, and my hair was yellow and spiky, post-punk prickly, just so now, and I was wearing my tight black jeans and my sexy Issey Miyake tuxedo-type top and she was wearing earrings big as Rosedale chandeliers, and that's because we'd just seen Subway, which is just too-too demi-monde Deco for words, and we'd realized that Christophe Lambert and Isabelle Adjani are just the fashion statements we want to make this week, I mean, as Tarzan, he brought nipples back, because of him I got my left tit pierced, well, not just because of him, Richard Harris in A Man Called Horse had something to do with it too, and so did the guy I saw one night at The Tool Box, all in leather with both tits pierced and a chain hanging down between them but two pierced tits and a chain is not knowing when to cease and desist, n'est-ce pas? and I don't know what I would have done with duo anyway, because this one little hole in my left nip where they put this one little gold stud, yeeps, it hurt just like Liz's nose, I have never had pain like that, but at least a tit can't catch cold, so the worst is finito, and it made Darla jealous beyond belief so she wanted to get a nose job because of Isabelle Adjani but the doctor told her she was too young, that she should wait until her cartilage had set or something, until she was like twenty-six or something, and he said there was nothing wrong with her nose anyway, that it wasn't very big anyway, and it's not, even if it isn't as small as Isabelle Adjani's, which is smaller than a jelly bean, so Darla took French lessons instead.

So over at Hazelton Lanes, we ran into Jason and Rick, poor us, and they were doing the usual, they were talking about the big gay dance at the Masonic Temple and all the dope they did and all the unmentionables they did and then they started talking about IT, The Disease, and who they knew who had it and who they knew who was going to get it and I just don't see how they can talk about it like that and then keep on doing what they do, I am speaking of sexual activity and drug abuse, and they start to get all wrinkly serious and like who needs it, wrinkles wreck the LOOK, unless you're DV, and Darla and I were just too bored for words and it certainly put Darla off her appetite and that's too-too gruesome because she just like recovered from anorexia and then those two started talking about the sixties, I mean they're old enough to remember them, and all I know about the sixties is paisley and that Janis Joplin had a fashion sense, I mean she was the Madonna of her day, and I also know, because Darla and I dragged ourselves to Woodstock out of duty to Jason, that no one else had any fashion sense at all, nada, I mean, shudder, natural hair and beads, when you saw that LOOK, well, you just wanted to look away.

So Darla and I left and I was feeling depressed, I knew I was just going to have to buy a Saint-Laurent at least and maybe a Hermès to get myself out of it, so I said that to Darla and she said, "What about your credit cards?" and I blew up at the bitch, but it was all copacetic lickety-split, I mean très vite, I mean I explained how those dizzy sixties queens had just put me off everything and Darla said, "You're jealous," and I blew up again and I said, "Jealous of what?" and she said, "That they have a good time," and I said, "Good time? good time? Darla, they are flirting with death. And it makes them wrinkly serious," and she said, "Safe sex is possible, you know," and I said, "Sex in the eighties is unsightly, it has no LOOK and that's all there is to it and every newspaper and even Dr. Ruth, well, tous les monde, they all make the recommendation that you choose your sex partners carefully and I for one am not choosing a sex partner until I know that he is the right one, I mean forever," and she said, "Well, roar away, aren't you just the Cowardly Lion?" and I didn't say anything because I wasn't sure what she was on about and then she said, "What if the right man has IT?" and I said, "It would be humanly impossible for the right man to have IT, because if he did, he would not be the right man and that's that. I am not about to care for an unhealthy person who got that way because he lacked self-discipline, nor am I about to care for the friends of Jason who are wasting away like Auschwitz or something because they could not control the placement of their orifices on the open market and that's that again, un point finale," and she said, "Well, wasn't that a fine little speech, Doris Day?" and I thought so too, but fuck you, Darla, for Doris Day.

And then she said, "I have AIDS."

We were on Bloor, I was heading for Holt's to look at the limited-edition leathers, I mean I was that depressed, and I stopped dead and I said, "What?" and even before I said it, it all made the most awful sense, the way Darla got sick about a year ago and could not be dragged out, not even to shop, and then started wasting away and would not eat, not even champagne truffles from Teuscher which are just the best chocolates in the whole world, oh God it all made the most awful sense and I thought all in a rush I thought IT'S NOT HER FAULT MAYBE IT'S NOT ANYBODY'S FAULT

MAYBE IT DOESN'T MATTER HOW OR WHY WHAT AM I
GOING TO DO WITHOUT HER THIS IS THE MOST AWFUL
PAIN IN ALL THE WORLD WORSE EVEN THAN THE TIT-
PIERCING OH GOD DARLA WHAT DO I SAY WHAT DO I DO
WHAT DO YOU DO WHAT DO WE DO I HAVE TO TALK TO
JASON.

She said it again, "I have AIDS."

And then she opened her purse and I thought HER ARM IS SO
SKINNY OH GOD and she took out a little package and she
handed it to me, a little cardboard box, and it said Ayds on it and
she said, "I hear it helps you lose weight," and that evil cunt started
laughing and I started laughing and I bought a $2,000 Claude
Montana leather jacket at Holt's and I don't know how I'm going
to pay for it but you only live once.

# KATHERINE GOVIER

# Brunswick Avenue

Everyone lives on Brunswick Avenue sooner or later. I did more than most, seven years at two addresses, a decade ago. I drove down Brunswick Avenue today and remembered that other September when I first stepped onto the street with my husband. We climbed the stairs of a house with a "Flat for Rent" sign in the window. A compact Chinese woman with an assessing eye came slowly to our knock. And when the transaction was completed, for the third floor rooms were exactly what we wanted, she patted my arm. "I'm Ivy. I like first name best."

I gave her mine; my husband was very shy. We worked back to back in our two rooms. For breaks we used to lie on the bed and discuss whose name would look better on the spine of a book. His was solid and rang true, but was, we agreed, a little easy to forget. We were happy at first, but after a while the place felt small.

Two years later Ivy let me have a larger apartment in another house. Friends helped me carry the bed, the table, the armchair, and twelve cartons of books across the street and up the stairs; after they finished, I gave them beer and sandwiches. When they left I was frankly, and for the first time in my life, living alone, and I was only beginning to understand what Brunswick Avenue would mean to me.

I still see that second apartment perfectly in my mind. Dark hardwood floors, warped to ridges which I felt with my bare feet as I walked them, claiming the place. Rooms running off a long narrow hallway which I planned to line with books. Facing west, on the front, a sitting room that was cool and dim during the day and briefly glamorized by the low lines of sun towards dusk. And a corner fireplace that actually worked.

That night I rolled my packing paper and burned it in the hearth. When the flames rose, I was ringed by their reflection in the window panes. I threw more and more paper on the flames, feeling the heat, until at last Dawn came pounding on the street door to ask if the house were on fire.

I let the conflagration die and went to the bedroom, where a bay window overhung the paved passageway between my house and the next. I fell asleep to the sound of wooden flutes wafting from a neighbour's window and woke the next morning to voices calling, doors slamming as people went to work. The haphazard division of Victorian houses into flats had created, on this block, a self-addressing world that had the feeling of a camp, struck each night on the same spot, wakened by its inhabitants' need to march – somewhere, anywhere – before resting again. I had come to be alone, but welcomed the borrowed sounds. They were a reminder that my solitary state was chosen, that other lives unrolled close by, that those lives and mine were not unaffected by one another.

From the beginning the Brunswick day fell easily over me, a loose, light garment in which I could hide or be revealed as I wished. As soon as I got up I put on my striped robe and went to the kitchen for coffee. Bearing a blue china cup I went from there to the porch off the back, which had morning sun and a view into the houses all around; that was where I worked at my typewriter. Tapping rapidly from the moment I sat, I could smell, in spring, the arms of the lilac bush scraping on the screen and in winter, vision blurred by plastic stretched over the windows for insulation, hear the drip of melting snow. If I raised my eyes from my work, I could see trees and more windows, alleys, and gardens and enjoy the little neighbourhood mysteries; the man who stored his motorcycle in his house and slept in his garage, the postman who made a regular morning trip up a back fire escape. I could see children smoking cigarettes and kicking heels against the back fences and my friends coming home in the evening with paper bags from the wine store.

"Come and sit on the porch with us!"

"Not now!" I'd wave them away. I wanted to be still and for them to move; I wanted to watch and not be seen. I had the habit of writing by then; I wrote every morning, through lunch. I took the afternoon off and began again after five when kitchen lights went on all around the square and dinners were cooking. I might have kept on until midnight if I hadn't been disturbed. But my friends were persistent. Sometimes they knocked at the door; if I didn't answer they walked right in.

"Come on, you have to eat."

Alarmed, I would jump from the chair and lie across my papers. My work was present and alive and obvious in that sunporch; it was on my skin; I was as if caught naked with a lover.

"OK, OK, let's go," I'd say, slipping the scattered pages into piles, bidding the story presence to fold up with them. And go out to chicken stew in Dawn's basement kitchen or something Hungarian at the Country-Style or just a beer at the Mug. They would have tales of irascible supervisors or humiliating auditions, whatever had happened to them that day. The work might have gone better without these interruptions, but then how would the world have come into it? Much later, with an inward apology to the Brunswick people, I would come back and put a scrap of their conversation in my notes. If they had surprised me in my lair, I caught them too. I was a member of the army encamped on that street, a member like any other, save that I was the one who stopped to write things down.

When my husband and I first chanced onto Brunswick, we were straight out of university in the west and innocent of the ways of these sophisticated urban gypsies. We knew where we wanted to be but not how to get there. Where we wanted to be was in the middle of things, where things happened. Ambition made our love conspiratorial; we alone knew how richly we deserved acknowledgement, not for anything we had done, because we had done nothing, but for everything we might do.

That first year we went upstairs together, shut the door and forgot the outside. We made love and argued, slammed doors, made up, and then made dinner. Our marriage was like a demanding self-obsessed house guest. Invited to parties, we neglected to go down; we said hello to our neighbours without realizing that they wanted to know us. But eventually the guest became a fixture; Hugh and I were released, at least partially, to the world at large.

In my daily, hopeful descents to the front door for mail I had noticed Dawn, stooped, graceful, weighted with long hair, holding conversations on the sidewalk. I had overheard words like "imagery" and "phantom," "inspiration" and "block." She had to be talking about art. One day I spoke to her.

"What do you do?" I said, which was in those days before definitions became firm a permissible question.

She danced. Well, actually she had a bad back and was giving up dancing and would probably study sculpture. In the meantime she was working as an artist's model. Nude, I had to assume. This allowed her the leisure for self-discovery. She said something about exorcising the ghosts of her childhood, during which she had been bedridden. I nodded as if this were the kind of answer offered a stranger every day, when in fact her boldness – not only did she pose without clothes, but she admitted she wanted to be an artist! – stunned me.

"And what do you do?" she asked, laying gentle grey eyes on mine and swaying on her long stem. As she stood, she rubbed her lower back and rolled her shoulders, as if working out a stiffness.

"I write."

"How exciting!" I could tell right away she wanted to know me. That was when my guilt began, for I was convinced that I lied. (I retain this conviction each time I say those words, some twelve years and three books later, which may imply something about me or simply impugn the craft, I don't know.) Back then although I did write I did not publish, and my claim seemed very weak indeed. I covered my confusion, however, by telling her a few things about the story I was working on, being sure I included the words "tone" and "voice" and talked a bit about the difficulties imposed by the first person narrator.

"Do you know Hannah?" said Dawn. Apparently a true, published writer (with a name I recognized) lived on the street. I gushed, but when introductions were offered I became cautious. Proximity was thrilling, but it was enough for the time being; my imagination leapt ahead to friendship and foresaw problems. I suppose I felt that writers claimed a territory; Hannah's and mine couldn't overlap. I asked more questions. I wanted to know about Hannah, but I was not prepared, not just yet, to know Hannah. When my conversation with Dawn ended, I rushed upstairs and told Hugh all about it. And after I did, I regretted that I had turned my discovery into something else that had to be shared in our cramped space under the sloping ceilings.

It was our second spring on Brunswick when Dawn made a beer stew and we went down to join her party. After that there were many nights on the porch in twilights soft and expansive after the sudden darknesses of winter. Elbows on our knees, bottles beside us, we sat and watched the street and talked more or less as Hugh and I had talked in private.

Our neighbours were like us, striving photographers, potters, film-makers, and graduate students in English or biology; a would-be actress who baked plasticine toys in her oven to sell at subway stops. Livings were put together from part-time teaching, grants, odd jobbing. Everyone was involved in rounds of submissions, auditions, applications; there were never any openings. We had all come from someplace else, and the city seemed to be a conspiracy to keep us out. How extravagantly we complained when a proposal or an exhibition by an unknown was ignored! What fools we thought the critics and custodians of culture! As the summer went on, the porch stoop changed from a place on the sidelines, a repose, to a high vantage point from which an urgent wave of change threatened to break.

Our voices carried across the street until 11 o'clock; then, after we wanted to go in, Hannah would come. Hannah had been, even to my cautious expectations, a disappointment. First, she was old. And then she had practically no conversation, except that which involved herself. She had followed her son, a draft dodger, to Canada; when he had taken amnesty and returned to New York, she was bitter. There was no going back for this veteran of many migrations and marriages. She had a bad heart, a catastrophic cough, and was frequently drunk. Furthermore, she seemed to find us dull.

It occurred to me that I did not understand Hannah. She showed me, once, the contents of her grease-stained knapsack. It had a pocket on either side to make it easier for her to find things. One side, labelled Beauty, had lipstick and scarves for her hair which she combed with her fingers. The other side, labelled Money, was usually empty. In between she kept a supply of self-addressed postcards which she gave away (sometimes with a stamp) to young men she desired, a coil notebook, and, always, a copy of her book, published years before to considerable notice. Hannah wanted people to sing, especially after midnight; unless she found those who were willing, she became hostile and incoherent and had to be led off to bed.

Expeditions to the tavern went and came back. Students pumped their bicycles south to the campus, and pan-handlers made their way up from Bloor Street. Young missionaries with slick hair came up from the Church Army House to ask us to join in their hymns. "Judgement is approaching," they said. "There is only a little time." But we did not want to be saved. Brunswick Avenue was there, moving more and more slowly as summer passed, a carousel in its last few revolutions. The suspense was exquisite; it hurt. I knew something was ending, but I did not know what, until the day Hugh's letter came. He'd been offered a teaching job in the Maritimes; he would take it. I decided to stay behind.

When Hugh left, it was as if a curtain parted; the world saw me and beckoned. Suddenly I knew everyone; after two years I was an old-timer on the street, along with Dawn and a biology student named Redfat. I listened well, and I had a quick way with a phrase; my witticisms were often quoted. The new apartment which Ivy had let me have was the most desirable on the block and added to my stature.

"There are two kinds of people," I remember saying. "There are landladies and then there are the rest of us." Ivy was a visible oppressor, walking in her slow, bandy-legged way from one property to another, wandering in and out of our doors without knocking. We joked about her ski pants with tabs under the heels, the maternity smock she wore long after the fact. And what did she think of us? Her habitually lowered brow did not lift when we spoke, although she still insisted on first names.

Perhaps it was this semblance of friendship that first made us angry with Ivy. Her bizarre habits ought to have produced more laughter than rage. She drove an old pink Cadillac with fins, in imitation of some fifties tycoon. The car rolled along Brunswick stopping at angles to the curb or even on the lawn when she visited a house. I used to find her downstairs in the morning going through our mail. She threw out all official correspondence, regardless of addressee. When once I protested, pulling a letter from the tax department out of the wastebasket, she shook her head.

"You don't want answer those people." A variation of this was "You don't want that man know where you are," which she delivered after sending away any official-looking person who should come looking for me.

"But Ivy, he was a friend."

"I just try help you." Hands went up – there was no accounting for my whims. I was frustrated, but she was enjoying our exchange. But even at her most jolly, the expression of suspicion did not move from her face. She gave nothing away, either avoiding questions or answering in proverbs. When had she come here? Who were the others who lived in her house?

"Ghosts tell no lies," she might say. If I persisted, she'd try to put me off with fake mistakes in English. "What's the matter, you have no sense of human?" was a favourite. The scattered details we discovered only made us wonder more.

The family, so far as we could tell, was extensive. Besides the two small boys, her sons, there was a young man who drove a post office truck and was sometimes "Uncle" sometimes "Brother." There were several sulky teenage girls, sisters or daughters, many "visitors" from China, a silent mother with a face like a walnut who crept up and down the street carrying small paper bags from the stores. A husband was occasionally mentioned but never appeared. Ivy seemed to be the provider for this complex establishment; indeed, she was its life force. She gardened in several backyards, kept rabbits for stew and chickens for eggs and had two dogs, the smallest of which was said to be trained to kill.

Ivy's domain was no less intimidating: we discovered by putting our knowledge together that she owned at least ten houses between Dupont and Bloor – numbers 300, 302, 304, and 306 being the ones where we lived. You could always point out Ivy's houses. Their open garages spewed bedsprings and random sinks, the roofs sagged, and the windows were grey with years of dirt. But there was always one redeeming feature – sunflowers by the porch or morning glories climbing the pillars, a certain grace in a turret or archway, something to inspire love.

We laughed, mind you, at the old houses' slow dissolve which seemed designed to thwart their owner. Ivy hated work; as well, she was cheap, careless, and had terrible luck. If, after procrastinating a decade, she finally painted a porch, the next day raccoons would eat through the roof over it, and the rain would ruin the job. If she replastered a ceiling, the plumbing on the floor above would leak through it. Ivy's handymen came out of the hotel tavern at the foot of the street; at least once I feared for the life of a pallid rubby on an unstable ladder outside my window. Ivy meanwhile complained of poverty and threatened to sell.

Although she was a millionaire, we were sure, she showed no sign of wealth aside from the Cadillac which usually sat in her driveway, windows open, with children playing in it. She lived in three rooms of such clutter that their purpose – dining, sleeping, sitting – was obscure. The largest was dominated by an iridescent tapestry of a moose glaring over a mountain lake. It was furnished with torn chairs, a card table covered with radio parts and dirty cutlery, and a couple of bicycles. In a doorway an ironing board stood, the perfect Ivy signature, indicating that some effort, albeit beside the point, was being made. It was the same every month when I delivered the rent.

I told my chums about the ironing board and got laughs for it. It was fun, during nights on the stoop, to speculate on the extent of Ivy's riches and why she lived like we did; or if, as she claimed, she weren't rich, who then was the secret slum landlord. It seems to me now a strange obsession. I suppose of all the mysteries before us, she was the one we could lay our fingers on; she was the aspect of this large and callous and thus far unresponsive city within our range. Because we weren't going anywhere, we butted our heads against the place where we had stopped; because she was a sign of our powerlessness, we began to hate her.

Of course without Hugh I had no money. I had to search for work and took it quite for granted when Ivy let my rent go unpaid. She brought me lettuce and beets and carrots from her garden; I hardly noticed. She asked me to go down to Queen Street with her to buy dented tins at a discount. Then she offered one of her dog's puppies to protect my person.

"Women living alone," she said, "got to be careful."

At that point, remembering her own absent husband, I realized that she was making friendly advances; she saw us as being in the same position. I was horrified. I did not want a killer dog; I did not want, in my wildest imagination, to be like Ivy.

I sold a piece of writing. I found a part-time job teaching, and then I sold another piece, this time to a magazine that asked me to do more writing for them. When winter came again, despite the fact that I was still in arrears, I complained of the cold in my apartment. Ivy came to check the radiators. She put her hand on their lukewarm ridges and then turned to me.

"You are too thin. You lose weight since your husband go. He send you money?"

"I'll get money of my own now."

She grimaced. "Men not fair to women who have money of their own, don't you think?"

If I thought, I wasn't saying. "Don't change the subject, Ivy. It's cold in here." But she saw the fault as mine. She offered to share a wild deer for the winter; I suppose its meat was to stoke my inner fires. "We buy one from the Indians, I take half, you take half, then I show you how to cook."

I gave up, laughing. "You're too smart for me, Ivy," I said and resolved to buy an electric heater, since she paid the hydro bill. We enjoyed our little game.

When finally I had the money to pay my rent, I took it to her door. It was a crisp winter evening and her boys were riding their bicycles under the streetlights. "Lovely night," I said to Ivy. "So peaceful." I felt much more a part of the world, now that I was earning. I suppose I looked triumphant, handing over the cheque.

"You think so?" She jerked the proffered orange slip of paper in toward her chest; running it between two fingers, she narrowed her eyes. "I don't think we have peace. I think we have war. Big trucks will push people off the street and there will be dead men every-where and no food. They even take the bicycles away from those kids." She raised her voice. "Boys! Boys!" and she made them put their bicycles in the garage and go indoors.

From what past these images came I was never to know. I don't think I cared where she learned to see conspiracies and disaster in a quiet city street full of gentle people, few of whom were hungry. But the lights came on as we stood there; suddenly I wanted to thank her for the Brunswick world that was a haven to me. I muttered a few words about liking my apartment, and then I was off.

My friendship with Ivy was becoming awkward. She disliked my knowing the others, as if she feared we would gang up against her. Her response to our nightly gatherings was to tell me tales about my fellows. This one stole furniture and that one pulled down light fixtures. Redfat was a bad man and very dirty; Hannah ought to be in a mental hospital. There were particles of truth in all of what she said, but Ivy knew me not at all if she thought I would abandon my friends for mere irresponsibility or vice.

Brunswick was at its height then. Looking back, I see mine as a nearly perfect life. I wonder how many of us have found its better? Sunlight fell through my back window in the morning and toward evening skimmed over the rooftops to enter the porch over the street. When good news came for me in the mail, there were three or four friends nearby to dance on the lawn in celebration. We were in and out of each other's apartments for teabags and money and records. We loved our tacky camp and all our possibilities. The street belonged to us for the time we were there. Years could go by without my wanting to leave, and years did.

The beginning of the end came with another summer – my fifth – and cockroaches. One day Redfat came out of his basement to say that he'd noticed some bugs in his oven. I went down into his dark kitchen and turned on the light. There was a general scuttle so fast I blinked; something dark on the walls, like a fine net, had dissolved in an instant. I looked closer. The things were everywhere, down behind the sink and taps, along the cracks of the kitchen counter, even in the rubber stripping along the fridge door.

"How can you stand it in here?" I asked.

"I never noticed," he said, shifting his feet. Chanting his mantra or sorting his dried weeds, he was oblivious to such detail.

"But Red —" I wailed. I didn't bother to explain what I knew. Because I lived above him and the other houses were attached, it would soon be evident he had roaches; we would all have roaches. In a week I found their traces, the black dust on shelves, transparent egg-cases in corners from which barely visible miniature versions crawled out to instant maturity. One day I reached in my kitchen cupboard for my blue cup and put my finger on a roach resting on the handle. I screamed and threw the cup across the room, smashing it.

Before that day in Redfat's kitchen, roaches had lived for me only in fable. I had heard they grew to the size of thumbs in Houston, and accepted that in certain New York hotels a few lazy black specimens could be seen by tourists. But these before me were small and brown and fast and successful beyond imagination. At first I attacked their numbers with spray insecticide. They increased. I tried boric acid. They thrived. My kitchen, with its crooked walls, old gas stove, and warped floorboards which were impossible to clean, was ideal for them.

Infestation gave my apartment a new and sinister identity. My quaint abode had gone over to another side of life. I had come from a cosmetic suburb where any show of human habitation from a neighbour was an affront; garbage cans, naked children, voices raised in anger, all like unpleasantness was carefully hidden. That was why Brunswick's gypsy-camp openness had charmed me so. But the vision of Red's kitchen stayed with me. I knew instantly that it was one thing to live in an eighty-year-old, patched and partitioned house among colourful eccentrics, and it was quite another to have bugs.

As it happened, the others were much like me. Roaches made our chic flats squalid; from this point urban poverty yawned before us, and we were on our way up, not down. Something had to be done. It took only days to discover that individual action was futile. Four of us went together to Ivy's door to demand she fumigate.

Demand, I say, and give away our mistake. Ivy stood half behind her door, her eyes hooking mine, her face more stubborn and blank with each word we spoke. To give in to a demand would have been beneath her dignity. If getting rid of the cockroaches had been our only aim, announcing helplessness and speaking ill of Red would have served us better. Perhaps because of my "friendship" with Ivy, I, more than the others, did understand, but I was too angry to take the easy way.

"Get rid of them," I said. "You have to."

She laughed. "Cockroaches very old. They been living one million years."

"Not in our houses," we said.

She shrugged. "They don't bite."

Assuring us that a little poisoned sugar along the baseboards (Poisoned sugar! What about my cats!) would do the trick, she closed the door in our faces.

Across the street, we gathered. Others were notified as they came home from work; the cockroach crisis would require a meeting of tenants. My apartment being the largest, I became the host. We would have none of Ivy's fatalism; there would be no giving up in the face of this threat to our homes. Human beings could not live in these conditions. There were laws about such things. We agreed to act; knowing all about Ivy's delays and half-hearted efforts, we would circumvent her and call in the authorities. And while we had their attention, we could ask for a few improvements in the houses – the water pressure was bad, we really needed some door bells, and none of our refrigerator freezing compartments was cold enough.

Dawn raised a point. She had given up sculpture by then and was following the Maharaji Ji; she was full of love for the world. "Ivy gives me lettuce," she said. "She doesn't raise the rent; she's my friend."

"Can you live off her lettuce? Are you a rabbit? Even her rabbits end up in the stew. If she cared about you, do you think she'd expect you to put up with all this?" I was persuasive, and Dawn was overruled.

I placed the first call myself the next morning. I'd been doing some writing for a newspaper and had learned how to deal with the city. I used a punchy phrase here, a suggested threat there, and all around a firm, determined voice. Within a week health inspectors had come and fumigation was ordered. After several sprayings the cockroaches were beaten; they died or moved on down the street. But there was more to come – inspectors from other city departments. Fire prevention, building, and zoning standards had to be met. There was a great flurry of action by the end of which Ivy was presented with a list of one hundred and eight improvements to make.

Well! That was action. We tenants had copies of this list. My apartment appeared as "Second floor south. Front room, inadequate ventilation. Bathroom unsafe, tiles cracked. Back porch uninhabitable, ceiling too low ..." We celebrated our victory, but I had a cold feeling; it was as if a loved one in perfect health had been taken in for examination and was assessed as having little chance of survival.

Ivy was given ninety days to make these repairs. Nothing happened during that time; that was no surprise. Next a more insistent demand, in the form of a poster with black lettering, was posted on the door of each faulty house. After one hundred and twenty days the houses would be deemed unfit for human habitation and would be closed. Face to face with this edict, we were given pause. "Will we have to move?" I said to the inspector, who was confidently pocketing his thumbtacks. He reassured me: these threats were always effective. I wanted to believe that, and indeed Ivy appeared to have capitulated. Estimators began to appear, examining chimneys and stairways and windows and then going away leaving all as before.

The poster curled and turned brown and fell off the door. Ivy disappeared. There were rumours that she was in China, in Florida, even in jail. One hundred and twenty days passed; the inspector came around, but he couldn't do anything, he said, until he could find Ivy. For one whole winter the pink Cadillac did not move, and rent was collected by sister/daughters or uncle/brothers.

It was a sullen spring day, as cold and damp as April can be in Toronto, when I walked up from Bloor to see a sun-tanned Ivy standing in her driveway. She hailed me, as she would have in old times. She didn't want to talk about Florida. Around her feet were cardboard cartons; she opened one to show me bags and bags of French-fried potatoes.

"They given away free," she said, "to non-profit organizations."

I could see the McCann's truck parked in front of the Church Army House and guessed that there had been a warehouse fire somewhere and that Ivy, along with the missionaries, was reaping the benefit. She was very pleased with her new phrase.

"Take some," she said, "I give them to you. I'm non-profit." She smiled wickedly. I couldn't ignore the challenge.

"Come on, Ivy, you went south for the winter while we sat here freezing in your apartments. You're rich."

"No," she said. "Not me. You people, you rich. Not me. Wait and see," she said, pressing half a dozen bags of potatoes into my arms, giving me her contradictory, sly grin. "Share them," she said. "Give some to Dawn." I went off with my arms full.

Perhaps Ivy thought that was the end of it: she could put down the revolt with evasion, climaxed by a bit of theatre. And she might well have been right. Some complicated legal procedure was said to be underway at City Hall, but we had lost interest. Tired of our campaign and perhaps a little ashamed, we were almost content to stop there. And why did we not? Partly because the grievance, though displaced, was real and partly because we couldn't: the dragging, seemingly ineffectual oxen of government were pulling, even though they could not be seen. The solution was to make a gesture: we took a collection and hired a lawyer. This man was eloquent on the subject of our rights, and he did something simple and wonderful. He asked us what we wanted. He asked each of us to lay out in detail the improvements we sought for our quarters. Then he took these demands away and had them typed.

So it was, one day I stood on the porch reading a new version of Brunswick Avenue, neat on bond with stapled pages. It was noon, and spring. The archway of branches over the street was still transparent, lightly touched with lemon-yellow buds. Sun made the gables and porches as sharp as pencil lines against the cardboard blue sky. Every brick on every house stood out in definition: I could have counted them. When I finished, I threw back my head and laughed aloud. It wasn't funny, it was just that I finally understood.

There was nothing wrong with Brunswick Avenue except that we had lived there too long, and for too long no one had asked us what we wanted. What we wanted: in other terms, the contents of Hannah's bag, Beauty and Money and Fame. But while those eluded us, here in such close quarters with others who strove, we would settle for new doorbells, freezer doors, plaster, and carpets; hotter water, fire escapes, and mailboxes. Snow shovelling in winter, outdoor lights in the parking lot, an intercom system, and a paint job. It had seemed reasonable enough, bit by bit. But pressed into type, under letterhead, I could see that it was not Brunswick Avenue at all, but a draft for another world.

In certain lights, I now have beauty and money and fame. I have published books (my ex-husband has published more) and I live in a house of my own. Occasionally I am invited to read from my works. A small number of people recognize my face from television. When I gave my notice on Brunswick it was nothing to apologize for. It was simply time to move on; I thought I might get married, I might even have children.

I wasn't the first to leave. Dawn had found our struggle too mundane and had gone to live with other converts to her religion. Redfat was evicted, Ivy's single scapegoat. His basement was rented to two members of a motorcycle group. With my house half empty, I was frightened. I heard noises above me in the night, and when I asked Ivy who was living there, she looked at me slyly. "Ghosts living there," she said.

That was why on moving day none of the old people were there to help me go; my new man waited out in front in his truck as I gave the key to the lesbian caterer who was taking over the fabulous apartment. I might have driven away without saying goodbye except that Ivy came down her driveway. I realized she'd been watching us load. Was she checking to see that I didn't take the light fixtures or throw paint on the floor? Perhaps. She saluted. I could not interpret the signal.

"You been living here long time," she said. "I will miss you."

Today as I drove down Brunswick I noticed our houses, numbers 300, 302, 304, and 306, had been renovated and were for sale. Could it be that at last the legions of witless inspectors had their way? Then I passed a tall, graceful woman leaning over a child on a bicycle, and her posture called back years before. The slight curve in the spine, the hair still long but now streaked brown and loosely tied. It was Dawn: recognizing her gave me a shock, as if I had unexpectedly run into a forgotten member of my family.

It had happened before: after I moved I had bumped into her on Avenue Road. She had renamed herself Halley after the comet and was wearing a sari. "I tried art," she had said then, "but it was too hard. I tried political action (she meant our tenants' union) but there was no love in it. Now He is giving me everything." I was angry then; today I realized that I always thought her silly.

I stopped, and she introduced me to her son. I asked Dawn what she was doing – the question that made us friends, that eventually set her to such pirouettes of self-examination and excuse, and that ultimately divided us.

"Nothing," she said carelessly and began to rub the boy's back as if he were a baby and needed to burp. The boy was ill, she said; she had just spent three weeks sleeping beside his hospital bed. I was unprepared and said something banal like perhaps he'll grow out of it. Her eyes, which always glowed, grew brighter with tears; perhaps not. We spoke a little longer, but he was whining and wanted to go home. I was out of my depth; I didn't know how to discuss this tragedy. Perhaps I was feeling a little outdone by my old friend.

"Do you live here again?" I said. I had been lonely over the years and had considered moving back myself, but it would have seemed like slipping.

"Oh no, I just come down to see Hannah," she said. "She's getting her old age money now. She hasn't got a thing, but she makes it look good. Like these pigeons she's a scavenger, but she does all right. Ivy won't take any rent."

"She still owns houses here then?"

"A few," said Dawn. I imagined her eyes to be full of accusations, and perhaps they were.

"The old life," I said lightly. "It was good at the time, but you'll not see me there again, not if I can help it."

Dawn said nothing. I stared at her and wondered if in her child she had found the perfect occupation, the one without compromise. "You're very brave," I said, or should have said.

She touched her hair. "I had no choice." And then, as she turned to go, "You've done well."

Did I imagine the distaste in her voice? Why did I not tell her I had no choice either? Of course, it wasn't true; I was very deliberate in my becoming. It was just that I wanted Brunswick Avenue to forgive me; I believed I was faithful to it. Apologies were definitely not in order, for after all I had done what the rest of us only talked about. But still she seemed superior; she made me feel unclean. Dawn had become content, and I was still greedy for more.

And that was not the worst of it, I realized as I faced her, all possible words draining from my throat. I thought of all we had said in our inexperience, our arrogance, about how beauty was bestowed by admiration, and money and fame got by compromise. She knew only too well what I had done; we had been that clever in our imaginings. If I had risen it was by using them; one of me required many of them in the background, living lives of pain and joy somehow more meaningful than my own. The battle with Ivy had been only a surface. The real battle was among us; it was the struggle to break out of the group, to have the power. If alliances were to be drawn now, it would be Dawn and Hannah and even Ivy against me. I was the other, the leech, the landlady. That was what she saw, and I saw her seeing it, and I had no way to contradict her.

I said goodbye to Dawn. I will run into her again on a street because that's the way this city is, but our long conversation over the years has closed. What she was, what they all were to me is over and done with. I have the stories, of course, but that is only half of it.

# NEIL BISSOONDATH

# Christmas Lunch

The little house was on a dingy street just off Bathurst and I was appalled at the thought of having Christmas lunch here, in this area through which I hurried late every Thursday night after doing my wash at the laundromat. The hosts were strangers and I had allowed my friend to drag me along only because I had nowhere else to go, nothing else to do, and it seemed wrong to spend all of a blustery Christmas day in a cold room with only a book for company.

The door – paint peeling and the wood visibly damp – was opened by a pot-bellied, middle-aged man wearing a white T-shirt and brown polyester pants, the kind that, at the merest hint of humidity, chafed the skin and gave a general feeling of discomfort.

"Merry Christmas," he said, taking my friend's hand. "Come in. Give me your coats."

My friend introduced me.

"From Trinidad too?" Raj, the host, inquired.

"Yes."

He had the look of a cane-cutter, gaunt of face but corpulent lower down. His handshake was shy and he looked strangely misplaced. He draped our damp coats over his arm and offered a drink.

My friend took a soft drink. "My stomach can't take anything hard, man. Still messed up."

"And you?" Raj nodded at me.

"Whatever you have," I said, still contemplating flight. "Rum and Coke?"

"Okay. Have a seat." He disappeared through a door from which flowed the almost viscous smell of sizzling curry and burnt garlic.

My friend introduced me to the others in the room. There, lounging barefooted on the floor next to the stereo, was side-burned Moses. Next to him, in an easy chair amateurishly covered in red vinyl, sat his wife, Pulmatee, a tiny woman of such anonymous aspect that she spent the entire afternoon disappearing into the background. On the red couch that squatted at right angles to Pulmatee's chair were the host's wife, Rani – a dour-faced woman who nodded at me and wrung her hands dry on a rag – and a young girl, a cousin of Rani's, who wiped a scowl from her face and flashed two prominent gold teeth at me.

The silence in the room was charged. It was clear that our arrival had interrupted a family dispute.

Rani, dabbing at her hands with the rag, said to Moses, "Anyway, is his business if he want to invite her. Let him feed her since he's the one who feeling sorry for her."

Moses shrugged and sipped his sweating beer.

Raj brought the drinks and, muttering, made me sit on the couch, scrunched between the perspiring Rani and the cold metal frame.

I thanked him and he mumbled an embarrassed "You're welcome," as if he had little occasion to say the words and was out of practice.

I lit a cigarette and Rani, heaving herself up with a grunt, ran to bring me an ashtray.

"Nothing like Trinidad hospitality at Christmas time, eh boy? Especially when you away from home." Moses flashed his white teeth and, unaware that he'd been addressing me, I got only an aftertaste of possibly unintentional sarcasm.

"Right," I said, fiddling with the cigarette, "nothing like it."

My friend said, "How the job going, Moses boy?"

Moses said, "Is not easy, man. You work from morning till night, you break your back, and these people never happy."

My friend said, "They don't know how to take it easy, you see, Moses. Everything for them is work, work, work. And the work never finish. I tell you, not only woman's work never done, eh. Back home, if you didn't want to work, you didn't work and that was that. But here ... how you could be happy living like this day in day out, eh? Tell me."

Moses couldn't tell him. They shook their heads sorrowfully.

I looked around the room, sensing a certain chaos, a disorder of things, that made me uncomfortable. In one corner stood a home-made stand, two wooden orange crates nailed together and painted a leery oak; on top of this had been placed a gaudy statuette of a woman, breasts exposed by the casual draping of her robe, entwined in plastic vines and topped by an artificial rose. In the opposite corner slouched a small tinsel Christmas tree which had seen several joyous seasons too many. Around its base was a plastic nativity scene: blue Mary, red Joseph, purple Jesus, green cow, and orange donkey. A faded red carpet covered the floor. The green walls had been haphazardly decorated with Christmas cards, some salvaged from past years, and incongruous framed postcards of the Hindu religious hierarchy. It was as if decoration meant less beautifying than simply taking up space, a dash of colour here and there.

Moses was still explaining to my friend why he found life in Toronto so terribly difficult when the front door opened and a fat woman of about twenty-six with pale, blotchy skin sauntered in singing at the top of her voice. All eyes fixed on her and, surprised, she broke off the song. "Why isn't anyone dancing?" she asked.

Moses, staring her in the eyes, grinned. "We waiting for you to start, Ann. Where your husband?"

"He's getting ready to go to his parents for dinner."

"You not going?"

She shook her stringy brown hair. "No, I don't want to see his parents." She spoke in a voice which told of an ongoing bitterness, a voice which asserted fact and discouraged further questions.

Rani and her cousin sighed pointedly and went into the kitchen. I nodded at Ann.

"What's your name?" she asked in a manner so familiar it was unsettling.

I told her and she gazed momentarily at me, as if trying to read my mind. Her eyes were tiny, and so dark it was as if they reaped an extra measure of shadow from the world. The circles under her eyes might not have been bags; they had the appearance of carefully applied mascara, but it was their very neatness that gave them away. The rest of her – from her unwashed hair to her scraggy silver evening shoes – was so rumpled, her rouge applied in so slapdash a manner, that the darkness under her eyes couldn't have been artificial: it was more instructive than an amused glance allowed.

She dropped herself onto the couch and crossed her legs, striking a masculine pose. Her powder-blue slacks gathered in folds of fat at her thighs and her unclean feet, encased in the thick straps of the evening shoes, wriggled to some private rhythm.

"What work you does do, Ann?" Moses asked in a leading voice.

"None," she replied. "I don't want any man to be my boss. Except my husband. If I have to go to work, I'll go into the oldest business. Prostitution. Because any other job is a kind of prostitution. You're still selling your body and what it can do."

"You want to work for me?" Moses asked mischievously.

Raj, standing next to him, blushed, embarrassed.

Ann, emotionless, said, "My husband knows some pimps who can break you in two." She sucked her teeth and looked away. Unexpectedly she said, "I'm from Newfoundland. I dream of going back there."

It was a strange declaration, offered almost in confession. It hung limply in the air; not even Moses knew what to do with it.

"You have any brothers or sisters?" Moses said at last.

Ann brightened visibly. "Eight brothers and seven sisters," she said proudly.

There were gasps of incredulity.

Moses said, "All-you never hear about birth control or what?"

"Newfoundland women don't like contraceptives, they think they're unnatural. And out there there's – or at least, there wasn't – no TV or cinema or anything. Nothing. All you could do in the evening was screw." She erupted into raucous laughter.

My friend snickered, embarrassed. Raj pretended to examine the stereo. Moses guffawed. I lit another cigarette. Rani and her cousin came to the door and listened; they were grinning.

"I mean, you wouldn't believe how beautiful it is," Ann continued, striking a match for her cigarette. "I love the country. Hunting. Fishing. When you pull in your lobster traps, you have fresh lobster. You don't have to buy anything. Everything's free. It's not like in this concrete hell full of lost souls."

The sudden bitterness took us by surprise. Again there was a silence, the shuffling of feet, the clearing of a throat.

Moses said, "But it must be a hard life out there, not so?"

"No, it's not," Ann said softly, studying her fingers, which lay interlaced on her lap. "It's beautiful. Imagine, getting up at ten, eleven o'clock in the morning, sleeping as late as you want, then going out to cut one or two cords of wood for your stove, a wood stove, of course. I dream of going back there. I hate this place ..." Her eyes filled with tears.

"Why you come here then?" Moses demanded, brushing aside Raj's restraining arm.

Ann passed her white knuckles across her eyes. "When I was fourteen, my parents tried to make me marry my uncle's son. I ran away."

"They wanted you to marry your first cousin?"

She nodded, and a tear dripped from the tip of her nose. "Oh

God, I want to go back," she moaned. "I hate living in Toronto.
Everybody's so cold, nobody cares about you."

"I care about you," Moses smirked.

"Whenever I think I'm getting adjusted to the place, something
happens to make me sad again."

"Like what?"

"Like my husband brings somebody home," she sniffled.

"Another woman?"

"No. I have to entertain his friends." Then she shook her head,
signalling she'd say no more. She said, "I've got to feed my baby,"
and rushed out the door.

"She lives upstairs," Moses said to my friend.

Rani wordlessly reached for the cigarette Ann had abandoned in
the ashtray and stubbed it out. Rani was not a smoker and the
crushed cigarette continued to smoulder.

Raj said, "Moses, you shouldn't ..."

"Oh Gawd, Raj man, just having a little fun, is all."

My friend, leaning against the wall, grunted noncommittally.
We exchanged glances; I couldn't read his face.

"I know," Raj whispered, "but don't push she too hard, she have
a lot of troubles."

Moses laughed. "Like she giving you something or what, boy?
How you sticking up so for she, eh? Ey, Rani, keep your eye on Ann
and your husband, you hear, girl?"

Rani sucked her teeth, gave him a harsh look, and disappeared
once more into the kitchen. Raj shook his head and looked at
Pulmatee. Pulmatee avoided his eyes; she was less unmoved than
removed.

"Anybody want a beer?" Moses asked, standing and dusting the
seat of his trousers.

"Come and eat," Rani called from the kitchen. "It getting late."

It would have been a good time to leave and I was about to ask
Raj for my coat when he took me roughly by the arm and half
pulled, half led, me into the kitchen.

It was a large room, three times the size of the living room, with a large window looking out onto the snowed-in backyard. There were few cupboards and the appliances – stove, fridge, both dappled with rust – appeared to have been inserted at random. Next to the fridge was an open closet in which several coats were hanging: a coat closet in the kitchen? Then I understood: in some inexplicable way, the rooms had switched purposes, the house had switched sides: what had once been the front was now the back, and vice versa.

The air, warm and damp, smelled strongly of curry, garlic, and burnt oil. Water condensed on my skin and a drop of perspiration tickled down my chest.

The table, standing in the middle of so spacious a room, seemed covered in a solitude strangely heightened by the knives and forks and plates that had been placed neatly in front of each chair. Raj directed me to a seat. I said, "Thank you," and this time he elected not to reply; he simply nodded, but still shyly.

When we were seated – Moses, muttering, managed to introduce a note of confusion into even so simple an act – Rani's cousin placed a platter of hot roti on the table. Then she giggled, covering her mouth with her hands. Moses, laughing, pointed to the platter: "That's a hot one, boy." Raj and my friend also laughed, as did Rani and, with restraint, Pulmatee. I didn't understand. Moses explained: "Look at the picture on the tablecloth." I saw an apple tree, a nude man retaining modesty with a leaf, a nude woman, breasts hidden by the hot platter, holding a half-eaten apple in her hand: a jaded Garden of Eden. "A real hot one," Moses giggled, creating the sound of someone choking.

Rani brought me a plate of curried chicken. She smiled the sugary smile of a grandmother and said, "We have plenty, so just ask if you want more, okay? Don't be shy."

The others had already started eating. No one spoke and for a long time the only sounds were those of violent mastication and heavy breathing, as if the meal were a tedious chore. Pulmatee,

Rani, and her cousin stood in front of the stove, looking at us eat and talking lowly to each other. I concentrated on my food, blocking out Raj's slurping and – after having witnessed the first – blinding myself to the periodic splashes of saliva from Moses's yawning munches.

I thought about Ann, wondering about the performance we had witnessed, about her husband and her baby, and the horrors of her life, which I could in no way conjure up. I wondered how long she'd lived in Toronto: she spoke with no accent. I would never have guessed she was from Newfoundland.

As if willed, the front door scraped open and Ann's voice, powerful yet weak and painfully theatrical, boomed into the kitchen: "Bye, darling. Love you. *Love you*."

Moses sneered, "He's a Chink."

Rani and her cousin cleared the dishes away. Raj belched three times and rubbed his stomach. We returned to the living room. It was the women's turn to eat and we left the kitchen to them. Ann was still at the open door, waving to her husband. Moses gave me a look which said that it was all for our benefit, a role conceived in mockery and executed in pantomime. Hearing us, she turned around and closed the door.

Moses howled: the zipper of her slacks was undone.

Ann, nonplussed, said, "Oh, how'd that happen?" She took hold of either side of the opening and, pretending to free the stuck pull, parted the zipper, revealing a pink panty. "Ooooh," she said in feigned horror.

Moses, grinning, offered to help. She accepted. He tugged gently at the zipper, taking his time, and after a few seconds of struggle pulled it up.

"Thank you very much," Ann said airily.

"You're welcome," Moses replied.

Ann indicated a wet spot on her T-shirt. "I have to change, the baby puked on me."

Raj, opening a door that had remained shut until now, said, "You can change in the bedroom, Ann."

Moses said, "Need more help, Ann?"

"Not this time, thanks." She looked offended.

Raj said, "The baby okay alone up there?"

"Yes, I can hear him if he cries." She closed the bedroom door behind her.

My friend laughed and said to Moses, "You better wash your hands quick, boy. You never know what she have inside them pants."

Rani came into the living room. "And you better throw away that glass you drinking from," she giggled.

Raj laughed weakly. I lit a cigarette. Ann came out of the bedroom and headed for the kitchen. Moses stopped her and indicated the drawing of a rum bottle on her clean T-shirt. "Is the rum good?" he asked.

She looked puzzled and then said with a naïve twitter, "Yes, very."

"Let me see," he said.

"It's good." Her voice hardened: she was losing control of the situation.

Moses said, "I want to feel it."

"No, I'm married."

"So what? I'm married too."

"You don't know my husband. If you knew him, then you could." She gave a hollow laugh and tried to walk past him. He seized her wrist. Without a word she slapped his hand and he released her. Looking hurt and irritated, she hurried into the kitchen.

Raj said, "Cool it, Moses. She gets angry sometimes. You harassing her too much."

Moses guffawed. "Like she really giving you something or what? What is it? You like big breasts? Where you does do it, up there or down here?"

"Oh shit, Moses." Raj gestured helplessly.

Suddenly Ann hurried out of the kitchen, a smile on her lips and tears in her eyes. She strode to the door and left the flat.

This time she didn't return.

I had another rum and Coke and then, faking illness, fled the house. A sense of dereliction arched through my head and switches of tension twitched down my back.

As I hurried away through the falling snow, I glanced back at the house with its walls of mismatched red brick and collapsing porch. Ann's flat on the second floor was in darkness. In the living-room window of Raj's flat, I saw Pulmatee. She was looking through the window at the snow. She looked sad.

# TIMOTHY FINDLEY

# A Gift of Mercy

When Minna Joyce first laid eyes on Stuart Bragg, she told herself to remain calm. This was back in 1975 when she was still in her waitress phase and working for a man whose name was Shirley Felton. Shirley ran what Minna called The Moribund Cafe on Queen Street West. It was really called the Morrison Cafe, because it was in the Morrison Hotel – a rummy dive for drunks and crazies, now defunct, on the north-east corner of Shaw and Queen. Minna had been working there since late July of the previous year and the reason she gave for taking such a job was that she had to keep her eye on the Queen Street Mental Health Centre, just across the road.

"You never know, my dear," she had said to one of her park-bench friends, "what they'll do behind your back." Also, there was the vaguest hope that her mother – the newly remarried Mrs. Harold Opie – might drift by one day and find her cast-off, screwed-up daughter working behind the counter in The Moribund Cafe – drop dead of shock and thus spare the world the continued menace of her presence. "And that, my dear, would be worth the price of admission!"

As to why Mrs. Harold Opie – the ex-Mrs. Galway Joyce –
might be adrift at all on Queen Street, only Minna Joyce could
imagine. Perhaps her cool stability was really less than it seemed
and she was looking for yet another masochist crazy enough to
marry her. Galway Joyce and Harold Opie had both been mad
enough to do so – and, from what Minna knew of her mother's most
recent marriage, Mister Opie was already on the way out the door.
But whatever the reason might be, Minna Joyce was content to
believe in its probability and dream of its eventuality.

Now in the depths of winter, Stuart Bragg had just walked
through the door and Minna – who was leaning down to place a cup
of coffee and a plastic spoon beneath the vacant stare of one of the
Moribund's regular customers – felt the draught and looked up to
see who might have entered.

There he was, and her body held its breath while her mind went
racing.

A blizzard was going on outside and Bragg had brought it with
him through the door. His hair was white with snow and he wore a
long, black coat. The storm raged up against the plate glass window
at his back and the way it blew, it looked as if it had pursued him,
eager to engulf him.

Bragg had the look of one who bore a message – lost and
uncertain as to whom the message must be given.

*Me*, said Minna's mind. *He's come here looking for me.*

But, of course, he hadn't. He was just another stranger in from
Queen Street and Minna was quickly reconciled to believing that
was good enough. Strangers were her specialty and those who were
pursued by storms and demons made the best strangers of all. She
herself had once been pursued by storms and demons, and, even
now, she was still in the process of firing at them over her shoulder
– her aim perfected after many years of practice. Only three or four
remained at her heels, and, of these, the most persistent were her
love of dark red wine and her passion for the written word. This
latter was a demon flashing sentences before her eyes with incom-
prehensible speed – and whose sibilant voice was lower than a
man's.

Bragg's eyes searched the restaurant for someone he could trust. Minna was used to this look. She saw it every day, when strangers walked in and were confronted by the faces of the regulars – the rummies and the drugged-out kids, the schizoids and the dead-eyed retainers whose job it was to sweep the snow and rake the leaves at the Queen Street Mental Health Centre. Bragg evaded all these people – caught Minna's eye and turned away from her.

*Wait*, she wanted to say to him. *I can help you.* Minna recognized the look in his eyes of unrequited sanity – the look of someone terrified of the light in a world lit up with stark bare bulbs. He even squinted, placing his hand along his forehead. Minna stepped forward – but Shirley was already marching down behind the counter.

"Yeah?" Shirley said to Bragg – using his dishrag, polishing the soiled Formica countertop, rearranging the packs of chewing gum piled beside the register. "What can I do you for?"

Minna listened, breathless.

*Please don't go away*, she was thinking. *Don't go away before we've made contact.*

"I need to make a call," said Bragg. "Have you got a telephone?"

"Sure I got a telephone," said Shirley, "but it ain't for public use. You wanta coffee instead?"

"Thank you, no," said Bragg. "I really do need to make a call." He was eyeing the telephone behind the counter just the way a man who is starving eyes the food on someone else's plate.

"Sorry," Shirley told him. "I got a policy here: no calls."

"Where, then? Where can I find a telephone?"

"'Cross the road in the Centre. Maybe there's a pay phone there."

"Thank you," said Bragg. And he turned to go.

*No*, said Minna. *You mustn't. We haven't met.*

But he was out the door and the storm was about to have its way with him.

Minna closed her eyes. Why were the lost so beautiful? She couldn't let him go.

"Wait!" she heard herself calling.

Shirley turned in her direction. "What the fuck's with you?" he said to her. "Didn't I tell you no one yells in the Morrison Cafe?"

But Minna was already reaching out for the handle of the door and barely heard him.

Out on the street she looked both ways and hurried to the corner. "Wait!" she shouted. (What if her mother could see her now?) Everything was white before her and blowing into her eyes. Peering through the snow, she saw the lights were about to change and she ran out, flat against the wind with her apron clinging to her legs like something desperate, begging to be rescued. Suddenly, there she was on the other side of Queen Street, blindly grabbing for the long, black sleeve of the departing stranger.

"Stop!" she yelled at him. "Stop!"

He turned, alarmed and tried to brush her off – but she dug her fingernails into the cloth and pulled up close to his arm.

The man was truly afraid of her; the look on his face was unmistakable and one she had seen a dozen times before. What had he done that she should have followed him – attacked him in such a panic?

"Please," he said, attempting to be civilized. "Don't."

There she was with her hand on his arm – a perfect stranger, standing in a blizzard out on Queen Street, wearing nothing but an apron over a magenta uniform – and *Minna* traced in thread across the pocket at her breast. And her hair was blowing across her face and he thought: *she's mad as a hatter – and beautiful as anyone I've ever seen.*

"All right," he said – giving in because it was so evident she wouldn't let go until she'd had her way. "Tell me what's wrong."

"Your name," she shouted at him – each word blown away in the wind. "Tell me your bloody name."

"What?" he shouted back at her. "What?"

Several people, fully cognizant of where they were and what they might be witnessing out in front of the Queen Street Mental Health Centre, huddled on the corner waiting for a streetcar. The way this man and woman were holding on to one another, they looked as if they were locked in a deadly struggle. But she was only waiting for his answer and he was only trying to prevent her from being swept away in the Queen Street traffic.

"Please," she shouted at him – right into his ear. "I have to know who you are!"

Bragg stepped back and stared at her as best he could through the storm. She was holding back the strands of her flowing hair and it was only then that he saw that she was smiling; laughing at her own audacity.

"Oh," he said. "I see."

Very slowly, he grinned, and three months later they were married.

By the time Minna died, the marriage had lasted just over twelve years. During the final months they had lived apart; Bragg in Toronto, Minna in Australia: *just about as far apart as a person can get, my dear*, she had said. *A gift of mercy for us both.*

Later, she had written in one of her final letters that it was more than likely fate was playing one of its better tricks when it devised this ending: terminating events before the thirteenth anniversary of their meeting on Queen Street. *What do people give each other after thirteen years?* she had written. *A baker's dozen of silver cups; one for each year they've remained on speaking terms? How do they celebrate? A game of Russian roulette? Thirteen guns and only one of them loaded? Yours or mine, Bragg? Yours or mine? We'll never know; for which I'm glad.*

One afternoon, after Bragg and Minna had been married for seven years and were living on Collier Street, Bragg came home and found a stranger in Minna's bed. This was in February of 1983.

Bragg had just gone into the bathroom where he was soaping his hands when he heard somebody cough. At first, he paid no attention, assuming it was Minna. But when the coughing contin-ued, and began to take on the characteristic sounds of someone who was choking, Bragg shut off the taps.

Instantly, there was silence – broken only by the last of the water curling down the drain. Bragg closed his eyes in order to concentrate. There had been too much of this, recently; too many phantom coughers – too much offstage laughter – too many voices behind his back. At its worst, this paranoia prompted him to wonder if Minna was trying to disrupt his life in order to gain some sort of mastery over him.

Pondering why Minna wanted to harm him always brought him back to his senses. No one had loved him more in all his life. *Still, people do the strangest things for love,* he would think, when he lay awake at four o'clock in the morning. *People have killed and people have died for love, though I'd rather not do either ...*

Bragg began to dry his fingers, one by one, with a Laura Ashley towel that Minna had given him for Christmas; a double set to go with the Bembridge paper in the bathroom – burgundy pearl-drop flowers with sprigs of dark blue leaves. Bragg would never have spent the money to buy such expensive towels – but Minna would, and had, and Bragg was secretly glad. He loved all things that had to do with water – bathrooms, bathtubs, basins; taps and showers and toilets. He loved the accoutrement of shaving gear and brushes – glass-stoppered bottles of cologne – soap that smelled of pine and cedar – steamy windows – toothbrush glasses ...

Bragg was looking in the mirror the way most people do who don't really want to see themselves – eyes askance, afraid of meeting other eyes. He was just about to duck his head and turn the taps back on to wash away the film of soap in the sink when the second bout of coughing began. Leaving the taps to do their work, Bragg went and stood in the hallway, drying his wrists and listening intently.

This time, the coughing did not abate.

The door to Bragg's own room stood ajar beside him, opposite the bathroom. He could see the comforting shapes of the cats where they lay asleep on his pillows: Morphine and Opium, named for their mother, Poppy, who had died on Queen Street. He could also see his wicker chair with its pile of folded laundry – the shirts and pyjamas he had ironed that morning.

Down at the end of the hall, where Minna's bedroom door was closed against a green satin shoe, the coughing became more violent.

Bragg stepped forward.

The green satin toe obtruded into the hallway, giving the impression someone was lurking there behind the door.

"Hello?" he said.

No one answered.

The coughing stopped.

Bragg screwed up his courage and – watching Minna's door as if he expected it to wield a knife – he approached it, holding his breath, until he was toe to toe with the green satin shoe.

He could see that no one was there – and he gave the door a push with his fingertips.

Lying on Minna's bed, more or less beneath the duvet – one foot and both hands sticking out – there was a tiny figure. It was small enough to be a child.

Bragg could not reconcile the dreadful coughing he had heard with what he saw. Two-Ton Tessie might have coughed like that. But not a child.

The room was lit with curtained light, and since the afternoon was drawing to a close, there was little enough of that to filter through the cotton drapes. The warm intensity of Minna's perfume greeted him briefly – riding past him on the draught from the open door. As soon as he moved into the room, however, he was overcome with the stench of someone exhaling gin and sweating nicotine.

To his left, the shape of Minna's blue Boston rocker stood between him and the windows. The coughing had altogether stopped – and had been replaced with the sound of laboured breathing. Bragg went over and opened the drapes and then – despite the February cold – he also opened the windows.

Turning towards the bed, he was able now to see that the shape he had thought might be that of a child was in fact the angular, sunken figure of someone very small and very old. Matted hair was spread across the pillows. Both hands, fisted, were raised above the figure's head. Halfway down the bed, the extruded foot was clothed in a filthy ankle sock.

Bragg went and stood as close to the bed as he could bear and he looked down into the face of a woman who was old and toothless.

Two small eyes looked up at him: terrified. Instantly, the fists descended and drew the duvet over the face – and a wailing sound began to rise from beneath the feathers.

"Help! Help! Man!" Bragg heard. Then; "Man! Man! Help!"

Bragg turned around and fled – not even stopping to close the door.

Standing outside the bathroom, he prayed the voice would go away before the neighbours called the police.

And indeed, it faded – though it did not stop.

Bragg leaned in against the wall.

"Oh, God," he muttered. "Please, not this again ..."

Conjuring up the woman's face – smelling the memory of gin and urine – hearing the woman's muffled voice – Bragg went into the bathroom, where he discovered, to his fury, he had not turned off the taps.

Banging them shut, he remained for a desperate moment, clutching the silver faucets. Then he let go and sighed. He looked up, helpless and resigned, met his own eyes in the mirror and smiled against his will.

"Better find somewhere to hide," he said out loud. "Minna has started another crusade on Queen Street."


They had lived on Queen Street long before then, in rooms above a restaurant. The restaurant was not the Morrison Cafe, but of another kind entirely: run by homosexuals and catering exclusively to gays. The clientele that hung about their doorstep was a trial at times. The very young were very beautiful and Bragg would turn away and walk around the block, attempting to gain control of himself.

For the most part, however, their life above the restaurant was centred on themselves – their love for one another and their work. While Bragg was busy writing in their dreadful little kitchen, Minna spent hours with her notebook, leaning along the window-sill, staring down at all the people walking in the street. Always, these people seemed to be inadequately dressed. Always, there seemed to be an inadequate number of umbrellas; was everyone, as always, mistaking April for spring?

Minna was not a waitress, now. That phase was over and the married phase had begun. Demon Number Two was hard at work in her and she was writing every day in her cloth-bound notebook. Bragg of the blizzard and the long black coat had turned out to be a budding writer, whose stories had already garnered him a name and a reputation for excellence. They were living on Queen Street not because Bragg had chosen it or even approved of the locale – but only because it seemed to be where Minna Joyce belonged.

Sometimes, early of a morning, the man across the street would come to his window and fling it up – and stand there shaking his fist and shouting obscenities every time a streetcar passed. One day, Minna had brought her notebook and her coffee to the window-sill, when she saw this man take off his clothes and fling them, item by item, onto the top of a streetcar stalled below him. What he wanted, so it seemed, was to get the streetcar's attention – but even now, with it stopped defenceless at his doorstep, the streetcar and its occupants remained oblivious.

Minna had not known what to do about this man. Certainly, she understood his desperation. There was nothing offensive about his nakedness – all its sexuality was masked in rage – and he himself made nothing of it. His clothing had simply become his arsenal – all he had of missiles in the moment. When the streetcar had at last departed, the man had retreated into his darkened room, and in the lulls between the passing traffic, Minna could hear him wailing like a child.

Two days later, Minna had taken up her post, prepared with pen in hand to continue the saga of the Man Who Hated Streetcars. His story already filled a dozen pages of her notebook.

The sky, that morning, was blue and full of promise. May Day was only a weekend away and the owner of the produce shop across the street had set out buckets of daffodils and tulips, paperwhites and carnations on the sidewalk. Women going to work in the office buildings on Bay Street wore their spring coats and colours. The students making their way towards Bathurst Street and Spadina Avenue wore an array of overalls and sweaters and rode an army of ten-speed bikes. Someone above her was playing a recording very loud of "Goodbye Yellow Brick Road." The sound of Elton John's voice had ridden through the whole of Bragg and Minna's winter, and there it was again, to get them into spring:

> *When are you gonna come down?*
> *When are you going to land?*
> *I should have stayed on the farm,*
> *I should have listened to my old man.*

Minna began to tap out the rhythms with her pen against her coffee mug.

> *You know you can't hold me forever,*
> *I didn't sign up with you.*
> *I'm not a present for your friends to open,*
> *This boy's too young to be singing the blues ...*

The man across the street appeared to be singing, too. Except that Minna knew better. The expression on his face was not quite right for singing a song, unless the song was *La Marseillaise*. His mouth was opening far too wide and his eyes were closed too tight. His neck and the muscles in his chest were scarlet and distended: alarming. All the while he sang or shouted, the poor man seemed to be fighting with his window – beating his fists against the latch and heaving his weight against the frame.

Minna stopped singing.

"Bragg?"

She stood up. Bragg didn't answer – locked in the other world beneath his fingers, mouthing the sentences he wrote.

Minna looked back across the road.

Up above, the music kept on spinning like a spider:

*... goodbye yellow brick road,*
*Where the dogs of society howl.*
*You can't plant me in your penthouse,*
*I'm going back to my plough.*

Down in the street, the traffic was piling up and a pair of streetcars had been surrounded by a horde of milk trucks and taxicabs. Nothing was able to move and the worst of it was, the man in the window had begun to panic. Perhaps he imagined the streetcars had come to parlay with him; make their peace and go away forever. But how could they hope to hear him if he couldn't open his window?

Minna could see he had failed altogether to budge the sash. Apparently, this was more than the man could bear, and she watched in horror as he ran away and returned with a baseball bat.

"Bragg?" she whispered. "Hurry ...!"

The man began to beat out all his panes of glass, and because the shards were falling to the sidewalk, people started to run for cover. Not an umbrella in sight.

"Stop!" Minna cried.

The man was climbing onto his window-sill.

In Minna's mind was the thought: *if only Bragg would come and help me ...* But Bragg had reached the climax of his story and was shaping it in perfect cadences, every word and every sentence judged against a count of syllables. He used a thesaurus for this and just at that moment he was looking for a two-beat word for *inhibition*.

Minna and the streetcar man, it seemed, were alone in their private vacuum.

"Stop!" she cried again.

To no avail.

By the time Bragg surfaced and at last appeared, the vacuum had been shattered.

Just as the man had risen onto his toes and leapt, Minna had put her hand through the glass in order to break his fall.

"What in the name of heaven did you think you were trying to do?" Bragg asked her in the Emergency Ward of St. Michael's Hospital. A doctor had wrapped a bandage around the stitches in her wrist – and Minna had been told to lie on her back for half an hour, until the sedation took effect.

"Stop him," she said, "of course."

Then she had looked away at the painted, peeling wall, closing her eyes and praying that Bragg had not been able to read her mind. *Stop him, of course*, is what she had said. But that was not quite true. In the moment, her hope had been that she would catch him; catch the man with her hand held out, the way you catch the rain.

While Minna gave the appearance of having fallen quietly to sleep, Bragg sat down on the iron chair beside the bed and took a slip of paper out of his pocket.

*Inhibition*, he read.

*Stricture*.

*Hindrance*.

*Restraint*.

None of these was right.

It took him roughly half an hour to decide. The word he chose was *impasse*.

Stuart Bragg's background provided him with money: just enough to buy a house – not enough to avoid a mortgage.

Shortly after the man had leapt to his death on Queen Street, Bragg began to think about a house where Minna would be safe from the influence of visible suicides and where the detritus of humanity wouldn't be on parade for her perusal every time she wandered to the window.

Bragg did not yet understand, back then, that Minna didn't "wander" anywhere. Nothing she did was done by chance and if he had only read her notebooks (not that she wanted him to) he would have discovered she was keeping meticulous track of how the people down on the street were faring. This was her journal of despair – but not her own despair. Somewhere, deep in the body of the notebook, written in a margin, were the words: *and what of me? I cannot articulate and have no desire to tell where I have been and where I am going. Surely this is dangerous. What am I hiding? When will it surface?*

But that was all there was of that. No conjecture. No predictions.

Nonetheless, Bragg had felt the urgency burgeoning in Minna's restlessness and he feared her growing habit of silence. Changing the milieu might not be the whole and only answer – but surely it must be part of it.

He, too, wanted to escape. He wanted trees and grass to re-enter his life. He wanted – even once a week – to make his way down the stairs and into the street without the ever-present threat of someone else's panic waiting to grab his sleeve. Or kill his cats.

Poppy, his aging Burmese female, had been driven under the traffic by a man with a stick, who was convinced all cats were spreading the devil's message in their scat. Two days later, Bragg announced he'd found a house on Collier Street, south of Rosedale, north of Bloor. It had three trees and a high board fence at the rear – and, across the road, a park.

Minna was urged, by dint of Bragg's enthusiasm, to go at least and take a look. "Give the house a chance to work its magic on you, Min," Bragg said. "It has the feel of a winner."

Minna was guarded about her reaction. The fact was, she liked it well enough – but it had two drawbacks she didn't want to discuss with Bragg. One was its proximity to Rosedale – Rosedale having been the scene of childhood traumas and, therefore, the only place in all of Toronto to which she had sworn she would never return. The other drawback to the house on Collier Street was its abundance of bedrooms: one too many for Minna to tolerate with any ease. She feared – had feared – would fear forever – Bragg's desertion of their mutual bed. But she couldn't say these things, and so it was that she gave her assent to the move and one month later, she and Bragg and the remaining cats moved in. Bragg's being able to afford it made it easier to reconcile. But Minna told herself that was not the end of Queen Street in her life.

Down in the kitchen, Minna was drinking her dark red wine and setting the table. A painted wooden tray, Bragg noted, had been lifted onto the counter and sat there waiting to be set. Somehow, the empty tray was like a threat, because it meant the woman in the bed was going to be fed up there, nurtured and urged to stay.

"What the hell is going on?" he said.

Minna said: "I'm making dinner. Any objection?" She was belligerent and defensive all at once. Bragg could see the bottle of Côtes-du-Rhône, sitting on the counter beside the empty tray, had been half emptied already.

"Yes, I have objections," he said – and got himself a glass. "I have objections to that woman's presence in your bedroom. Who the hell is she?"

Minna put her hand out and lifted the Côtes-du-Rhône out of Bragg's way just as he was about to reach for it. "Why not open a bottle of your own?" she said. "I'm keeping track of how much I drink," she added – and filled her glass.

Bragg went and rummaged in the corner cupboard where he found a bottle of Beaujolais and two more bottles of Côtes-du-Rhône. Choosing the Beaujolais, he found the corkscrew, still with Minna's cork impaled on it.

Minna, holding her drink and cigarette in one hand, was standing at the stove and stirring something in a pot with the other. Her back was to him. All the while Bragg was opening the Beaujolais, he was watching Minna's back to see what it would tell him.

Nothing.

At last, having filled his glass, he said: "you haven't answered my question, Minna. Who is that woman in your bed?"

"Her name is Elizabeth Doyle," said Minna. "Calls herself Libby."

Bragg found Minna's cigarettes – took one and lighted it. "And?" he said.

"And what?"

"Oh, for Christ's sake!" he exploded – spilling his wine. "Who the hell is she? What the fuck is she doing here?"

Minna laid down the wooden spoon and walked across to the painted tray. She began to lay out silver and a napkin on its blue and yellow birds. Her voice was shaking when she answered – but she resisted raising it.

"I found her on Queen Street," she said as evenly as possible. "Standing in the rain."

Bragg gave a sigh and sat at the table.

Minna turned and looked at him.

"It's all right, Bragg," she said. "She's perfectly harmless."

"I'm glad to hear it," said Bragg. "After you've fed her, what then?"

"She'll more than likely go back to sleep," said Minna. "I would, if I was her. I don't think she's had a decent sleep in ninety years." She set a wine glass next to a pepper grinder on the tray and looked around for an extra salt shaker. "My guess is, she's homeless – but she won't admit it."

"Did she admit she was a lush?" Bragg asked.

Minna paused and then went on with her search. "Maybe if I was living on the street I'd be a lush, too," she said.

"You'd be a lot of things, wouldn't you. *If*," said Bragg. He was absolutely furious because he felt the trap of reason closing around him. Surely, all of this would end with Minna saying *only a monster would have left her there* ...

"Where will you sleep?" he said.

Minna didn't hesitate a second.

"Why, with you, of course."

Bragg crushed out his cigarette and pinched another one – lighting it at once. He got up, retrieved the bottle of Beaujolais and sat down. He finished the wine already in his glass and filled the glass again.

"It doesn't make sense," said Bragg. "Bringing home strangers. It's crazy."

"I brought you home from Queen Street," she said.

Bragg did not utter.

Minna filled her glass and then said: "why is it crazy? What would you have done? Leave her there?"

"I wouldn't have been on Queen Street to begin with," said Bragg, "if I were you. I wouldn't even be there if I were me. What the hell were you doing?"

"Research."

This was true. Bragg knew that. Minna's book was going to be all about the denizens of Queen Street.

Then he said something cruel – wishing he wasn't saying it – saying it anyway. "What makes you think you have to do research, Minna? Tell me what it is you don't already know about these people."

Minna turned away – got down three large plates and put them in the oven to warm them.

"Aren't you going to answer me?" said Bragg – pressing his luck.

"Answer you about what?"

"Your goddamned research, Minna. Your goddamned research and your goddamned need to throw yourself under the wheels of that woman upstairs."

"I ..."

"What's there to know about these goddamned people you don't already know? They're crazy, Minna. They're *crazy!*" He was almost yelling.

"So – they're crazy," she said. She still didn't want to raise her voice. She only wanted this to end.

"Then why don't you go and live with them – instead of bringing them back here?"

"Why should I do that, Bragg?"

"Because you're one of them, that's why. You and the goddamned Morrison Cafe."

Minna subsided. Everything turned to ice inside her.

"Fine," she said. "I'm one of them. That settles it."

Nothing more was said.

Bragg sat out the interim while Minna took Libby Doyle her tray – and he drank another glass of wine.

When Minna came down about five minutes later, she got out another tray and began to set it with silver.

"What are you up to, now?" said Bragg – alarmed.

"Nothing unusual," said Minna. "I just thought I'd take my dinner upstairs. Eat with my own kind. That sort of thing. That's all." She plonked another bottle of Côtes-du-Rhône on the tray.

Bragg said: "I'm not going to let you do this, Minna. That woman is going to leave this house and you are going to return to your senses."

He stood up and almost knocked his wine glass over. Minna watched him carefully. Maybe she was secretly glad he was doing this. She couldn't tell. But she didn't challenge him – and when he made his move to the door, she didn't try to stop him.

Like anyone growing up knowing there was money in the bank, Bragg had never given it a lot of thought. Perhaps if he had been of another generation – the one emerging in the 1980s, for instance – he might have found more delight in money than he did; far more joy in having it – far more anguish when it disappeared. But having come of age in the 1960s, Bragg's relations with money were indifferent: cordial enough if a dividend passed his way, but unconcerned if riches eluded him.

*I've never felt I was writing for money*, he was to say much later on. He wrote to make his living, he told a journalist, not to make his fortune. His work was well if not highly regarded. Whenever a new

Bragg piece appeared, his severest critics – other writers – always said: the best is yet to come. He wrote short novels and he wrote long stories – a paradox for which he had no explanation. The first of his stories – still regarded as his best – had already been published before the advent of Minna in his life.

The thing about Bragg that gave his writing its "voice" was his savage sense of humour – laughter that only reached the page; he had no gift for laughter in his life. Bragg himself – though he shunned the practice, even the thought of analysis – was perfectly aware of the written humour's source. All his life he had known he was set aside from the comfortable mass by the fact of his homosexuality.

Some who where close to him – one of his brothers, one of his aunts – had forgiven him. Most of those close to him had not. Bragg well knew he need not be "forgiven"; he knew that "forgiveness" in the given view could only be construed as a kind of arrogance. *What kind of person* – Bragg had allowed a character beneath his hand to ask – *would think it appropriate to confer forgiveness on a chap for being born?* After all, Bragg had a cousin who was retarded and an aunt who was schizophrenic. Had anyone forgiven them? If they had, Bragg might have hauled out a gun and shot them for their impertinence. Still, he recognized the impulse in his brother and his aunt to be forgiving. They had been nurtured in the Church, where forgiveness had no connection to understanding. Bragg's other brother and their father had urged him to seek a "cure." His mother, long since dead, had been convinced the sin was in her. His birth had, therefore, been a punishment laid upon her immortal soul. So much, Bragg concluded, for the gentle mercy of God.

So this was his private fund of rage: the rage that produced his written humour – and the rage, by most accounts, that saved his writing from the spoils of too much darkness.

One day, however, Bragg would free the bitch inside him – or the bitch inside him would cut her leash, break loose and savage the neighbours. But he didn't know that yet. He still contained her on the page – where she was always confined to barking through the mouths of those Bragg least resembled in his private being. He did not believe in writing as revenge.

Minna Joyce could not let go of Queen Street West. Or perhaps it was that Queen Street West would not let go of Minna Joyce. She had gone there to take up residence with a sense of mission. When that had been, she could not recall, probably because she had gone there so often in her mind before she had sought out lodgings there and jobs. More than likely the move had taken place in 1971 or '72. This would be after her parents had divorced and Minna was in her early twenties.

The Galway Joyces and their only remaining child had lived in the depths of Rosedale up on Douglas Drive beyond the Glen Road Bridge. They had lived there all of Minna's life and during the time when her sister, Alma, had been carried off by a burst appendix. *Carried off* had been Galway Joyce's phrase. Mrs. Joyce – whose first name was Lue Anne – had been more forthright and more unforgiving: the doctors had done it and that was that. They had failed to gauge the progress of Alma's condition and they had *let her die before relief could reach her*. Minna had been nine when Alma died and Alma had been eleven and, again in Lue Anne's words, *the First-Prize Winner of all the children ever born*. In Minna's words, she grew up after Alma's death as "the First-Prize Winner, my dear, of all the unwanted children ever born." But that was fine, in Minna's terms, because it meant she would never have to feel obliged to love her parents.

Queen Street West and, in fact, the whole of Parkdale offered a world of unwanted people – the only people Minna felt any affection for. They lived in the shadow of the Queen Street Mental Health Centre, either having been discharged from its vast and innumerable wards or waiting to enter them. Minna took rooms in several houses – one and then another – moving according to her whims and work. She spent some time as a clerk in a retail outlet selling bathroom fixtures; then as a dispatcher for a taxi company;

then behind the counter in a porno shop, where the magazine covers finally got her down and then, at last, as Shirley Felton's boisterous and rebellious waitress in The Moribund Cafe. And all this while, she was pursued by her storms and demons – red wine and writing consuming all her free time.

Red wine and writing – and people-watching.

The crazies touched and moved her beyond all others: the way they walked, the way they stood, the way they tried to speak. *Just to be seen, Bragg. Just to be seen and heard and acknowledged. That's what they wanted. Witness. Not to be forgotten.*

"Where am I now?" they would say to her. "Can you tell me where I am?"

Minna would listen and she would tell them: "here."

It was the only answer any of them ever understood and no one else had ever said it to them. *Here is where you are: with me.* Everyone else was always saying to them: "you're on Queen Street."

Over time – in spite of everything, including love of Bragg and love of life – Minna could not abandon the crazies and the winos out on Queen Street. She couldn't stay away from *here.* She tried, but it was a true addiction: something in the nerve ends needing a constant fix. She kept going back for more. This way, she had encountered Libby Doyle, who was now upstairs, about to be evicted from the only bed she had known in over a year.

Soaked with rain and standing in an alley down behind the Marmax Bargain Centre, Libby Doyle had been drinking gin from a bottle concealed in one of her Eaton's shopping bags. She had worn an old dark dress at least four sizes too large and a pair of children's yellow rubber boots. Her hair was only partly covered with a green plastic triangle Minna soon perceived was the scissored corner of a garbage bag and she had been singing songs. "Don't Sit Under The Apple Tree" had been one of them. "Paper Doll" had been another. "I'll Be Around" and "You'll Never Know." War songs from her heyday.

Looking at her, Minna had decided her heyday must have been terrific. What an extraordinary face she had – Elizabeth Doyle, with wide-set eyes and high-pitched bones – a raging beauty, back in 1942. And now what other people would call a hag.

"Can I drink with you?" Minna said.

"You can, indeed," said Libby Doyle and offered her gin at once, the way all rubbies do. "Do you know where we can get another?"

Minna said: "yes, I do" and drank from the bottle – hating gin, but doing it for Libby's sake.

After her third or fourth *pull on the tit* (as Libby Doyle described it) Minna said: "there's a pub round the corner we can go to." She really wanted just to get Libby in somewhere and out of the rain. But Libby said: "they kick me out of pubs. It's 'cause I always sing."

Minna said: "then I'll take you home."

"I'm home right here," said Libby Doyle. And she indicated the alley filled with large-sized cardboard packing crates from the Marmax Bargain Centre.

"No," said Minna. "I mean, I'll take you home with me."

"Oh," said Libby Doyle. "I suppose you wouldn't have a glass I could drink from, would you?"

"Yes," said Minna. "I have lots of glasses."

"Good," said Libby Doyle. "These goddamned bottles are always breaking my teeth."

Minna laughed and they made their way to the curb with all of Libby's shopping bags and Minna hailed a cab and brought the old woman home to Collier Street.

Nothing was said along the way until they were stopped for a light on Markham Street and Libby, wiping the window clear of steam, peered out and said, with perfect sobriety and without a trace of envy: "my daughter lives in that house there; the one with all the windows."

Minna looked and saw a perfectly restored brick house set back beyond a wooden deck. A cat was staring down from a lighted room on the second floor

"The cat's name is Rosie," said Libby Doyle. And they drove away.

After an extended silence, Minna heard footsteps on the staircase: Libby's first – Bragg's second. Then she heard Bragg speaking in the hallway. "Stay there, Mrs. Doyle," he said. "If you move an inch, I'll call the police." Then he pushed open the kitchen door and let it swing closed behind him. Minna blinked. Bragg's arms were filled with a wild array of plastic carry-all bags and little boxes and bits of clothing. What had he done to Libby Doyle? "May I just show you," he said, "before I transport your lady friend back to Queen Street, how she has repaid your hospitality?" He said this with an icy coldness and then he began to dismantle the array of goods in his arms – tersely naming every item as he set it down on the kitchen table. "One pair of satin shoes," he said. "Green. One blue cotton dress. One wool jacket. Three pairs of freshly laundered men's underwear – mine," he said. "One knitted jersey – mine. Your old watch. Your photograph of me in its silver frame. One jar of olives – god knows where that came from – one bottle of aspirin – and this –"

Bragg held out the long silver cord of Minna's French dressing gown.

Minna sat frozen.

Bragg didn't understand. He thought her stillness signified that she had learned her lesson: crazy bag ladies steal.

But that was not what had frozen her.

"I'm taking her back," said Bragg. "To the Marmax Bargain Centre where you found her. And, by the way, be grateful she didn't kill us in our sleep." He threw a switchblade knife on the table.

Minna still did not move.

Bragg went back into the hall and Minna listened to him hustling the old woman out through the front door and down the walk to his little car and then she heard the car doors slam – one, two – and the whole world drive away. Or so it seemed.

Minna blinked and poured herself another glass of Côtes-du-Rhône.

She reached out and touched the silver cord and lifted it up and held it against her cheek.

Minna tried to banish the picture the silver cord had conjured when Bragg first threw it down: the image – vivid as the photograph of Bragg in his silver frame – of Libby Doyle hanging by her neck in the Marmax Bargain Centre's alley – free at last of her storms and demons.

"I almost saved her," she said out loud. "He simply doesn't understand." She thought of Shirley Felton and his goddamned telephone down at The Moribund Cafe – and the day Bragg had entered her life. "I got a policy," Shirley had said to him. "No calls."

Now, Stuart Bragg had become like that: no one is allowed to call for help.

Back in 1964, when Minna Joyce was in her seventeenth year, Lue Anne, her mother, had had her committed briefly – because she had broken all her family's traditions of silence, propriety and submission. Yelling fits had overcome the child in the worst of places: streetcars and schoolrooms – Britnell's Book Store – Eaton's and Simpsons – church. It had been a nightmare time for everyone concerned, though no one – least of all Lue Anne Joyce – had seemed to understand it was a nightmare most of all for Minna. Minna knew that in the depths of her mother's being she was offering up the child she did not want to the same profession that had killed the child she loved. Minna's committal was nothing less, she surmised, than revenge.

Emerging sedated and sedate at seventeen, Minna had launched herself upon the adult world in a ship as sleek and silent as a deadly submarine. Until her parents were separated and she was able, at last, to leave their Rosedale house and take up life elsewhere – Minna had remained in view upon the surface. But once the divorce was final and all the silverware and Spode and all the securities had been divided, Minna had submerged and gone to live in a rooming-house on Foxley Street in Parkdale. This, for Minna, was a perfect haven – centred in the dark of Crazyland.

Foxley Street ran between Dovercourt and Ossington, both of which provided escape routes via public transport out of the danger zone. Walking every evening in the twilight, wearing her duffel coat and tam, Minna strolled at ease beneath the trees, that spring, across the wide and burgeoning lawns of the Queen Street Mental Health Centre. Whenever she spoke, she spoke to squirrels. If she sang, it was always under her breath. She never yelled, she never cursed and she never once flung herself beneath the heels of authority. Quietly, with dignity and calm, she lay beneath the surface of her tranquillizers, plotting the overthrow of all the conniving mothers in the world – and all the sentimental, ineffectual fathers – not to mention all the obedient, deadly doctors.

It was also then that Minna Joyce began to plot the overthrow of silence.

When Bragg returned that night – he was not alone. Something in that day's events had impelled him to do a thing he had never done before in all the years of his marriage to Minna Joyce.

After leaving Libby Doyle on the pavement, roughly speaking just about where the Man Who Hated Streetcars had died – he drove back to Yonge Street and up to Dundas, where he parked his car in a parking lot and went inside a bar he had heard of long ago. It was called The Cockatoo.

Round about two o'clock that morning, Bragg arrived at Collier Street with a lad called Donald Murray, whom he led inside the house and up the stairs and into his bed

Minna's door was open and about an hour later – far down the tunnel of the hallway – she saw the shape of Donald Murray as he passed into the bathroom.

*There*, she thought. *It's done. We've come full circle from the day we met and now our lives will never be the same.*

She was thinking of what Bragg had told her about that call he had wanted to place from The Moribund Cafe.

"I was going to phone a man I'd met and make him a gift of my virginity."

So much for Shirley Felton's policy.

When she slept that night, in all her dreams Minna was yelling *STOP! STOP! STOP!* at the top of her voice on Queen Street in the snow.

# NORMAN LEVINE

# Because of the War

I left Canada in 1949 and went to England because of the eighteen months I lived there during the war. I met my wife because of the war. She was evacuated to Cornwall from London. She also had a weakness for displaced Europeans who had left their country. And I am European – one generation removed. For almost twenty-seven years we were happily married, raised a family, then she became ill and died.

Soon after that the writing stopped. I'd go out in the morning to get the *Times*, do shopping, cook something to eat. Then go for long walks. Or I would sit in the front room, look out of the window, and listen to the wind, the clock, the gulls. The evenings were the most difficult.

After seven months I realized I couldn't go on like this. So I came back to Canada, to Toronto. A city I had never lived in before. I came mid-February (two months before a new book was to be published ... it was the last thing I read to her in manuscript). I like

Canadian winters. But after two weeks in Toronto I didn't want to go out.

I would only leave this room to walk to the corner store and buy two packs of cigarillos. And mail my letters. Then I would go to Ziggy's supermarket. The neat piles of fruit and vegetables. Such lovely colours. And in sizes I wasn't used to. The cheeses from all over. The different bread, bagel, salami, hot dogs – what abundance. Equipped with this I stayed inside, cooked, listened to the radio, made cups of coffee, smoked the cigarillos, and wrote letters to England, Holland, and Switzerland. I like a foreign city. But there was something here that made me uneasy every time I went out.

My publisher had got me this apartment. A large bare room on the seventh floor in the centre of Toronto. It looked shabby from the outside but one wall was all glass. I watched passenger jets, high-rise office buildings, clusters of bare trees, and some magnificent sunsets. It was even more impressive at night. The lights inside the glass buildings were left on. They made the city look wealthy, full of glitter, like tall passenger liners anchored close together in the dark.

On my first day I went to a bank on Bloor Street to open an account. A small grey-haired woman with glasses came to the counter. "What is your job?"

I told her.

She lowered her head and mumbled.

"Unemployed?"

"No."

As she wrote my name, address, and other particulars, I could see she didn't believe I was in work. I wondered why. I had on a new winter coat. I was wearing a tie, a clean shirt, a dark suit. I had good shoes.

I walked to the Eaton Centre. From the outside it reminded me of Kew Gardens – one greenhouse above another. And seeing people moving sideways on the escalators – like something from "Things to Come."

I had come to get a telephone. And when I came out, with the telephone, I was on a frozen side-street. I didn't know where north was. So I asked a woman in a fur coat.

"Don't talk to me," she shouted angrily, waving her hand. "Go away, go away – just walk along –"

I did walk along. The panhandlers kept asking. "Can you spare a quarter?" "Any change sir?" Then told me to have a good day or else to take care. The cold wind blew loose newspapers down Yonge Street. It looked shabby and raw.

But inside it was different.

I'd come in from the cold to this well-heated building. Though the room was warm the air was dry. The toothbrush I'd left wet at night was like chalk next morning. And when I left out a piece of sliced bread ... In the morning I woke to a high-pitched sound. It was the dry bread drying even more.

In those first weeks I went for walks. And discovered a large Chinese section, a Portuguese, Italian, Polish, Jewish, Greek ... with their restaurants, bakeries, butchers, bookstores, and banks.

On a cold morning I walked into a district of large houses, wide lawns, a small park. Icicles were hanging from the roofs. And on the lawns the snow had a frozen crust. It was garbage day. The garbage cans, and the tied black-green plastic bags, were on the snow at the edge of the lawns. In the road steam was rising from the manholes.

Because of the ice I was walking slowly through the park when I saw a red bird fly to a young tree. This small red bird in this frozen landscape looked exotic. I was watching this bird when three large dogs appeared. They attacked the garbage cans, ripped the plastic bags, and foraged. They did this, from lawn to frozen lawn, without making a sound. Then went away leaving garbage scattered and exposed.

Some days I gave myself destinations.

One afternoon I decided to walk to the Art Gallery of Ontario. At a busy intersection I had to wait for the lights to change. I looked up and saw a black squirrel on a telephone wire slowly crossing above the crowded street. No one else seemed to take any notice.

Because I saw the squirrel get across and because the sun was shining, I said to the man waiting beside me.

"Isn't this a lovely day?"

"You too," he replied.

Late on a Saturday, I went and bought a paperback of *Heart of Darkness*. Then walked back through fresh snow to the apartment. As the elevator started it began to vibrate. At the top it stopped. The door remained shut. I pressed number seven button again. It went to the bottom. And stopped. The elevator door still wouldn't open. I tried all the buttons, the switches. Nothing happened except the lights went out. It was then that I realized I was trapped.

I began to call out.

I don't know how long I was there. The air had become stale. I thought: how awkward it will be if I die here. Finally someone did hear me. "OK fellah," I could hear him on the other side. "Don't worry. I'll get the fire department. They will have you out in a matter of minutes." And they did. They forced the door open. I was at the bottom of the shaft. And climbed out into the light and the cold air.

That's how I met Nick, the superintendent of the apartment. He was standing with the firemen. He looked distressed. "Not my fault. I start work yesterday. I no work weekend. Not my fault."

"Of course it's not your fault," I said.

After that Nick and I talked whenever we saw each other. His wife had left him. He had custody of their son. When he left for school in the morning, I watched them wave and smile until the boy finally turned the corner. Nick told me he was Yugoslavian. That he grew up with the Germans in his country. "I see people die. I see people hang. These things I cannot forget.

"I work for the two sisters. They need to fix here plenty. But they no like to spend money."

The two sisters came from France after the war and spoke English with a French accent. They owned the apartment and ran it from an office on the second floor. Every morning – Monday to

Friday at ten – I'd go down to see if I had any mail. And be greeted by smiles and good mornings from one of the sisters. "Please sit down. A cup of coffee?"

Edith, the older one, despite her straight grey hair, looked the younger. She was tall, slim, with dark eyes deeply set. She had a long intelligent face. But there was something awkward about her presence. Both sisters were generous, sociable. And both were elegantly dressed.

"These shoes," Edith said, stepping out of one and going easily back into it. "I went to Paris to get them."

"I too go to Paris for my clothes," said Miriam.

She was stocky: blue eyes, black hair, a round face. She smiled a lot and liked to talk. But often when she started to tell a story she would forget the ending and stop in mid-sentence with a startled look.

Edith was separated with two children. Miriam was divorced with two children. They thought I was too much on my own.

"You won't meet people staying in," Miriam said, "or going for walks by yourself. Go to dances. Go to political meetings. Join something –" She forgot what she was going to say. Then in a flat voice said, "In this business you can tell a lot about a person from their luggage."

At the end of March I met Mrs. Kronick. She lived on the floor below. A small Jewish woman, seventy-eight, a widow. She came with her husband from Poland after the First World War. He died ten years ago. She had a son, a doctor, in Vancouver. But he rarely came to see her. Mrs. Kronick was still a striking woman, very independent. And she looked after herself. Every time I saw her she wore a different hat. But she couldn't tolerate the cold. I was in the lobby, waiting for the elevator, when she walked in from the outside. Her face was pale, her eyes watering.

"It's a Garden of Eden," she said trying to catch her breath. "A Garden of Eden."

"What have you been doing, Mrs. Kronick?"

She was silent. Then quietly said, "Sewing shrouds."

"It's an honour," she added quickly. "Not everyone gets asked."

Next morning Edith knocked on the door of my apartment.

"Did you see what they did in the elevator?"

"No."

"Come, I'll show you."

On the inside of the elevator I saw, scratched on the metal, a badly drawn swastika. And on the inside of the elevator door: *Kill Jews.*

"They don't like us," she said.

Edith's student-daughter told me. "My mother wears dresses from Dior. She has a woman to help her in the house. But she can't throw away a small piece of cheese. She will wrap it up and save it. She also saves brown paper bags that she gets from shopping – to use again. It's because of what happened to her in the war."

Both sisters were delighted with Nick.

"He is so much better than the last one," Miriam said. "He never stops working."

"The last one was too old," said Edith. "He came from the Ukraine. After forty years here – he was still in the Ukraine."

"You must come and meet our friend Henry," Miriam said. "He is very intelligent. Come for brunch next Sunday." And wrote an address and drew a simple map. "Do you think you will be able to find your way?"

"In the war," I said, "I found my way to Leipzig."

On Sunday I took the subway north and travelled as far as it could go. Then began to walk. I had not seen a Canadian spring in thirty years and I had forgotten how colourful the trees were. The flowering crab-apple's pink and crimson; the horse chestnut with its miniature white Christmas trees. And all kinds of maples.

I was walking through a suburb, several cars were beside each house, but no sidewalks.

I walked on the road.

A car drove up, on the opposite side, and stopped. A man got out. He stared at me. Perhaps because I was walking. As I came opposite I called out. "Why didn't they build sidewalks?"

"I'll only be a minute," he said nervously. And ran inside the nearest house.

"This is Hannah," Miriam said.

And I was introduced to a handsome woman in her late fifties: thinning red hair, brown eyes, high cheekbones, a pleasant face, but there was a certain arrogance.

The man opposite was Henry, a professor of Russian at the university. He was wearing jeans and a blue sports shirt. I felt over-dressed in a grey suit. Miriam had on an expensive-looking sack dress in pastel colours. Edith had gone to New York for the weekend. In the other room the table was set.

We were sitting in the adjoining room. A blue Chagall of flowers was on the wall. And faded photographs of young women with attractive faces in old-fashioned clothes.

Henry was around my age. He spoke English with an accent. I told him that he looked very fit.

"I go jogging every morning. I play tennis. I swim. You realize you are the only Canadian here. Hannah comes from Poland. She came just after the war. I came a few years later. What Russian writers do you like?"

"Chekhov and Turgenev."

He smiled. "And what modern ones?"

"Babel, Mandelstam, Akhmatova."

"Yes," he said and kept smiling.

I felt my credentials were being examined.

"I have not long come back from Moscow," he said. "The status of a writer in Russia today is determined if he is allowed to visit the West. It is the highest accolade. It is higher than getting your book published."

And I remembered a Russian writer who came to see me in England. He was hitch-hiking. And it was pouring with rain.

"What are you doing?" I asked him.

"Right now, I'm doing an article on suicide in Dostoevsky. Then I will lecture on it."

We went to the other room and sat around the table. In front of each plate there were wine glasses and tall thin glasses with a yellow rose in them.

Miriam came in with a platter of bagels and croissants.

"Don't let them get cold," she called out, "they are delicious."

I sat next to Hannah. She told me she was leaving tomorrow for Israel. "I know a lot of people but I don't like staying with friends or relatives. I will stay in a hotel. My mother told me: Guests and fish stink after three days."

Miriam poured wine into the glasses.

"Why," Hannah asked, "is it so difficult at our age to find another person?"

"Once you have been married," Henry said, "when you meet someone who has also been married, you are both carrying trailers with you. It is this that makes it difficult."

"But people do marry again," Miriam said.

Then Hannah told us how someone she knew got out from Eastern Europe. "He was running across the border when he heard a whistle. He didn't turn around. He kept running. Then he heard the whistle again. He kept running. He expected shots. When he got to the other side he heard the whistle again. And saw it was a bird."

Hannah took a croissant.

"I don't know why," she said, "but people from Europe that I meet in Canada seem to be smaller. I don't mean in size."

"Because in Europe," Henry said, "things are small and intimate, therefore the importance of a person is exaggerated. And over there people talk better."

Miriam brought in ice cream with a hot chocolate sauce. Then waited until she had everyone's attention. "Today," she said with a smile, "I would like us to talk about happiness."

"You cannot generalize about happiness," Henry said. "What is true for one person is not true for another."

"With the truth you can go around the world," Hannah said. "My mother told me that."

"What is happiness for you?" Miriam asked.

"Moments," I said. "You're lucky when they come."

"For me," said Miriam, "it is getting to know another person."

"But Miriam, don't you agree," I said, "that it is impossible, really, to know anyone else at all. At the most it is just speculation."

"It's living with another person," Hannah said. "That's what people can't do without. Once you've had that you want it again."

"On a visit to a mental hospital," I said, "I met a patient. She was in there a long time. She was in there because she was always happy. If someone she liked died. She laughed."

Miriam suddenly stood up. "Such a nice day," she smiled. "Why don't we go for a walk."

So we did, the four of us. We walked on the road in the sunshine. Then Hannah said she had to leave as she had to pack. And Henry became restless. He said to me: "Can I drive you to where you live?"

When he had gone to get the car Miriam said. "Henry must be lonely. He is always the last one to leave a party."

The book came out and the publisher arranged a promotion tour. Everywhere I was taken to be interviewed there was a young rabbi ahead of me. He was being interviewed because he claimed to be "an authority on Death." There was also a singer making the same tour. In Vancouver she said, I love Vancouver. In Calgary, I love Calgary. I love Ottawa, I love Montreal ... it's beautiful, beautiful. A man from the States said: "I fell in love with Canada. I changed my nationality. I'm going to die here." People were going around saying "I ... I ... I ..." At the end of the week I felt I had given enough radio and TV interviews to satisfy a minor Head of State. But when an article appeared in the *Globe* I had a phone call.

"Do you remember Archie Carter from McGill?"

"Of course," I said, recognizing his voice and seeing a tall man with dark straight hair, thin lips, a sharp nose, a sharp jaw. He used to be an athlete, then something happened, for he had a limp. In our last year at McGill, Archie Carter started a small recording business. He got me to interview visitors as if they were visiting celebrities. Then they would buy the record to take home. In return Archie let me make recordings of the poems of Thomas Hardy.

"Can you come and see me, or are you busy?"

"Of course I'll come."

"Today?"

"Yes."

He gave me his address.

It brought me to an expensive high-rise opposite a grove of young birches. A doorman, his war medals on a pale blue uniform, saluted me.

I pressed the button outside Archie's door. He called out. "Prepare yourself for a shock." "I'm not the same either," I shouted back. When he opened the door I didn't recognize him. He was bald. He had put on weight. All those sharp features were gone. Only his voice was the same. And I wondered what he was seeing in my face.

We shook hands. He led me into a room with a glass wall overlooking the birches. He limped more than I remembered.

"What would you like to drink? I only have Italian wine. But it's a good one."

He came back from the kitchen with two glasses of red wine. We drank in silence.

"I have three daughters," I said. "When they were small a friend from London, a painter, would come to see us once a year. When he arrived he would give the three of them five pounds in separate envelopes. The last time he came he only had two envelopes. He had forgotten the youngest. So he quickly asked me for an envelope and a piece of paper. As I went to get them the youngest ran into another room. I could hear her crying. I thought she was crying because he had forgotten her. So I went in to tell her that people often forget ... But the tears were trickling down her face. And she was sobbing. *He's got old. He's got old.*"

"I'm not a failure," Archie said.

"In the end Archie we're all failures."

"Oh, I don't know about that. Do you like the wine?"

"Yes."

"I'm in love with Italy," he said. "The food, the climate. Everything. I go there every two years ... I got this foot in Italy. I was leading my company. A mortar bomb hit me. They had to remove the ankle."

"What happened after McGill?"

"I taught English for a while. Then I began to paint. I'll show you the paintings later." He paused. "Of course I'm mad." And paused again to see what I would say. I said nothing. "When it's bad it's just boring. It was the pain from the wound that brought it on. The first time was in the hospital ship going back from Italy to England. The next time was fifteen years ago."

"What happened –?"

He hesitated. "It's because I have an economic theory that I believe will cure the world's economic problems." He hesitated again and smiled. He had a pleasant smile. "I believe we wouldn't have inflation or unemployment or high prices – things would be more abundant and we would be a lot happier – if people didn't *gyp* one another."

"Did they put you into a mental hospital for that?"

"I went to Lakefield," he said, "before McGill. Some of my friends are ambassadors – people like that – scattered all over. I called up Cairo, Amsterdam, London – and told them about this theory."

"That still doesn't seem bad enough to be put away."

"But I called them at two in the morning. Some of them became concerned and called the police. It was the police who brought me in ... I thought at this point I was a genius. The hospital I was in was full of people who thought they were geniuses."

He filled the glasses with more wine.

"A nurse in the hospital tried to make me pee. She got a jug full of water and emptied it into an empty jug. So I could see and hear it. She kept repeating this. I still couldn't go. But the other patients, who had been watching, all wet their beds.

"I have invented a word-game that I intend to put on the market. I still think I'm not a failure, you know. But I must not forget. I must call this number." And he took out an envelope. And dialled very determinedly. "There is a studio going. And I must get this woman before she lets it to someone else."

He let the phone ring a long time before he hung up.

"What was I saying?"

"What happened after you came out of hospital?"

"I began to paint. My shrink quite likes them." He brought several small canvases from his bedroom. They were gentle landscapes of fields and trees by a river. "What do you think?"

"I like the colours."

"I better phone that woman or else that studio will go. And I need a studio."

He dialled. No response.

"Remind me to try again."

"Yes," I said.

"It's good you are in Toronto. We have lots to talk about."

"I'm going to England," I said.

He looked disappointed.

"But I'm coming back."

I got up. "I'll ring when I get back."

"Fine. I better call that woman again."

He took out the envelope. We shook hands. And I left him dialling the number.

On the way back I saw Mrs. Kronick.

"What have you been doing?" I asked.

"I was walking down Yonge Street,' she said, "and I thought of the people I knew who are dead. What have I done with my life?"

I didn't know what to answer.

"You have a son," I said.

"Yes," she said gently. "That's what I have done with my life."

The two sisters continued to ask me to small parties that they arranged for people separated or divorced. But I met Helen in the supermarket. I could not find the roasted peanuts in their shells. She was standing near by. I asked her. And she walked over to show me where they were.

She was tall. Light blue eyes, a small fine nose, a small mouth, colour in her cheeks, short blonde hair with a fringe. She smiled easily and had a pleasant voice. Because I detected a trace of an English accent in it I said.

"Where in England are you from?"

"Devon – from Exeter."

"How long have you been here?"

"Thirty-four years."

"I've not long come from England."

The next time I saw her was in a small cemetery. I was coming from my publisher. She was arranging flowers by a stone. "I don't come here often," she said. "It's my husband's birthday."

"Shall we go and have some coffee?"

"My car is here," she said. "Why don't we go home."

There were oil paintings on the wall, books, and black-and-white photographs of a handsome-looking man.

"He was a very private person," she said. "It's almost four years. He had come back from a business trip when he had a heart attack."

She made me a cheese and tomato sandwich.

"I met Jimmy during the war. He was with the RCAF. We got married when the war was over and he brought me to Toronto. Then Jimmy's father died. And he had to run the family business. We had a very good marriage for almost thirty years."

Then she told me about her early life in England. How she was brought up by two grandmothers. The one in the city ran a theatre. The other, in the country, was a farmer's wife.

"Why don't you write it down," I said. "It would make a good book."

"I wouldn't know how to go about it."

"Talk into a tape recorder.'

"I can talk to you," she said. "Leave me a photograph. That will help."

"No, I'll come up."

That's how it started. Twice a week I would leave the apartment and go there in the late afternoon. She would give me a drink. And talk into the tape. And I would ask her questions and she would answer. Then she would give me dinner. And do another hour of talking into the tape.

One evening there was a thunderstorm.

"Why not stay the night," she said. "There's a bed in the spare room or you can sleep with me."

As I got into bed she said.

"I bruise easily."

Later she said. "I wanted you to know that you had a choice."

Did I have a choice, I wondered.

It was very pleasant having breakfast together. Then walking in the early morning, down Yonge Street.

After two weeks Helen said. "Why don't you move in here. One room could be your study and where you work."

"I'll have to go to England first and settle things. Then I'll come back."

"The sooner the better," she said.

The two sisters decided to buy a small coffee and cake store for their children. But the children were hardly there. Only Edith and Miriam. And they seemed to be enjoying themselves. As I came in Edith said. "You must have a croissant. They are the best in Toronto ..."

"Did you know Nick will be leaving us?"

"No," I said. "But why?"

"He takes too many days off. He doesn't do his work."

Miriam came in. "You're just the person I want to see. We are having a small party on Saturday night. There will be some interesting people. Henry will be there –"

"I have come to say goodbye."

"I don't like goodbyes," said Edith.

"Ella Fitzgerald used to sing," I said:

*Every time we say goodbye*
*I die, a little.*
*Every time we say goodbye*
*I wonder why, a little.*

"That's Lamartine," Edith said. *"Chaque fois qu'on se dit, au revoir, Je meurs un peu* – imagine being in a store like this in Toronto and quoting Lamartine."

"I'm sure that in small stores in Toronto – Czechs are quoting from Czech writers. Italians, Hungarians, are doing the same. The Portuguese here are quoting from Portuguese poets –" when I noticed grey airplanes in the sky. I could see them from the store window. They were coming in all directions. I counted a Dakota, six Mustangs with their clipped wings, two Bostons, a Lightning, a Tiger Moth, another Dakota.

"They're airplanes from the Second World War," I said.

"It must be from a museum," Miriam said in her flat voice.

I watched the low flying planes. They looked so slow. Then they began to circle as if they were going to land.

I went outside to watch the airplanes and saw Nick coming across the car park. He was carrying a loaded shopping bag from the supermarket. I wanted to tell him about the airplanes. But he had his face down. As he came closer I could see tears in his eyes. I thought it was because he had lost his job.

"Tito is dead," he said. And walked by.

The airplanes had disappeared. There was not a trace of their presence. Only a seagull flew low between two high-rises.

I was walking by the store that showed the time in the capitals of Europe when I saw Mrs. Kronick on her way back to the apartment. She had on a smart black-and-white suit and a large black hat.

"I'm leaving, Mrs. Kronick."

She looked at me for a while. Then said.

"When I leave a person. I don't care if I never see them again."

"But what about those you love?"

"Of course," she said, "with those you love there's always regret."

On Yonge Street, opposite the main library, I stopped a taxi. It took me to the airport.

# GWENDOLYN MACEWEN

# House of the Whale

Of course I was never a whale; I was an Eagle. This prison is a cage for the biggest bird of all. I'm waiting for them to work their justice, you see, and while I'm waiting I'm writing to you, Aaron, good friend, joker. The hours pass quickly here, strange to say; I have all kinds of diversions. The nice fat guard with the bulbous nose and the starfish wart at the tip often greets me as he makes his rounds. I make a point of waiting at the front of the cell when I know he's coming. And then there's Mario in the next cell who taps out fascinating rhythms at night with his fingernails against the walls.

I don't have an eraser with me, Aaron, so any mistakes I make will have to stay as they are, and when the pencil wears down, that will be that.

I can't help thinking how young I still am – 23. Twenty-three. Can I tell you about my life again? It was normal at first. I wrenched my mother's legs apart and tore out of her belly, trailing my sweet house of flesh behind me. I lay on a whaleskin blanket and watched the water; I sucked milk; I cried. I was wrapped up in thick bearskin in winter. I was bathed in the salt water of the sea. My mother was taller than all the mountains from where I lay.

There were the Ravens and the Eagles. You already know which I was. When I was old enough to take notice of things around me, I saw the half-mile line of our houses facing the waters of Hecate Strait. And I saw the severe line of the totems behind them, guarding the village, facing the sea – some of them vertical graves for the dead chiefs of old. Some totems, even then, had fallen, but our Eagle still looked down on us from the top of the highest one, presiding over the angular boats on the beach, the rotting cedar dugouts and black poplar skiffs. (Someone ages before had suggested getting motors for them – the boats, that is – and the old men of the village almost died.)

I was turned over to my uncle's care after I passed infancy, and he spoke to me in the Skittegan tongue and told me tales in the big cedar-plank house. I've long since forgotten the language, you know that, but the stories remain with me, for stories are pictures, not words. I learned about the Raven, the Bear, the Salmon-Eater and the Volcano Woman – just as your children someday will learn all about Moses or Joshua or Christ.

I never knew my father; after planting me in my mother's belly he left to go and work in the Commercial Fisheries on the mainland. He forsook the wooden hooks and cuttlefish for the Canneries – who could blame him? Secretly, I admired him and all those who left the island to seek a fortune elsewhere, to hook Fate through the gills. But he never came back.

Our numbers had once been in the thousands but had dwindled to hundreds. My grandfather, who was very old, remembered the smallpox that once stripped the islands almost clean. He remembered how the chiefs of the people were made to work in the white man's industries with the other men of the tribe, regardless of their rank; he remembered how the last symbols of authority were taken away from the chiefs and *shamans*. A chief once asked the leader of the white men if he might be taken to *their* island, England, to speak with the great white princess, Victoria – but he was refused.

Sometimes I heard my grandfather cursing under his breath the Canneries and hop fields and apple orchards on the mainland. I think he secretly wished that the Sacred-One-Standing-and-Moving who reclined on a copper box supporting the pillar that held the world up would shift his position and let the whole damn mess fall down.

When I was young some of our people still carved argillite to earn extra money. It was a dying art even then, but the little slate figures always brought something on the commercial market. The Slatechuk quarry up Slatechuk creek was not far from Skidegate; and there was an almost inexhaustible supply of the beautiful black stone, which got shaped into the countless figures of our myths. I remember having seen Louis Collison, the last of the great carvers, when I was still a child. I watched his steady gnarled hands creating figures and animals even I didn't know about, and I used to imagine that there was another Louis Collison, a little man, who lived inside the argillite and worked it from the inside out.

(The fine line, Aaron, between what is living and what is dead ... what do I mean, exactly? That party you took me to once in that rich lady's house where everyone was admiring her latest artistic acquisition – a *genuine Haida* argillite sculpture. It illustrated the myth of Rhpisunt, the woman who slept with a bear and later on bore cubs, and became the Bear Mother. Well, there were Rhpisunt and the bear screwing away in the black slate; Rhpisunt lay on her back, legs up, straddling the beast, her head thrown back and her jaws wide open with delight – and Mrs. What's-Her-Name kept babbling on and on about the 'symbolic' meaning of the carving until I got mad and butted in and told her it was obviously a bear screwing a woman, nothing more, nothing less. She looked upset, and I was a little drunk and couldn't resist adding, "You see, I too am *genuine Haida*." And as the party wore on I kept looking back at the elaborate mantelpiece and the cool little slate sculpture, and it was dead, Aaron, it had *died* – do you see?)

My mother wove baskets sometimes and each twist and knot in the straw was another year toward her death. And she sometimes lit the candlefish, the *oolakan* by night, and we sat around its light, the light of the sea, the light of its living flesh. Sometimes the old *shaman* would join us, with his dyed feathers and rattles, and do magic. I saw souls and spirits rising from his twisted pipe; I saw all he intended me to see, though most of the people left in the village laughed at him, secretly of course.

My grandfather was so well versed in our legends and myths that he was always the man sought out by the myth-hunters – museum researchers and writers from the mainland – to give the Haida version of such-and-such a tale. My last memory of him, in fact, is of him leaning back in his chair and smoking his pipe ecstatically and telling the tale of Gunarh to the little portable tape recorder that whirred beside him. Every researcher went away believing he alone had the authentic version of such-and-such a myth, straight from the Haida's mouth – but what none of them ever knew was that grandfather altered the tales with each re-telling. "It'll give them something to fight about in their books," he said. The older he got, the more he garbled the tales, shaking with wicked laughter in his big denim overalls when the little men with tape recorders and notebooks went away.

Does he think of me now, I wonder? Is he still alive, or is he lying in a little Skidegate grave after a good Christian burial – a picture of an eagle on the marble headstone as a last reminder of the totem of his people? Is he celebrating his last *potlache* before the gates of heaven; and has the *shaman* drummed his long dugout through waves of clouds? Are the ceremonial fires burning now, and is my grandfather throwing in his most precious possessions – his blue denim overalls, his pipe?

(Remember, Aaron, how amazed you were when I first told you about the *potlache*? "Why didn't the chiefs just *exhibit* their wealth?" you argued, and I told you they felt they could prove their wealth better by demonstrating how much of it they could *destroy*. Then you laughed, and said you thought the *potlache* had to be the most perfect parody of capitalism and consumer society you'd ever heard of. "What happened," you asked, "if a chief threw away everything he owned and ended up a poor man?" And I explained how there were ways of becoming rich again – for instance, the bankrupt chief could send some sort of gift to a rival chief, knowing that the returned favour had to be greater than the original one. It was always a matter of etiquette among our people to outdo another man's generosity.)

Anyway, I lie here and imagine grandfather celebrating a heavenly *potlache* – (heaven is the only place he'll ever celebrate it, for it was forbidden long ago by the government here on earth) – and the great Christian gates are opening for him now, and behind him the charred remains of his pipe and his blue denims bear witness to the last *potlache* of all.

Some of my childhood playmates were children of the white teacher and doctor of Skidegate, and I taught them how to play *Sin*, where you shuffle marked sticks under a mat and try to guess their positions. They got sunned up in summer until their skins were as copper as mine; we sat beneath the totems and compared our histories; we sat by the boats and argued about God. I read a lot; I think I must have read every book in the Mission School. By the time I was fifteen I'd been to the mainland twice and come back with blankets, potato money, and booze for the old *shaman*.

I began to long for the mainland, to see Vancouver, the forests of Sitka spruce in the north, mountains, railroads, lumber camps where Tsimsyan and Niskae workers felled trees and smashed pulp. My uncle had nothing to say when I announced that I was going to go and work at "the edge of the world" – but my grandfather put up a terrific fight, accusing me of wanting to desert my people for the white man's world, accusing my mother of having given birth to a feeble-spirited fool because on the day of my birth she accepted the white man's pain-killer and lay in "the sleep like death" when I came from her loins. And then he went into a long rambling tale of a day the white doctor invited the *shaman* in to witness his magic, and the *shaman* saw how everything in the doctor's room was magic white, to ward off evil spirits from sick flesh, and he saw many knives and prongs shining like the backs of salmon and laid out in neat rows on a white sheet; from this he understood that the ceremony wouldn't work unless the magical pattern of the instruments was perfect. Then the doctor put the sick man into the death-sleep, and the *shaman* meanwhile tried to slip the sick soul into his bone-box, but he couldn't because the doctor's magic was too powerful to be interfered with. It was only when the doctor laid out exactly four knives and four prongs onto another white sheet, that the *shaman* realized the doctor had stolen the sacred number four from us to work his magic.

I worked north in a lumber camp for a while; we were clearing a patch of forest for an airplane base. In one year I don't know how many trees I killed – too many, and I found myself whispering "Sorry, tree" every time I felled another one. For *that* I should be in prison – wouldn't you think? Wasn't it worse to destroy all those trees than do what I did? Oh well, I can see you're laughing in your beer now, and I don't blame you. Anyway, I really wanted to tell you about Jake and the other guys in the bunkhouse, and what a great bunch they were. I learned a lot about girls and things from them, and since I didn't have any stories of my own like that to tell them, I told them the myth of Gunarh – you know the one; you said the first part of it is a lot like a Greek myth – and all the guys gathered round, and Jake's mouth was hanging open by the time I got to the part about Gunarh's wife eating nothing but the genitals of male seals...

   "Then she took a lover," I went on, "and her husband discovered her infidelity and made a plan."

   "Yea, yea, go on, he made a *plan*!" gasped Jake.

   "He –"

   "SHADDUP YOU GUYS, I'M TRYING TO LISTEN!"

   "When they were asleep after a hard night, the lover and the wife ..."

   "Hear that, guys – a HARD night!"

   "Jake will ya SHADDUP!"

   " – Gunarh came in and discovered them together. He killed the lover and cut off his head and his –"

   "Jesus CHRIST!"

"Jake will ya SHADDUP!"

" – and put them on the table ..."

"Put *what* on the table?"

"It ain't the *head*, boys!"

"Jesus CHRIST!"

"So the next morning his wife found her lover gone, and she went to the table for breakfast – you remember what she usually ate – and instead of ..."

"O no! I'm sick, you guys, I'm sick!"

"SHADDUP!"

" – well, she ate *them* instead."

"Jake, will ya lie down if you can't take it?"

I never did finish the story, because they went on and on all night about what Gunarh's wife ate for breakfast, and Jake kept waking up and swearing he was never going to listen to one of my stories again, because it was for sure all Indians had pretty dirty minds to think up things like that.

Almost before I knew it, my year was up and I was on a train heading for Vancouver; the raw gash I'd made in the forest fell back behind me.

At first I spent a week in Vancouver watching the people carry the city back and forth in little paper bags; I stayed in a strange room with a shape like a big creamy whale in the cracked plaster on the ceiling, and curtains coloured a kind of boxcar red which hung limply and never moved. I drank a lot and had some women and spent more money than I intended, and after standing three mornings in a row in a line-up in the Unemployment Office, I bumped into you, Aaron, remember, and that was the beginning of our friendship. You had a funny way of looking at a person a little off-centre, so I was always shuffling to the left to place myself in your line of focus. I can't remember exactly what we first talked about; all I know is, within an hour we'd decided to hitch-hike to Toronto, and that was that. At first I hesitated, until you turned to me, staring intently at my left ear, and said, "Lucas George, you don't want to go back to Skidegate, you're coming east." And it was that careless insight of yours that threw me. You always knew me well, my friend. You knew a lot, in fact – and sometimes I was sure you kept about fifty percent of your brain hidden because it complicated your life. You were always a little ahead of yourself – was that the reason for your nervousness, your impatience? You could always tell me what I was thinking, too. You told me I was naive and you liked me for that. You predicted horrible things for me, and you were right. You said my only destiny was to lose myself, to become neither Indian nor white but a kind of grey nothing, floating between two worlds. Your voice was always sad when you spoke like that...

Hey Aaron, do you still go through doors so quickly that no one remembers seeing you open them first?

My grandfather's tales, if he's still alive, are growing taller in Skidegate. My mother's baskets, if she's still alive, are getting more and more complicated – and the salmon are skinnier every season. My time's running out, and I'd better finish this letter fast.

You were silent in B.C. but you talked all the way through Alberta and Saskatchewan; we slept through Manitoba and woke up in Ontario. The shadows of the totems followed me, growing longer as the days of my life grew longer. The yellow miles we covered were nothing, and time was even less.

"Lucas," you turned to me, "I forgot to tell you something. In B.C. you were still something. Here, you won't even exist. You'll live on the sweet circumference of things, looking into the centre; you'll be less than a shadow or a ghost. Thought you'd like to know."

"Thanks for nothing," I said. "Anyway, how do *you* know?"

"I live there too, on the circumference," you said.

"What do you do, exactly?"

"I'm an intellectual bum," you answered. "I do manual work to keep my body alive. Sometimes I work above the city, sometimes I work below the city, depending on the weather. Skyscrapers, ditches, subways, you name it, I'm there ..."

Aaron, I only have a minute left before they turn the lights out for the night. I wanted to ask you...

Too late, they're out.


"Well," you said, the first day we were in the city, "Welcome to the House of the Whale, Lucas George."

"What do you mean?" I said.

"Didn't you tell me about Gunarh and how he went to the bottom of the sea to rescue his wife who was in the House of the Whale?"

"Yes, but –"

"Well, I'm telling you *this* is the House of the Whale, this city, this place. Ask me no questions and I'll tell you no lies. This. This is where you'll find your *psyche*."

"My *what?*"

"This is where you'll find what you're looking for."

"But, Aaron, I'm not looking for anything really!"

"Oh yes you are ..."

We stood looking at City Hall with its great curving mothering arms protecting a small concrete bubble between them. Behind us was Bay Street and I turned and let my eyes roll down the narrow canyon toward the lake. "That's the Wall Street of Toronto," you said. "Street of Money, Street of Walls. Don't worry about it; you'll never work there."

"So what's down there?" I asked, and you pointed a finger down the Street of Walls and said, "That's where the whales live, Lucas George. You know all about them, the submerged giants, the supernatural ones ..."

"The whales in our stories were gods," I protested. And you laughed.

"I wish I could tell you that this city was just another myth, but it's not. It smacks too much of reality."

"Well *what else*!' I cried, exasperated with you. "First it's a whale house, then you want it to be a myth – couldn't it just be a city, for heaven's sake?"

"Precisely. That's precisely what it is. Let's have coffee."

We walked past the City Hall and I asked you what the little concrete bubble was for.

"Why that's the egg, the seed," you said.

"Of *what?*"

"Why, Lucas George, I'm surprised at you! Of the *whale*, of course! Come on!"

"Looks like a clamshell to me," I said. "Did I ever explain to you where mankind came from, Aaron? A clamshell, half open, with all the little faces peering out ..."

"I'll buy that," you said. "It's a clamshell. Come on!"

I got a job in construction, working on the high beams of a bank that was going up downtown. "Heights don't bother you Indians at all, do they?" the foreman asked me. "No," I said. "We like tall things."

He told me they needed some riveting work done on the top, and some guys that had gone up couldn't take it – it was too high even for them. So I went up, and the cold steel felt strange against my skin and I sensed long tremors in the giant skeleton of the bank, and it was as though the building was alive, shivering, with bones and sinews and tendons, with a life of its own. I didn't trust it, but I went up and up and there was wind all around me. The city seemed to fall away and the voices of the few men who accompanied me sounded strangely hollow and unreal in the high air. There were four of us – a tosser to heat the rivets and throw them to the catcher who caught them in a tin cup and lowered them with tongs into their holds – a riveter who forced them in with his gun, and a bucker to hold a metal plate on one end of the hole. They told me their names as the elevator took us to the top – Joe, Charlie, Amodeo. I was the bucker.

Amodeo offered me a hand when we first stepped out onto a beam, but I couldn't accept it, although the first minute up there was awful. I watched how Amodeo moved; he was small and agile and treated the beams as though they were solid ground. His smile was swift and confident. I *did* take his hand later, but only to shake it after I had crossed the first beam. I kept telling myself that my people were the People of the Eagle so I of all men should have no fear to walk where the eagles fly. Nevertheless when we ate lunch, the sandwich fell down into my stomach a long long way as though my stomach was still on the ground somewhere, and my throat was the elevator that had carried us up.

I found that holding the metal plate over the rivet holes gave me a kind of support and I was feeling confident and almost happy until the riveter came along and aimed his gun and WHIRR-TA-TA-TAT, WHIRR-TA-TA-TAT! My spine was jangling and every notch in it felt like a metal disc vibrating against another metal disc.

After a while, though, I got the knack of applying all sorts of pressure to the plate to counteract some of the vibration. And when the first day was over I was awed to think I was still alive. The next day I imagined that the bank was a huge totem, or the strong man Aemaelk who holds the world up, and I started to like the work.

I didn't see you much those days for I was tired every night, but once I remember we sat over coffee in a restaurant and there was an odd shaky light in your eyes, and you looked sick. A man at a nearby table was gazing out onto the street, dipping a finger from time to time into his coffee and sucking it. I asked you why he was so sad. "He's not a whale," you answered.

"Then what is he?" I asked.

"He's a little salmon all the whales are going to eat," you said. "Like you, like me."

"Where are you working now, Aaron?"

"In a sewer. You go up, Lucas, and I go down. It fits. Right now I'm a mole and you're the eagle."

Aaron, I've got to finish this letter right now. I don't have time to write all I wanted to, because my trial's coming up and I already know how it's going to turn out. I didn't have time to say much about the three years I spent here, about losing the job, about wandering around the city without money, about drinking, about fooling around, about everything falling round me like the totems falling, about getting into that argument in the tavern, and the fat man who called me a dirty Indian, about how I took him outside into a lane and beat him black and blue and seeing his blood coming out and suddenly he was dead. You know it all anyway, there's no point telling it again. Listen, Aaron, what I want to know now is:

Is my grandfather still telling lies to the history-hunters in Skidegate?

Are the moles and the eagles and the whales coming out of the sewers and subways and buildings now it's spring?

Have all the totems on my island fallen, or do some still stand?

Will they stick my head up high on a cedar tree like they did to Gunarh?

Will the Street of Walls fall down one day like the totems?

What did you say I would find in the House of the Whale, Aaron? Aaron? Aaron?

# CARY FAGAN

# Figuring Her Commission

"I don't see how you add the figures up to ten dollars," he said. "I don't see that at all."

They sat together in the bright subway car, their seats facing backwards so that they could see the tunnel pulling away as the train left the station. He was tall and lean, a narrow head and rough skin. His hair was too long for the new fashion and his moustache drooped past the corners of his mouth. Over an imitation silk shirt he wore a black vest that hung on his shoulders as he leaned forward, his elbows pointing on his knees, his fingers winding and unwinding. She sat next to him, straight upright in a pink dress. She had a round face covered in pale freckles and wispy hair.

The train lurched to a halt at Dundas. A young man got in, with a straggly student's beard, the kind friends make fun of. He sat down opposite the two and pulled a book out of his back pocket.

"I'm sure it's ten dollars," she said. "That's my commission today." Her faint voice hardly carried.

He watched through the back window of the car and pulled in his lips. "I sold three boxes today," he said. "You got me two of them, right? How could that be ten dollars? " He spoke in a deliberate manner, without raising his voice, as if he wanted to make sure that every word came out perfectly.

"It's got to be," she insisted, and then, as if to prove her point, "I need ten dollars more to buy that pair of shoes."

The student looked up from his book.

"Look," the man said, making a sharp movement with his hand. "We'll work this out. I sold three boxes today, and you got me two of them on the phone. Correct? At two dollars a box, that's four dollars commission for you. I don't see any way it could be ten dollars."

"It can't be only four dollars," she said, looking down at the floor and pouting.

He breathed in audibly, the expression on his face slightly changing, hardening. He turned his head away from her for a moment, then turned it back. Patience. "You got two boxes. I get five dollars a box, you get two dollars a box. That is four dollars owing to you."

"I got three boxes."

"What?"

"I did. I got three boxes today."

"Well, I only saw two."

"I put it on your desk."

He spoke slowly, exactly. "Then perhaps you got three. If that is the case it will be on my desk tomorrow. But that makes six dollars, not ten."

She rubbed her nose with her hand. "I just don't want to be ripped off."

"Who is ripping you off?"

She studied her feet, pointing her toes together. "Nobody."

"You work for me, don't you? So if somebody's ripping you off it has to be me. Are you accusing me of cheating you?"

He glanced over at the student. The student looked down at his book. "Yes, you are accusing me. It makes me very angry.

Everything you get comes from me. Those six dollars you wouldn't have earned without me. And you are accusing me of stealing. Accusing!" He formed the word like a nail in his mouth.

"No, I'm not," she said, her voice fainter than before.

"We will discuss this later," he said. "After I have had an hour to relax. I am in no condition to talk about this anymore right now."

"Okay."

They sat in the subway car, not speaking. The train stopped at Bloor and the doors opened. A girl and a boy carrying roller skates over their shoulders got in and walked to the front of the car. On the boy's head was a cap with a pair of golden wings on it. The student turned a page in his book. The doors closed and the train jerked forward.

She said, "I'm owed one box from last week."

"When? I paid you last week."

"I only got paid for one box on Wednesday, but I got two."

He remained silent a moment, calculating. "Perhaps I do owe you one for Wednesday. The box for Ferguson. That means I owe you eight dollars at the most. But not ten."

"And you owe me one for the week before."

"No I don't."

"Yes you do."

"What was the name?"

She giggled. "I can't remember."

"Look," he gripped the side of the seat with his hand. "You know I don't keep a written record of who gets what, I don't write everything down. There's no proof. We always figure things out."

"I just don't want to get ripped off," she said.

He turned away, checking himself, holding his body still. "You are accusing me again. I can't believe it."

"I'm not."

"Now I am very, very angry," he said, his voice rising just a little. "You better not talk about it anymore. That is my advice to you. You see that seat over there? I am so angry I want to punch that seat with my fist."

She shrugged. "Why don't you punch the wall beside you," she said helpfully.

"Because," he spoke as if she were very young or very stupid, "if I punch the wall I will hurt my hand."

"I think my commission is ten dollars."

"Did you not hear me? I said we won't discuss this anymore now. I am saying this for your benefit. We will figure it out later. You don't know how angry you have made me."

She looked into her lap.

"I wasn't accusing you," she said.

"Move over," he said with disgust, waving her away with his hand. "Just move over." She obeyed, shifting herself over to the window.

The train shunted from station to station. St. Clair. Davisville. Eglinton.

"Danny," she said, "I got a hole in these shoes."

"I'm not talking right now."

"Okay, Danny."

The train stopped at Lawrence and the doors slid open. She was looking out of the window. He got up quickly and went out through the doors. Not noticing him leave for a moment, she had to scurry after him before the doors closed.

The student watched them leave, turning his head to see them until the train pulled out of the station. The boy with the winged cap was spinning the wheels of his roller skate with one hand.

# CYNTHIA FLOOD

# Beatrice

My parents died stupidly in a car crash when I was fourteen. No one was surprised to learn that the fault was my father's. I already knew he was ineffectual, that he and my mother were soft and blurry instead of clear-edged and definite like the parents of the popular boys at school. I would watch as these beings emerged from their glossy cars on prize days and at half-terms and strode to meet their offspring, and then would see our old Morris coming slowly round the curve of the drive, my father peering through the windshield – of course the wipers were not working – and looking as though he had never visited this part of England before. Their deaths and my grief were a drama in the school. "Speeding, I suppose?" the boys asked admiringly, when such questions could decently be put. I said, "Yes," because I could not bear the truth, that my father had caused the crash by driving too slowly. Soon however the drama heightened. I was to leave the school, leave England, and go to Canada to live with my mother's sister, my Aunt Beatrice. The éclat of this news carried me through almost to the end of term when everyone lost interest in Hugh Proctor for the simple reason, apparent to all except myself, that I wasn't going to be back and they were. I felt even worse than just after the funeral, yet I never dreamt of trying to get out of going to Canada. Arrangements had been made. I was most miserable. In this state I boarded the plane that flew me to Malton Airport near Toronto in August 1959.

Nineteen years ago. More than half my life. Perhaps more than half my life is over now? Do workaholic lawyers make old bones? Do not-quite-alcoholic lawyers? My daughter, my daughter, think of her, at the very beginning of her life. Think of her lying up there on the fourth floor of the hospital, dark-haired, rosy in her rosy blanket in that odd plastic container they put new babies in. Imagine being able to say My daughter. (Do you have any children? Yes, I have a daughter.) I wonder if my parents felt anything like this when I was born. If they did I wasn't worth it. I have a feeling my mother would have liked a girl. She always loved her sister Beatrice very much. Admired her. "Beatie was always the one for doing things. We all thought it was so brave of her to go off on her own like that, after the War. Get this war over, and I'll be 'off to Canada to have adventures,' she always said. And then she really did it." How many times at home did I hear variations of this speech.

Aunt Beatie. The first clear understanding of her, after a month or so of dislocation and muddle in the new country. I am in a large meeting hall. Hundreds of people on cheap wooden chairs. Banners. Posters. Too much smoke, too few ashtrays. In front of the platform stretches a huge hand-painted paper banner reading Fair Play For Cuba. On the platform a fat, sweating young man is describing the evils of prostitution in pre-revolution Havana. This is not the first political meeting I have been to with Aunt Beatie. Already in one month with her I have heard more about politics than in the entire rest of my life, but still the main point has simply not sunk in. Tonight it does. The young man says quietly, "Now all that is changing," and these plain words make the crowd clap and cheer. But those people in Cuba are Communists, I think. Then these people are too. Then Aunt Beatie is. But she can't be a Red, she's my aunt. I turn and look at her. My body trembles with the power of what I have finally understood. She is folding her hands in her lap again, smiling gently. She could be a teacher at a girls' school. Curly pepper-and-salt hair, neat features, pale skin, glasses; a dark blue cotton dress, white summer sandals; composed, reserved, calm, what the hell is the word to describe that I-am-my-own-person air? There she is, and everything about her says she should be at the village concert to raise money for the restoration of the Norman arches in the church. But instead she's here cheering for some pinko peasants in a hot messy little country somewhere off the coast of the States.

Not that I expressed all that to myself then. All I could get clear that night was that I was in the charge of a Red and did not know what to do. I remember thinking I should run out of the hall and go to the police. All of which provides illustration of the subtle and complex ways in which ideology is transmitted. My parents had never discussed politics. I do not remember anything that could remotely be described as a political discussion at school, nor a history lesson that either (a) went beyond the Wars of the Roses or (b) dealt with those wars in anything except a first-there-was-this-battle-and-then-there-was-that-battle way. Yet from some unseen nipple I had sucked and absorbed and made my own every single conservative notion a fourteen-year-old boy could possibly have. I was profoundly shocked, the more so because Aunt Beatie was a woman.

Of course I did not go to the police. I stayed where I was, and in fact I lived with Aunt Beatie for over ten years.

I would be embarrassed to say how long a time went by before I gave any thought to the effect my sudden eruption into her life must have had on Aunt Beatie. My other relatives in England and the family lawyer had told me that I should be grateful to her for offering to provide a home for me. I obediently thanked her shortly after my arrival. But it still seemed to me that she had simply done the correct thing and there was nothing to be so impressed by. After all, I was only fourteen and could scarcely live on my own, could I? And she was family, wasn't she? After a while around the revolutionary party and around Harbord Collegiate, I learned that these to me logical sequences of thought were not at all so to others. Fourteen-year-olds could and did live on their own and blood ties meant very little to some people. These however were what I thought of as people with funny names. Thinking of them that way helped me to counter my sense of utter alienation. An uptight middle-class English schoolboy, late fifties model, dumped into the polyglot polychrome ferment of a downtown Toronto high school whose high standards were the springboard out of the ghetto, on to the campus, up the hill – I would have found Mars easier. I see I have again wandered away from Aunt Beatie, unable to resist talking about myself. Yet it was she who enabled me to make it at Harbord. I think she thought it was her responsibility. As a matter of fact I think her ideas about her responsibility for me weren't that different from mine, for all her revolutionary politics. I didn't know then how hard it can be just to do the correct thing.

Serious revolutionaries work very hard. Most have jobs or families or school or some combination thereof, and on top of that have a load of political activities that would break the back of a Percheron. Aunt Beatie got home from work (she was the supervisor of a pool of forty typists at the telephone company) around five-fifteen. We had dinner at half past. She would then leave for, say, a six o'clock executive meeting of the revolutionary group she belonged to. (Our, her, apartment was west of Spadina and north of College, near her group's headquarters – also near those of many other left-wing groups, for they all seemed to hole up in the same part of the city.) This meeting would last until perhaps half past seven. She and others would then leave for the political assignment/event of the evening: union meeting, branch meeting, outside group meeting, film series, lecture series, picket, fundraiser, whatever. She would get home about eleven and work for an hour or so before bed – revise an article or speech, do the books for some organization, read a couple of Marxist papers. We got up no later than six-thirty in the mornings, and sometimes Aunt Beatie would rise earlier to finish some task. This went on five days a week. Weekends were sometimes lighter, sometimes a lot heavier. She had to attend two-day conferences or series of classes, or sell the revolutionary press, or go on sub-drives. So I suddenly had to be included in this jam-packed schedule.

At the beginning especially I must have been an awful chore. I could dress myself and make my own bed, period. I had never cooked, cleaned, shopped, laundered, budgeted, and I despised these kinds of work because women did them. I truly thought Aunt Beatie was joking when she told me to set the table, turn on the oven, take out the garbage. Disbelief phased into outrage and there was confrontation. Of course I hadn't a hope against Aunt Beatie. Any woman who had been organizer of a large urban branch of a Trotskyist organization throughout the Cold War would have made short work of me and my adolescent sexism, and Aunt Beatie did so. By Christmas of 1959 I could prepare an adequate dinner and iron my shirts quite well. By the time I left high school I was an accomplished houseworker and in fact I made extra money in university by doing housework. I don't do it now, of course, Robyn doesn't like me to. It makes her feel funny to see me cleaning the floor. I know why, but we don't talk about it.

So Aunt Beatie had to train me as a co-inhabitant of her apartment. That took up her time and energy. She had to re-educate me about education, and so did that. I thought school was silly and boring. In my defence I will say that I can't think of a more awful bunch of teachers than those at the school in England my parents had mortgaged themselves to send me to. She also had to try to teach me to take my life seriously. I had no thought of what I might do when I was finished with school. I had no special bent to direct me. I suppose I had thought the grownups would suggest something when the time came. Aunt Beatie would not tolerate this aimless drifting. She made me talk about what I was learning in school. She argued with me. She suggested things I should ask my teachers. She criticized my papers after they were handed back to me. (Not before, because if I incorporated any suggestion of hers it would mean that the paper wasn't wholly my work and therefore the mark I got wouldn't really be mine either.) She got it into my head that as a minimal goal I must learn to do some sort of saleable labour so that I would not be dependent on anyone. She was of course firmly in favour of all forms of social assistance, unemployment insurance, etc., but to work was clearly best. I don't know whether it was the Marxism or the North Country-ish self-reliance which said that more strongly in her. It doesn't matter I suppose. Though it would have, to her. She hated political sloppiness.

Have I made her sound cold and strict? There was more than that. Once, soon after I arrived, she made us pancakes for Sunday breakfast. I had never seen or eaten such things and said I would rather have toast. I'm sure I said it in my snottiest oh-you-colonial tones, too, but she got the underneath sense. My homesickness and grief made this unfamiliar food just too much for me to take that morning. She put the batter in the fridge, kissed me warmly, and made me a pile of toast. Then she got me to take the toaster apart and clean out the crumbs, and I felt much better. Later on in that hard first year in Canada, at Harbord, I was struggling with Latin. In England I had learned to decline nouns using a certain order of cases, and in Canada another order was used; it sounds a small thing, but for a kid at school it's not. I kept making stupid mistakes in my translations because of this change. Aunt Beatie came home unexpectedly early one evening from a meeting and found me crying over my homework. She ignored my humiliation and got me to explain the problem. We discussed it while my face dried. The act of explaining helped. Time of course did the rest. A few weeks later Aunt Beatie said, "You know, Hugh, there's no shame in a man's crying. The tear ducts are presumably there to be used, eh? Crying's sometimes a good way to clear out your feelings. For man or woman." And she went on to something else.

I cried this morning when my daughter was born. I am wordless to say what I felt when she emerged from Robyn in that final quick bloody rush. She lay, small yet substantial, in the doctor's arms, gently moving her hands and feet. She gave that low cry and her eyes looked right through my head and past it through to some realm I don't even know about. What can you do with emotions of such power but let them have their way, and cry as they possess you?

That Aunt Beatie had an emotional and sexual life never occurred to me either. Like most teenagers entranced and obsessed and agonized by their emerging sexuality, I was revolted by the notion of anyone over perhaps twenty-five engaged in sex. Aunt Beatie was in her mid-thirties. She was my aunt. She was not married. Three taboos. If I'd been older I might have wondered how on earth she would find the time to get involved with anyone, or speculated about the quantities of men available who would appeal to a woman revolutionary. But I wasn't and didn't; so I was shocked one night when I got up to go to the bathroom and glanced in at Aunt Beatie's open bedroom door as I went past. There she was in her bed all right, but not reading as I had expected. She lay naked, with her back to me, in the arms of an equally naked comrade who had been at the meeting held in our living-room earlier that evening. They did not see me. On the way back from the bathroom (I did not flush, because of the noise) I stood by her door, terrified lest they should notice me passing it. I considered lying on the floor and crawling past. My embarrassment then achieved indescribable heights as I realized, from the passionate (though muted) sounds they were now making, that I could probably do the Highland fling in the doorway and they wouldn't notice. I slipped past, and back to my own empty couch. Aunt Beatie's was the first live unclothed female body I had ever seen. The curved pale line of hip-waist-back affected me powerfully, and I lay awake and active for some time.

Next morning at breakfast Aunt Beatie was calm and cheerful as usual. Comrade Stan ate his porridge and boiled egg placidly at our table as he had frequently done before. I had assumed that he and indeed any other visitors we had did their sleeping on the couch in the living-room; I felt much older than the day before and at the same time I felt silly and inexperienced. And I felt wicked because I had been aroused by my aunt. I got off to school as fast as possible. I think I was then sixteen.

Perhaps it was this incident that led me to look consciously at the people with whom Aunt Beatie spent her life when she was not at her job. To this point they had been simply "the comrades," a group of adults who were part of the backdrop of my life. The foreground increasingly was filled with other kids at school and by school activities I was finally getting into, having lost the worst of my English accent and having gotten rid of my ties and grey flannel trousers. I was an all-right student, not terrific but more than holding my own, and I had a mild aptitude for debate, which a fanatical coach was insisting that I develop. I looked forward to school now instead of dreading it. The idea of going to university was becoming interesting. But these comrades now, these people with whom my Aunt Beatie evidently had far deeper and more complex relations than I had understood, what were they really like? I passed them in review. I made no discoveries about their respective sex lives like that I'd made about Stan's, but I did reach one very solid conclusion: my Aunt Beatie was the best of the bunch by a wide margin.

The women – remember this was the very early sixties – generally fell into two categories: the housewife-helper of the bigshot Marxist, and the socialist sexpot. The men were more varied (there were far more of them of course). Thin hungry-looking office workers. Pudgy, brooding students. Elderly men with dried skins who walked softly so as not to wake the black-lung cough. Downwardly mobile envoys from Rosedale: these affected strange raiment, black capes and such. Big construction workers, their hands permanently crusted with chalky stuff. Literary types who always wanted to have forums on Christopher Caudwell instead of on the latest CCL convention.

Aunt Beatie's singularity and decorum set her off from the other women, and she was straightforward and truthful in a way that most of the leadership males weren't. There was no bombast in her.

When she said, "I hate the bosses," she meant it literally. She loathed her own boss – he was fifteen years younger than she and earned a third more – and she loathed all bosses. The passion with which she said these things was striking in the context of her general reserve.

When the women's liberation movement erupted into the branch, new kinds of women began to join. I suppose that for the first time in her years of commitment to the revolution Aunt Beatie had comrades she could really talk to. She was intensely admired by some of these younger women. They made her almost a matriarchal cult-figure for a while. They all wore jeans or pants, of course, and one day Aunt Beatie appeared at the hall wearing a neat denim pantsuit. They literally cheered her. "I've wanted to do it for years," she said, smiling. (Later she led and won a battle at work over wearing pants on the job.) After that she wore skirts and dresses only. Of course the political crush on her did not last. (Everything contains within it the seeds of its own destruction.) She was found to be sexually prudish, secretive, and too loyal to male organizational structures. All that came later, though.

One of the few issues on which many comrades openly criticized Aunt Beatie was her treatment of me. (Of course, no one spoke ill of her directly to me; but I overheard, guessed, saw enough to know that my aunt was ruthless in internal party struggle and that numerous members of the branch bore the scars to prove it.) They thought, and said, that she should be actively encouraging me to participate in revolutionary politics – join the youth group, write for the paper, and so on. There was a rough faction-fight in the branch during the mid-sixties (again and once again the "question of the NDP"), and I believe that some comrades then rumoured it that Aunt Beatie's own commitment to the party must be weakening, for otherwise would she not urge me to join? Some of the comrades were themselves red diaper babies. As infants they had slept on registration tables in meeting halls while their parents spoke and argued and raised funds for this and that leftist cause in the late thirties and during the war. As children they had helped to run off innumerable leaflets on the Gestetner in the basement. Now as teenagers or young adults they were getting their own files opened by the RCMP and finding their own way around the changing left in Toronto. They couldn't understand her refusal to pressure me. Aunt Beatie's reasons were as usual clear in her own mind.

"Hugh, your job now is to get through school and get trained at something. I've no patience with these young ones who're up half the night selling the press and then fail their Christmas exams. And then what? All to do again, or else sponge off their parents for years. Young workers, that's different. I wish we had more of them, the branch is middle-aged, mostly. But you do your work. When you're through there's time enough to get involved in the movement, and you'll be some use then because you'll know how to apply yourself. If you decide for the revolution, that is." But of course she never doubted that I would. And although I didn't join the youth group I was a regular at the party hall. I helped stuff envelopes and do phonings after my homework was done. I read two or three Marxist papers a week. I went round with the collection buckets or sold buttons at rallies on the weekends. Being a radical at Harbord was not remarkable. There was even a certain cachet to it, useful with girls.

I wonder what I will do about my daughter. Will she hate me when she grows up for having pushed her in one direction or another? Is it possible not to push? Is it desirable? Even if you don't actively push, isn't it obvious that given your inescapable example the child will get a very clear message about where you think the right road lies? But I don't want her on this road. I can't bear it if she hates me. I didn't know love could erupt this fast. Yesterday she was simply The Baby, and now she herself is here and thinking of her makes me ache. Aunt Beatie never had a baby. I certainly never hated her, although I have felt very miserable because of her.

She approved when I decided to go to university. Money for this was not a major problem because of the insurance arrangements my father had made. Typically, they were muddled and had taken some sorting out by the lawyer, but they paid for my education. Off I went to U. of T. in the fall of 1964. My four years there saw the rising of the student and black civil rights movements in the States, the radicalization spilling into Canada, the beginnings of the movements for women's liberation and against the Vietnam war. Big things began to happen inside Aunt Beatie's group and in all radical organizations in the country. She was busier than ever, and so was I. I took an honours degree in history and finally "did" the Wars of the Roses in a way that made some sense. I was on the UC debating team and then on the Varsity team. I began to think about being a lawyer.

It is hard to explain my political life during those years, yet important to me; there are distinctions I must make. I was not inactive. I went as usual to all the major events Aunt Beatie's organization put on: the Russian Revolution banquets and the May Day banquets, the New Year's parties, the Labour Day picnics. I went frequently to the weekly forums. When leaders of the Fourth International from Europe or South America came on speaking tours I went to hear them, and I went to all the major demonstrations on the various issues which those turbulent years cast up. I see that my choice of words has said it all: "I went to." I was not part of, not involved in. I don't think Aunt Beatie saw that. There were more things happening, so I turned up at more things, so she took that as a deepening commitment.

I see that I have reached that part of my own life story which I find so unsatisfying in so many biographies and autobiographies: the change-over from youth to adult. The years of early and middle childhood are always clearly described, for the colours of those first designs on the mind and heart never fade. Things get more complex in adolescence. Then suddenly there is the grownup, saying and doing things that sound boringly like the things all other grownups say and do. I cannot in my own mind pinpoint a month or even a year in which the shift took place. All I know is that when I left high school I took it for granted that after some further education I would move into radical politics in a committed and active way, and when I graduated from university I knew, submergedly, that I would not do so. I did not yet verbalize this to myself. Later, I found out that the comrades' analysis was that my convictions had been sapped by petty-bourgeois academia. They thought that my history and political science and economics professors, conservatives and liberals to a man (and come to think of it, they were without exception men) had overwhelmed my elementary understanding of Marxism with the sophistication of ruling class ideology. I was defensively angry when I first heard this. Then I realized that it was after all a very commonsense explanation for my change, so I considered it carefully. I still don't think that was the reason.

No. That's too cerebral. On the level of argumentation, theory analysis, I could, I can, still say that the Marxist world-view makes infinitely more sense than any other. When I go into the courtroom the class lines are so clear to me they're like a coloured overlay on a page of print. Sometimes in the courtroom I'm on one side and sometimes on the other, but those lines are burning clear. But. I think what was missing in me was some element of conviction. Confidence? Maybe that's the word, confidence. Aunt Beatie had so much of that. She didn't rely on other people's approval. She did what she did, she was sure. I wasn't. For all I knew about the potential of the working class, about strategy and tactics, the contradictions within capitalism intensifying to the point of rupture, the links between and among the various groupings of the oppressed, the role of the vanguard party, the role of the trade union movement – I still didn't hold it in my heart of hearts that it would work.

I can hear everything you would say to that, Aunt Beatie, but I'm sorry, it's me that wants to say my say now as I never did to you. Well then, why didn't I have that confidence, that conviction? Why you and not me? Does the root cause wriggle all the way back to that boy in the English school feeling inadequate because his parents were not like others? Well, back further, why did he/I feel that way? Or does it go back to the night I learned that Aunt Beatie was a Red and I didn't run and fetch what I didn't then know was the class enemy, a cop, to save me from her? Action, being active. That was Aunt Beatie but it is not me. I am more of a re-actor. Is that a middle-class trait, finally? Is there then a class-based explanation of why my feelings (not my head) were inadequate for the revolution? Or is all this just a fancy rationalization of political cowardice?

I've spent a lot of time and gone to the bottom of a great many bottles trying to find out, but I still haven't.

In some ways I am rather pleased with what I did do when I finally admitted to myself that I was not going to join the revolutionary party. Unlike many people I can think of, including some so-called radical lawyers (there is no such animal in my opinion), I have not pretended. I have not clad myself in trendy dishevelled garb and set up shop in a downtown reno and boasted about "only" charging two-thirds as much as straight lawyers do. No. I went through law school working as hard as I could, and did well enough so that I first articled with and then joined one of Toronto's more prestigious firms. Not obviously one to which birth in the right family is the door-key, but a very good one. There are quantities of partners, all with solidly WASP names like Galbraith and Twining and Mortimer, and I expect that Proctor will fit in very nicely in a few years' time. I wear three-piece suits and dark socks. My hair is neither so short as to make me appear sexually repressed nor so long as to look fashionable. Until Robyn and I were married I lived on nearly the top floor of an expensive high-rise at Bloor and Yonge. We now have a smallish house in the nether reaches of Rosedale. I know the block I want to live on in Forest Hill, and presumably at some point we will do so.

In fact I suppose that I have become almost exactly what my parents thought they wanted me to be. They cannot have imagined, though, that I would subscribe to half a dozen radical papers from around the world or that I would be known to many lefty groups in town as an almost sure hit for money every fund drive. (I won't let my name be used publicly as a donor or endorser, though, and there are now a few groups to which I will no longer give.) What a joke it is, what a joke I am. I wonder if my daughter will ever laugh at it with me. Maybe she will just think I am funny, and laugh at me, myself, instead. Serve me right.

Aunt Beatie. What did she think of all this? The thing was that I never levelled with her. I never said, "Aunt Beatie, I need to explain myself to you. Let's make a pot of Earl Grey and sit down and talk with one another the way we used to." Maybe if I had she would have known the answer? No, I don't think so. Outside her lexicon. Too healthy. I suppose my direction must have become clear to her as my law school years went by. I went to fewer party events. My Marxist papers from Europe and elsewhere lay in piles with their wrappers still on. I pleaded overwork. I did really have a lot of it to do, and that was always a valid reason for her; still I think she sensed what was happening. The day I came home from writing my last examination I met her at the door of the apartment – she was naturally on her way to a meeting – and she asked me how it had gone. "Fine," I said, "I think I aced it." "That's good, Hugh," she said. She looked at me very hard. "I hope you're going to use what you have learned in the defence of the poor and the oppressed. I hope so." And she went off, but not, I think, before she had observed that I could not meet her gaze. Actually I've become a bit of a specialist in insurance litigation.

When I was called to the Bar, of course she was there. And she came to my glossy new apartment sometimes for dinner, and admired my new furniture, and I made steak-and-kidney pie for her and we laughed and talked almost like old times. And of course she came to my wedding. Shortly after I had found Robyn (I went on a rather systematic search for a wife after I'd been with the firm for almost four years), I took her to meet Aunt Beatie. Robyn was horribly uncomfortable. Aunt Beatie still lived in the same third-floor walk-up in the same dingy building and I don't think Robyn had been in that part of Toronto or in such a building once in her life. Aunt Beatie was fine. She had made Eccles cakes for tea. She looked tenderly at Robyn and joined with enthusiasm in discussing plans for the wedding. Robyn was telling her about the brides-maids' dresses when the phone rang. We listened while Aunt Beatie delivered some terse comments on the line of the French CP in May '68 to a comrade who was preparing an educational on the student movement. She came back to the sofa all set to revert immediately to green sashes and ivory lace, but Robyn had some trouble adjusting herself. She is a very conventional woman, which I suppose is largely why I chose her. She is the ultimate in presentability. That's why she made no argument when I started the custom of having Aunt Beatie for dinner with us regularly twice a month. After the meal I would take Aunt Beatie in here to the library, and pour her a Drambuie or the evening's Scotch. Then she would fill me in on all the news of the left. I was beginning to build up a collection of biographies and autobiographies of leading Marxists, and she liked to look at these and talk about them as well. I think Robyn was both bored and intimidated on these occasions, but since Aunt Beatie was my aunt and utterly respectable in dress and behaviour apart from her politics, she did not object. Once I heard her on the phone talking to a friend. "His aunt's here," she said, "you know, the one I told you about. The Real Radical." I felt anger and amusement at the same time.

So there was no final cleavage between us, no scene in which she told me what a craven lickspittle sellout I was. I think she loved me. I was family. And I think she had a profound belief that people do what they have to. Though she would say that was too mecha-nistic.

Aunt Beatie's dead. She died of a heart attack three weeks ago. She never looked ill. She kept her trim figure and upright posture and air of composed assurance into middle age. Her hair was greyer and her skin was drier and she wore her glasses all the time instead of most of the time; those were the only changes I saw. The doctor said, however, driving nails of pain into me with each cliché, that she was all used up and her heart was worn right out.

I bitterly regret that she died before my daughter was born. Perhaps I thought that the gift of a great-niece or -nephew would be a recompense I could make her for myself? Selfish again.

But one thing I can and will do. The name we had planned if the child was a girl was Kimberley Anne. I never liked Kimberley – I don't approve of the growing custom of giving children the names of places or things, like Chelsea and Flower – but Robyn is very fond of it. Anne is Robyn's mother's second name; it's all right by me. But one of those two names must go now.

Out with you, false Kimberley or pallid Anne. Make way for Beatrice.

Goodbye, Aunt Beatrice. It's all I can do.

# DIONNE BRAND

# At the Lisbon Plate

The sky in the autumn is full of telephone and telegraph wires; it is not like sitting in the Portuguese bar on Kensington in the summer, outside – the beer smell, the forgetful waiter. I wonder what happened to Rosa. She was about forty and wore a tight black dress, her face appliquéd with something I could barely identify as life. Her false mole, the one she wore beside her mouth, shifted every day and faded by evening. She had a look that was familiar to me. Possibly she had lived in Angola or Mozambique and was accustomed to Black women. so she looked at me kindly, colonially.

"Do you have fish, Rosa?" I would ask.

"Oh yes, good Portuguese fish."

"From the lake or from the sea."

"Ah the sea, of course."

This would be our conversation every time I would come to the bar, her "of course" informing me of her status in our relationship.

My life was on the upswing, and whenever that happened I went to the bar on Kensington. That was usually in the summertime. After twenty years and half my life in this city I still have to wait for the summertime to get into a good mood. My body refuses to appreciate dull, grey days. Truthfully, let me not fool you, my life was neither up nor down, which for me is an upswing and I don't take chances, I celebrate what little there is. Which is why I come to this bar. This is my refuge, as it is. I believe in contradictions.

So Rosa ran from Angola and Mozambique. Well, well! By the looks of it she'd come down a peg or two. At the Lisbon Plate, Rosa seems quite ordinary, quite different from the woman who entertained in the European drawing rooms in Luanda and Lorenços Marques. Then, she gave orders to Black women, whom she called 'as pretinhas.' Then, she minced over to the little consul from Lisbon and the general, whose family was from Oporto and whom she made promise to give her a little gun for her protection when the trouble started.

I figured anyone who left Angola was on the other side, on the run. Rosa did have a kind enough look, personally. The wholesale merchant she was married to or his general manager, whom she slept with from time to time, had to leave. So, Rosa left too. This does not absolve Rosa however. I'm sure that she acquired her plumpness like a bed bug, sucking a little blood here, a little there.

As I've said, my life was on the upswing. Most other times it was a bitch. But I had spent two successive days with no major setbacks. Nobody called me about money, nobody hurt my feelings, and I didn't wake up feeling shaky in the stomach about how this world was going. And, I had twenty clear bucks to come to the bar. This is my refuge. It is where I can be invisible or, if not invisible, at least drunk. Drinking makes me introspective, if not suicidal. In these moments I have often looked at myself from the third floor window of the furniture store across from the bar. Rheumy-eyed, I have seen a woman sitting there whom I recognize as myself. A Black woman, legs apart, chin resting in the palm of her hand, amusement and revulsion travelling across her face in uneasy companionship; the years have taken a bit of the tightness out of my skin but the expression has not changed, searching and uneasy, haunted like a plantation house. Surrounded by the likes of Rosa and her *compadres*. A woman in enemy territory.

It has struck me more than once that a little more than a century ago I may have been Rosa's slave and not more that twenty-five years ago, her maid, whom she maimed, playing with the little gun that she got from the general from Oporto. My present existence is mere chance, luck, syzygy.

Rosa's brother, Joao the priest, was now living in New Jersey. He used to live in Toronto, but before that he lived in Angola. One day, in a village there, during the liberation war, two whites were kidnapped and the others, including Rosa's brother, the priest, went into the village and gunned down a lot of people – women, children, to death, everything. He told this story to Maria de Conseçao, my friend, and she told me. Women and children, everything. People think that saying women and children were killed makes the crime more disgusting. I was sorry that Maria de Conseçao told me, because whenever I think about it I see Joao the priest confiding this crime as if he relished it, rather than repented it. I think Maria de Conseçao told me the story just to get rid of it. It's the kind of story which occurs to you when you're doing something pleasant and it's the kind of story you can't get rid of. I've kept it.

I am not a cynical woman under ordinary circumstances, but if you sit here long enough anyone can see how what appears to be ordinary, isn't.

For, on the other hand, I look like a woman I met many years ago. As old as dirt, she sat at a roadside waiting her time, an ivory pipe stuck in her withered lips and naked as she was born. That woman had stories, more lucid than mine and more frightening for that.

The day I met her, her bones were black powder and her fingers crept along my arm causing me to shiver. She was a dangerous woman. I knew it the moment I saw her and I should have left her sitting there, the old grave-digger. But no. Me, I had to go and look.

I had to follow that sack of dust into places I had no right being. Me, I had to look where she pointed. She wanted to show me her condiments and her books. I thought nothing of it. Why not humour an old woman, I said in my mind. They were old as ashes. All tied up and knotted in a piece of cloth and, when she opened it up, you would not believe the rattling and the odour, all musty and sweet. A bone here and a fingernail there. They looked like they'd been sitting in mud for centuries, like her. When it came to the books, it was before they had pages and the writing was with stones, which the old thing threw on the ground and read to me. I never laughed so much as I laughed at her jokes, not to mention her stories which made me cry so much I swore I'd turn to saltwater myself. It was one of her stories which led me here, in search of something I will recognize, once I see it.

But back to things that we can understand, because I want to forget that harridan in the road and her unpleasantness.

Today I am waiting for Elaine, as usual. She likes to make entrances of the type that white girls make in movies. The truth is she's always getting away from something or someone. She is always promising too much and escaping, which is why we get along. I never believe a promise and I, myself, am in constant flight.

Elaine is a mysterious one. Two days ago she told me to meet her here at one o'clock. I've been sitting here ever since. I know that she'll turn up a new woman. She'll say that she's moving to Tanzania to find her roots. She'll have her head tied in a wrap and she'll have gold bracelets running up her arms. She'll be learning Swahili, she'll show me new words like 'jambo' and she'll be annoyed if I don't agree to go with her. Elaine wants to be a queen in ancient Mali or Songhai. A rich woman with gold and land.

The bar has a limited view of Kensington market. Across the street from it there's a parkette, in the centre of which there is a statue of Cristobal Colon. Columbus, the carpetbagger. It's most appropriate that they should put his stoney arse right where I can see it. I know bitterness doesn't become me, but that son of a bitch will get his soon enough too. The smell from the market doesn't bother me. I've been here before, me and the old lady. We know the price of things. Which is why I feel safe in telling stories here. They will be sure to find me. For fish you must have bait; for some people you must have blood. Spread the truth around enough, and you must dig up a few liars.

In the summertime, I come to the bar practically every day. After my first beer I'm willing to talk to anyone. I'm willing to reveal myself entirely. Which is a dirty habit, since it has made me quite a few enemies. Try not to acquire it. The knots in my head loosen up and I may start telling stories about my family.

I keep getting mixed up with old ladies; for instance, I have an old aunt, she used to be beautiful. Not in the real sense, but in that sense that you had to be, some years ago. Hair slicked back to bring out the Spanish and hide the African. You could not resemble your mother or your father. This would only prove your guilt. This aunt went mad in later years. I think that it must have been from so much self-denial or, given the way that it turned out ...

Anyway, when I was a child we used to go to their house. It was made of stone and there was a garden around it. A thick green black garden. A forest. My aunt worked in the garden every day, pruning and digging. There was deep red hibiscus to the far right wall. The soil was black and loose and damp and piled around the roots of roses and xoras and anthuriums and orchids. In the daylight, the garden was black and bright; in the night, it was shadowy and dark. Only my aunt was allowed to step into the garden. At the edges, shading the forest-garden were great calabash mango trees. Their massive trunks and roots gave refuge from my aunt when she climbed into a rage after merely looking at us all day. She would run after us screaming, "Beasts! Worthless beasts!" Her rage having not subsided, she would grab us and scrub us, as if to take the black out of our skins. Her results would never please her. Out we would come five still bright-black little girls, blackness intent on our skins. She would punish us by having us stand utterly still, dressed in stiffly starched dresses.

Elaine never reveals herself and she is the most frustrating storyteller. She handles a story as if stories were scarce. "Well," she says, as she sits down at the table. Then she pauses, far too long a pause, through which I say, in my mind, "I'm going to last out this pause." Then quickly getting upset, I say, "For god's sake, tell me." Then I have to drag it out of her, in the middle of which I say, "Forget it I don't want to hear," then she drops what she thinks is the sinker and I nonchalantly say, "Is that it?" to which she swears that never again would she tell me a story. The truth is that Elaine picks up on great stories, but the way she tells them makes people suffer. I, on the other hand, am quite plain. Particularly when I'm in my waters. Drink, I mean. I've noticed I'm prepared to risk anything. But truthfully, what makes a good story if not for the indiscretions we reveal, the admissions of being human. In this way, I will tell you some of my life; though I must admit that some of it is fiction, not much mind you, but what is lie, I do not live through with any less tragedy. Anyway, these are not state secrets, people live the way that they have to and handle what they can. But don't expect any of the old woman's tales. There are things that you know and things that you tell. Well, soon and very soon, as they say.

Listen, I can drink half a bottle of whisky and refuse to fall down. It's from looking at Rosa that I get drunk and it's from looking at Rosa that I refuse to fall down. I was a woman with a face like a baby before I met Rosa, a face waiting to hold impressions.

I saw the little minx toddle over to the statue of Columbus, the piss-face in the parkette, and kiss his feet. Everyone has their rituals, I see. And then, before her mirror, deciding which side to put the mole on. Her face as dry as a powder. Perfuming herself in her bedroom in Lorenços Marques, licking the oil off that greasy merchant of hers. Even though the weather must have been bad for her, she stuck it out until they were driven away. It's that face that Rosa used cursing those "sons of bitches in the bush," when the trouble started. "When the trouble started," indeed. These European sons of bitches always say "when the trouble started" when *their* life in the colonies begins to get miserable.

I never think of murder. I find it too intimate and there's a smell in the autumn that I do not like. I can always tell. The first breath of the fall. It distracts me from everyone. I will turn down the most lucrative dinner invitation to go around like a bloodhound smelling the fall. Making sure and making excuses, suggesting and insinuating that the summer is not over. But of course, as soon as I get a whiff of that smell I know. It's the autumn. Then the winter comes in, as green and fresh as spring and I know that I have to wait another ten months for the old woman's prophecy to come true. That hag by the road doesn't know what she gave me and what an effort I must make to see it through. On top of that, I have to carry around her juju belt full of perfidious mixtures and insolent smells and her secrets. Her secrets. My god, you don't know what a soft pain in the chest they give me. I grow as withered as the old hag with their moaning. She's ground them up like seasoning and she's told me to wear them close to my skin, like a poultice. I thought nothing of it at first. A little perfume, I said, a little luxury. I now notice that I cannot take the juju off. I lift up my camisole and have a look. It's hardly me there anymore. There's a hole like a cave with an echo.

The old hag hates the winter too; says it dries her skin out. God knows she's no more than dust, but vain as hell. She migrates like a soucouyant in the winter, goes back to the tropics, says she must mine the Sargasso for bones and suicides. I must say, I envy the old bagsnatcher. Though she's promised me her memories, her maps and her flight plans, when it's over. Until then, I wait and keep watch here, frozen like a lizard in Blue Mountain, while she suns her quaily self in some old slave port.

At this bar, as I have my first beer and wait for the African princess, Elaine, I discover substantive philosophical arguments concerning murder. The beauty is, I have a lot of time. I have watched myself here, waiting. A woman so old her skin turned to water, her eyes blazing like a dead candle. I'm starting to resemble that bag of dust, the longer I live.

Now they have a man waiting on tables at the bar. I suppose the pay must be better. Elaine says he resembles Rosa except for her beauty mole and her breasts. It doesn't matter how Rosa looks in her disguises, I am doomed to follow her like a bloodhound after a thief. He is quite forgetful. Twenty minutes ago I asked him for another beer and up to now he hasn't brought it. Elaine's the one who got me into beer drinking anyway. In the old days – before the great mother old soul in the road and before I sussed out Rosa and her paramour, Elaine and I used to roam the streets together, looking. The old bone digger must have spotted my vacant look then. Elaine, on the other hand, had very definite ideas. Even then Elaine was looking for a rich African to help her make her triumphal return to the motherland.

Still, a rumour went around that Elaine and I were lovers. It wouldn't have bothered either of us if it were true at the time or if it wasn't said in such a malicious way. But it was because of how we acted. Simply, we didn't defer to the men around and we didn't sleep with them, or else when we did we weren't their slaves forever or even for a while. So both factions, those we slept with and those we didn't, started the rumour that we were lovers. Actually, Elaine and I laughed at the rumours. We liked to think of ourselves as free spirits and realists. We never attempted to dispel the rumours; it would have taken far too much of a commitment to do that. It would be a full time job of subjecting yourself to any prick on two legs. And anyway if the nastiest thing that they could say about you is that you loved another woman, well...

Elaine and I would take the last bus home, bags full of unopened beer, or pay a taxi, after I had persuaded her that the man she was looking at was too disgusting to sleep with, just for a ride home. Elaine takes the practical to the absurd sometimes.

We've been to other bars. Elaine looked for the bars, she scouted all the hangouts. She determined the ambience, the crowd, and then she asked me to meet her there. There's no accounting for her taste. I'd get to the appointed bar and it would be the grungiest, with the most oily food, the most vulgar horrible men and a jukebox with music selected especially to insult women. This was during Elaine's nationalist phase. Everything was culture, rootsy. The truth is, I only followed Elaine to see if I could shake the old woman's stories or, alternately, if I could find the something for her and get her off my back. It's not that I don't like the old schemer. At first I didn't mind her, but then she started to invade me like a spirit. So I started to drink. You get drunk enough and you think you can forget, but you get even greater visions. At the beginning of any evening the old woman's stories are a blip on the horizon; thirteen ounces into a bottle of scotch or four pints of beer later the stories are as lurid as a butcher's block.

I had the fever for two days and dreamt that the stove had caught afire. My big sister was just standing there as I tried furiously to douse the fire which kept getting bigger and bigger. Finally, my sister dragged the stove from the wall and with a knowledgeable air, put the fire out. When I woke up, I heard that the stock exchange in Santiago had been blown up by a bomb in a suitcase and that some group called the communist fighting cell had declared war on NATO by destroying troop supply lines in Belgium. Just as I was thinking of Patrice Lumumba. For you Patrice! From this I surmised that my dreams have effects. Though, they seem somewhat unruly. They escape me. They have fires in them and they destine at an unknown and precipitous pace.

I followed Elaine through her phases, though there were some that she hid from me. Now we come to this bar, where we cannot understand the language most of the time. Here Elaine plans the possibilities of living grandly and, if not, famously. As for me, I tolerate her dreams because when Elaine found this bar I knew it was my greatest opportunity. All of the signs were there. The expatriates from the colonial wars, the money changers and the skin dealers, the whip handlers, the coffle makers and the boatswains. Their faces leathery from the African sun and the tropical winter. They were swilling beer like day had no end. Rosa was in her glory, being pawed and pinched. Of course, they didn't notice me in my new shape. Heavens, I didn't notice me. It scared the hell out of me when the juju surged to my head and I was a thin smoke over the Lisbon Plate. What a night! They said things that shocked even me, things worse than Joao, the priest. The old-timers boasted about how many piezas de indias they could pack into a ship for a bauble or a gun. The young soldiers talked about the joys of filling a black with bullets and stuffing a black cunt with dynamite. Then they gathered around Columbus, the whoremaster, and sang a few old songs. The old woman and I watched the night's revelry with sadness, the caves in our chest rattling the echo of unkindness, but I noticed the old woman smiling as she counted them, pointing and circling with her hand, over and over again, mumbling "jingay, jingay, where you dey, where you dey, where you dey, spirit nah go away." Before you know it, I was mumbling along with her too, "jingay, jingay, where you dey." We stayed with them all night, counting and mumbling. Now, all I have to do is choose the day and the spot and it's done. The old woman loves fanfare and flourish, so it will have to be spectacular. If Elaine knew what a find this bar was, she'd charge me money.

Elaine never cared for Rosa one way or the other, which is where Elaine and I are different. Some people would have no effect on her whatsoever. This way she remained friends with everyone. Me, I hate you or I love you. Always getting into fights, always adding enemies to my lists. Which is why I'll never get any place, as they say. But Elaine will. Elaine, sadly, is a drunk without vision. I unfortunately, am a drunk with ideas. Which is probably why the old woman chose me to be her steed.

I pride myself with keeping my ear to the ground. I read the news and I listen to the radio every day, even if it is the same news. I look for nuances, changes in the patter. It came to me the other night, when listening to the news. One Polish priest had been killed and the press was going wild. At the same time, I don't know how many African labourers got killed and, besides that, fell to their deaths from third floor police detention rooms in Johannesburg; and all that the scribes talked about was how moderate the Broderbond is. We should be grateful I suppose.

It occurred to me that death, its frequency, causes, sequence and application to written history, favours, even anticipates, certain latitudes. The number of mourners, their enthusiasms, their entertainments, their widows' weeds, all mapped by a cartographer well schooled in pre-Galileo geography. I'm waxing. Don't stop me. I couldn't tell you the things I know.

Meanwhile back at the bar, still waiting for Elaine to surface, there have been several interesting developments. Speaking of politics. First, I hear that the entire bourgeoisie of Bolivia is dead. It was on the radio not more than half an hour ago. The deaths are not significant in and of themselves. What is interesting is that only a few days ago, when I heard that president Suazo was kidnapped in La Paz and that there was possibly a coup, I said in my mind, that the entire bourgeoisie should perish. It was the Bolivian army who killed Ernesto Che Guevara, you see. They put his body in the newspapers with their smiles. Now, I hear the news that the entire bourgeoisie of Bolivia is dead. Of course from this I learned that as I become more and more of a spirit, I have more and more possibilities. First Santiago and Belgium and now Bolivia.

Second, and most, most important, the big white boy has arrived here. He's ordered a beer from Rosa's brother. The last time I saw them, I was lying in the hold of a great ship leaving Conakry for the new world. It was just a glimpse, but I remember as if it were yesterday. I am a woman with a lot of time and I have waited, like shrimp wait for tide. I have waited, like dirt waits for worms. That hell-hole stank of my own flesh before I left it, its walls mottled with my spittle and waste. For days I lived with my body rotting and the glare of those eyes keeping me alive, as I begged to die and follow my carcass. This is the story the old road woman told me. Days and days and night and nights, dreaming death like a loved one; but those hellish eyes kept me alive and dreadfully human until reaching a port in the new world. His pitiless hands placed me on a block of wood like a yoke, when my carcass could not stand any more for the worms had eaten my soul. Running, running a long journey over hot bush, I found a cliff one day at the top of an island and jumped – jumped into the jagged blue water of an ocean, swimming, swimming to Conakry.

Elaine has also arrived and disappeared again, she's always disappearing into the bar to make phone calls. I never get an explanation of these phone calls mainly because I simply continue with my story. But I have the feeling, as the afternoon progresses into evening, and as different moods cross Elaine's face after every phone call, that some crisis is being made, fought and resolved. I have a feeling that Elaine needs my stories as a curtain for her equally spyish dramas.

The big white boy was sitting with his dog. I did not see his face at first, but I recognized him as you would recognize your hands. His hair was cut with one patch down the middle. He was wearing black and moaning as he sat there smoking weed. Like Rosa, he had fallen on his luck. I heard him say this.

"I don't have nobody, no friends, I ain't got no love, no nothing, just my dog."

He was blond. At least, that was the colour of his hair presently. I felt for him the compassion of a warship, the maudlin sentiment of a boot stepping on a face. He said this to Rosa, who gave him an unsympathetic look as she picked her teeth. I'm not fooled by their lack of affection for each other. They are like an alligator and a parasite. I felt like rushing to his throat, but something held me back. The old woman's burning hand. I've seen him and Rosa whispering behind my back. What would a punk ku klux klansman and a washed-up ex-colonial siren have in common. Except me and the old lady. I suppose they're wondering who I am. Wonder away you carrion! I wonder if they recognize me as quickly as I, them. I saw them do their ablutions on the foot of the statue in the parkette. How lovingly they fondled his bloody hands. They have their rituals, but I've lived longer than they.

Listen, I neglected to say that my old aunt of the forest has gone mad. She told my sister, and indeed the whole town of Monas Bay, that on Easter Sunday of 1979, this year, jesus christ had descended from the heavens and entered her bedroom and had been there ever since. She had had a vision. After days of fasting and kneeling on the mourning ground, she had entered a desert where nothing grew. No water and inedible shrubs. The sun's heat gave the air a glassiness upon looking into the distance. Then she saw christ. He was withered and young as a boy of twenty. Christ and my aunt conversed for many days and planned to marry three years from the time of their meeting. They would have a son who would grow to be the new christ. My aunt related this incident to any one who would listen and cursed into hell and damnation anyone who did not believe. Few, needless to say, didn't. Anyone with a vision was helpful in bad times and people said that at least she had the guts to have a vision, which was not like the politicians in those parts.

Even my aunt's garden had descended into sand and tough shrub. It had become like the desert of her vision. She no longer made any attempt to grow plants, she said that armageddon was at hand anyway. Her bedroom, she turned into a shrine on the very day of her meeting with christ. On the wall hung bits of cardboard with glossy photographs of her fiancé cut out of the *Plain Truth*, and candles burnt endlessly in the four corners of the shrine. Sundry chaplets of jumbie beads, plastic and ivory maneuvered themselves on the windows and bedposts. My aunt knows that some people think that she is mad; so, in the style of her affianced, she prays for their salvation. If she is mad ... Which is a debate that I will never personally enter, having seen far too much in my short life and knowing that if you live in places with temporary electricity and plenty of hard work, jesus christ (if not god) is extant. Not to mention that, the last time that I saw her, she stood at what was once the gate to the forest garden and was now dead wire, wearing a washed-out flowered dress and her last remaining tooth, even though she was only a woman of fifty, and told me that the land taxes for the forest and the stone house was paid up or would be as soon as she went to town. This, to me, attested to her sanity. Come hell or high water, as they say, though these might be the obvious causes of her madness, if she were mad, they were certainly legal. Anyway, if she is mad, her vision is clearly not the cause of it.

Rather it has made her quite sane. At any rate she no longer uses face powder.

This trick that I learned in Bolivia and the dream in Santiago has set me to thinking. She, the old poui stick, is not the only one who can have plans. The dear old lady only gave me seven red hot peppers and told me to write their names seven times on seven scraps of paper. Then put the seven pieces of paper into the seven red hot peppers and throw them into seven latrines. This, she said, would do for them. This and sprinkling guinea pepper in front of their door every morning. Then, she said, I should wait for the rest. The old hag is smart, but she never anticipated the times or perhaps that's what she means.

Elaine thinks I'm taking things too far, of course. But, I cannot stand this endless waiting. I've practically turned into a spirit with all this dreadfulness around the Lisbon Plate. I want to get back to my life and forget this old woman and her glamorous ideas. So, what must be done, must be done. Elaine's on her way to Zaire, at any moment anyway. I think she's landed Mobutu Sese Seku.

For now I've taken to hiding things from her. She doesn't care about anything. Each time I mention it she says, "Oh for god's sake, forget them." As if it's that easy. You tell me! When there's a quaily skinned battle-axe riding on your shoulder and whispering in your ear. Well fine, if Elaine can have her secret telephone calls, and I don't think that I mentioned her disappearances, I can have my secret fires too. She can't say that I didn't try to warn her.

Wait! Well, I'll be damned! They're coming in like flies, old one. I eavesdrop on conversations here. I listen for plots, hints. You never know what these people are up for. This way, I amuse myself and scout for my opportunity. Listen,

"Camus' *Outsider* can be interpreted as the ultimate alienation!"

Ha! Did you hear that? Now, literature! Jesus. That's the one who looks like a professor, all scruffy and sensitive. If the truth be known several hundred years ago he made up the phrase "Dark Ages," then he attached himself to an expedition around the Bight of Benin from which, as the cruder of his sea company packed human cargo into the hold of their ship, he rifled the gold statues and masks and he then created a "museum of primitive art" to store them. Since his true love was phrase-making he made up "museum of primitive art," elaborating his former success, "Dark Ages." Never trust white men who look sensitive. They're the worst kind of phonies. They want the best of both worlds. Compared to him, the big white boy looks like a saint.

Anyway, alienation, my ass! Camus! Camus wrote a novel about a European, *un pied noir*, killing an Arab on a beach outside Algiers. He works it so that the sun gets into the European's eyes (they have their rituals) and the heat and his emotionlessness to his mother's dying and all this. But killing an Arab, pumping successive bullets into an Arab is not and never has been an alienating experience for a European. It was not unusual. It need not symbolize any alienation from one's being or anything like that. It was customary in Algeria, so how come all this high shit about Camus. Didn't it ever strike you that Meursault was a European and the Arab on the beach was an Arab? And the Arab was an Arab, but this European was Mersault.

You want to hear a story? Let me tell you a real story. I have no art for phraseology, I'll warn you.

Ahmed. Ahmed. Ahmed. Ahmed came to the beach with Ousmane to get away. The town, stiffly hot, drove him from the bicycle factory, making an excuse to his boss. Headache, my little brother has a headache three days now. He needs the salt air. The grimy hands of the boss closed around a dry cigar in the tin can ashtray. "Ahmed, if you leave I don't pay for the week. That's it. That's it you hear." Ahmed retreating, feeling free already, sweat trickling and drying under his chin. He would go to the beach, Ousmane was waiting for him, the sand would be damp, Ousmane was at the corner, he held his flute anxiously looking up and down the narrow street. His face lit up as he saw Ahmed. "You got away, good Ahmed," running beside Ahmed's bicycle. Ousmane climbed onto the handle bars. Ahmed pedalled in the hot silence toward the beach. Nearing the sea, their legs and arms eased from the tension of the town. Ousmane's bare feet leapt from the makeshift seat at the same time that Ahmed braked. They headed for their favourite rock wheeling and lifting the bicycle through the sand, hot and stinging. Already he felt tranquil as the thin wind shaking the flowers. He dropped the bicycle, raced Ousmane to the water, crushing softly underfoot the vine and silky mangrove. Ahmed and Ousmane fell into the sea fully clothed, he washing away the sticky oil of the bicycle shop, Ousmane drowning his headache. Then they lay beside the rock, talking and falling asleep.

Ousmane awakening, felt hungry; his dungarees, still damp, felt steamy on his legs. Shading his eyes from the sun which had narrowed the shadow of the rock, his headache came back. He stood up, lifted his flute and played a tune he'd made over and over again as if to tame the ache in his head. After a while he wandered down the beach, looking for a foodseller.

Ahmed, Ahmed. Ahmed awoke, feeling Ousmane's absence at the same moment that he heard an explosion close to his ear. Ahmed felt his eyes taking an eternity to open into the glassy haze of the afternoon. A blurred white form wobbling in the heat's haze. Sound exploded on the other side of Ahmed. He barely raised his body, shielding his eyes as he made out the white form of a European. Far out in the ocean a steamer was passing. The sand around Ahmed pulsated with the heat and the loud ringing in his ears. Ousmane! Run!

Ahmed's vision pinpointed the white's face, the toothpick between the white's teeth and lip moving. The gun transfixed his arms. Beneath a veil of brine and tears, his eyes were blinded; they watched the steamer's latitude longingly. "Born slackers!" Ahmed's chest sprang back, tendrilled. "Born liars!" A pump of blood exploded in his left side. "Born criminals!" Sheets of flame poured down his ribs. "Born ...!" Ahmed!

That is what happened! And as for Camus. Murderer.

This is it baby. The old woman has given the go-ahead. Now that they're all gathered – Rosa, the big white boy, the professor, the money-changers and the skin dealers, the whip handlers, the coffle makers and the boatswains, the old timers and the young soldiers. I'm going to kill them. I'll tell them I have something to sell. That'll get them going; it always has. Then we'll strangle them. It'll be a night for the old woman to remember. That'll make up for it. Then that'll be the end of it.

We chained them around the statue of Cristobal Colon, the prick head. The old woman and I slashed his face to ribbons then we chewed on the stones and spit them into the eyes of the gathering. When that was over and they were all jumping and screaming, the old woman drew out her most potent juju and sprayed them all with oceans of blood which, she said, she had carried for centuries.

"En't is blood all you like?!" she whispered in their ears maliciously.

Then we sang "jingay ..." and made them call out everything that they had done over and over again, as they choked on the oceans of blood from the old hag's juju. Then we marinated them in hot peppers, like the old woman wanted. What an everlasting sweet night we had. The old woman was so happy, she laughed until her belly burst.

When Elaine returned from her continuous phone call, I convinced her to stuff the bodies in her trunk to Zaire. It wasn't easy, as she almost could not see me and kept saying how much my face had changed. I promised her the Queendom and riches of Songhai. She bought it. The old lady has promised me her big big juju, so this is where the African princess and I must part. I'm off to see my new love and companion, the old hag of a banyan tree.

Endnote: "Ahmed's death" is intended to echo and counterpoint the corresponding scene in *L'Étranger* and therefore echoes the language of the Penguin edition, English language translation.

## SHIRLEY FAESSLER

# Maybe Later It Will Come Back to My Mind

"Lady! Lady!" An old man in a wheelchair at the far end of the corridor was beckoning me. I was standing at the elevator preoccupied with thoughts of my father, whom I was visiting at the Jewish Home for the Aged, and had not noticed the old man before. I took my finger from the UP button and went to him.

"Good morning," he said, adjusting his yarmulka. "You got somebody here?"

"My father," I said.

"Where is he?"

"On the fifth floor."

"That's in the hospital part, no?"

"Yes. He's recovering from an operation. And I've only got time for a short visit with him," I added warily. I had been trapped so often before. I had been prevailed on to make calls to delinquent sons, daughters, grandchildren; I had made trips to the kitchen with complaints about the menu; I had been asked to rustle up a doctor for somebody, a nurse, an orderly – and I was bound this morning not to become involved as I had only a short time to spend with my father.

The elevator came to the door. "Excuse me," I said. "My father's waiting for me."

"So he'll wait a little minute," he said. "I want you should do me a little favour first."

"If I can, and providing it doesn't take too long."

Instead of saying what he wanted of me, he kept me waiting – quite deliberately, I could tell. He kept me waiting while he searched his pockets, brought out a match, struck it on his chair, and held the flame to his stump of a cigar. Even after he got it going, he sat puffing away and slapping at the ashes on his vest.

A second elevator came to the floor. I was disposed to leave him, and took a few steps toward it.

"Wait a minute," he said. "What are you in such a hurry? Your father wouldn't run away. All I want is you shall take me out in the garden." He cocked an eye at me. "Easy, no?"

I looked at the old man, taking him into account for the first time. During visits to my father I had encountered dozens of old men in wheelchairs, also old ladies in wheelchairs. I had spent the time of day with them in hallways, in sitting-rooms, and had done errands for many of them. I had been thanked, excessively so, for a trifling service like addressing an envelope. For making a telephone call I had been blessed. But this man – there was something odd about him. I had never been addressed with such peremptoriness, such lack of regard for my own affairs. There was something about him that took me back. Where had I seen him? I looked at the old man, studying him. Broad face, heavy-lidded eyes, hooked nose, thick torso, and short legs, his feet barely reaching the footrest of his chair.

"What are you looking?" he said, bringing me up short. "You never saw an old man before? Go behind better, and give me a little push," he said in Yiddish. "The Messiah will come first before I'll come out in the garden."

Ah, now I had it! Now I knew who he was!

"Is your name Layevsky? Myer Layevsky?"

He closed an eye at me. "How did you know?"

"I used to work for you. A long time ago, about thirty years ago. I was your office lady; my name was Miss Rotstein. I worked for you nine months, and you fired me. Do you remember me?"

He wagged his big head. "From this I shall remember you? God willing I shall have so many years left how many girls I fired. So I fired you. On this account you wouldn't take me out in the garden?"

"Oh, don't be –" I was about to say don't be silly. Fancy saying don't be silly to Myer Layevsky.

I wheeled him to the lobby, and once outside the glass portals, carefully down the ramp.

"How's your son?" I asked.

He turned full face to me. "My Israel? A very important man," he said, giving equal emphasis to each word. "A very big doctor in the States."

"And Mrs. Layevsky, how's she?"

He turned, facing front. "Dead. A healthy woman crippled by arthritis. Ten years younger than me. I always had in my mind the *Molochamovis* will come for me first, but it turned out different. Take me over there by the big tree."

I settled him by the big tree. "And you don't remember me? I was only sixteen, and now I'm a married woman with two grown children, so I must have changed a lot. But you should remember me. You gave me a week's holiday; I took an extra few days, and when I came back, you had another girl in my place. Now do you remember?"

"Ask me riddles," he said, again in Yiddish. "Do me a favour and go to your father," he said, using the familiar thou instead of the formal you, with which he had first addressed me. "Maybe later it will come back to my mind."

My father was in the armchair beside his bed, reading a newspaper. "Pa! You'll never guess who I saw downstairs. Remember Myer Layevsky, the man I used to work for?"

My father removed his eyeglasses. "I remember him very well. And also how you hid under the bed from him when he came to find out why you didn't come in to work one morning. Correct?"

My father had it wrong. He was confusing Myer Layevsky with Mr. Teitlbaum, the comforter manufacturer, from whom I *had* hidden under the bed.

"You've got it wrong, Pa," I said. "You're thinking of Teitlbaum, the comforter manufacturer. But how did you know I hid under the bed? Ma swore she wouldn't tell you."

"Maybe a little bird told me," he said. "Now I remember. It seems to me you got another job that summer. Correct?"

"That's right. For a toy factory, remember? Three days after I quit Imperial Comforters I went to work for a toy factory, in the Kewpie doll section. I wanted to stay on, but you wouldn't let me. You made me go back to commercial school. But I went only six weeks of my second term, and you let me quit. Then I went to work for Layevsky, the man I saw downstairs –"

"I let you quit Commercial? This I don't remember, but if you say so, maybe you remember better." He sighed reminiscently. "You always had your own way with me. Whatever you wanted you accomplished."

Like fun I'd always had my own way with him. For one thing, I never wanted to go to Commercial. My plan, after being passed out of Grade VIII, King Edward School, was to go with my best girlfriend, Lizzie Stitsky, to Harbord Collegiate, but my father wouldn't cough up the money for books. So I had to go instead to commercial school, where the books were free and the course took only two years. I loathed the sight of that dismal building, the dreary classroom, the drabs I was thrown in with, and went every morning five days a week with a resentful, heavy heart, and my lunch in a paper bag.

Sure, he let me quit Commercial after only six weeks of my second term, but not through any understanding on his part, or sympathy: I swung him around through a trick, a bit of chicanery.

Everything had gone wrong for me that Monday of my seventh week. I had gone to bed the night before with a bag of hot salt pressed against my cheek to ease a toothache, and Monday morning after a troubled night's sleep my cheek was inflamed, and the brassière I had washed the night before was still wet. When the noon bell rang, I was as miserable as I had ever been in my life. When I tried to get at my lunch, my desk drawer was jammed. Propping my feet against the legs of the desk, I gave the drawer a terrific yank. It shot out suddenly, knocking me back and landing overturned in my lap. Everything spilled to the floor, pencils, pads, erasers, books. I scrabbled around collecting my things, and returning them to the drawer, noticed a man's handkerchief, dirty, clotted, and stuck in the right-hand corner. I had never got the drawer more than partially open before, so it must have been there all these weeks side by side with my lunch. My tooth began to ache again. I fled the room, and that night at supper, screwed up enough courage to tell my father I would not be returning to Commercial.

He reared. "Why?" he wanted to know.

"Because I found something in my desk."

"What did you find?"

I made no answer; I knew under cross-examination my case would be lost. He insisted on knowing; he kept badgering me. "A dead mouse?"

"Worse."

"What worse?" he persisted, getting angry.

"Don't ask me, Pa." On the inspiration of the moment, I turned my inflamed cheek to him and said, "I'm ashamed to talk about it."

And my father, sensing that the object had something to do with sex, stopped questioning me. I had won. I knew he'd never let me quit on account of a dirty hankie in my desk.

A week later, through an ad in the paper reading *Girl Wanted, Easy Work, Easy Hours, Good Pay*, I went to work for Myer Layevsky. Myer Layevsky was sitting in a swivel chair at a cluttered roll-top desk in his two-by-four office when I came to be interviewed for the job. His hat was on the back of his head, and in his mouth a dead cigar. He swivelled around, and closing one eye, inspected me with the open one.

"You're a Jewish girl, no?"

"Yes."

"I had already a few people looking for the job, but I didn't made up my mind yet." He pointed to a beat-up typewriter. "You know how to typewrite?"

"Yes."

"So if I'll give you a letter, you'll be able to take down?" He rooted around the desk and came up with several lots of file cards, each bound with a rubber band. "Customers," he said. "I sell goods on time. You heard about that joke a dollar down and a dollar when you ketch me? This is my business."

He extracted one lot of cards and put them aside. "Deadbeats," he said, screwing both eyes shut and shaking his head. "Deadbeats. From this bunch nobody comes in to pay. I have to collect myself. Sometimes I even have to go and pull back the goods, so this bunch you can forget about." He went on to the other cards. "This bunch is something difference," he said fondly. "Good customers, honest people which they come in regular with a payment. So this is what you shall do. A customer comes in the office with a payment? First you'll take the money. Next you'll find out the name. Then you'll make a receipt, mark down on the card the payment, and keep up to date the balance." He struck a match on the desk and put it to his cigar. "Easy, no?"

"Another thing which I didn't mention it yet," he said. "Sometimes it happens a cash customer falls in the office for a pair sheets, a pair towels, a little rug, a lace panel, something – so come in the back, I'll show you my stockroom."

I was taken by surprise when he stood up, to see how short he was. Sitting, he looked like a giant of a man. But the bulk of him was all in his torso; his legs were short and bowed, and he stood barely over five feet, and loping in baggy pants to the stockroom he looked like a comic mimicking someone's walk.

Except for a conglomeration of stuff piled in a corner of the stockroom, everything was in order, price-tagged, and easy to get at.

"This mishmush," he said, indicating the heaped-up pile, "is pulled goods from deadbeats which they didn't pay. So if a poor woman comes in the office with cash money for a pair secondhand sheets, a pair secondhand towels, a lace panel, something, let her pick out and give her for lest than regular price. Give her for half. A really poor woman, give her for a little lest than half."

Right away I panicked. "How will I know a real poor woman from only a poor one?"

"You got a pair eyes, no?" He snapped off the overhead light. "So that's all. You'll come in tomorrow half past eight."

"An office job," said Ma when I gave her my news. "Wait till Pa hears."

When Pa heard, the first thing he said was, "How much a week?"

"I forgot to ask, Pa."

"Very smart. The first thing you do," he lectured me, "is to ask how much. If he mentions a figure not satisfactory, you ask for more. The way you handled, you'll have to take whatever he gives. But it's not too late yet. You didn't sign no contract, so tomorrow before you'll even sit down or take off your coat, you'll ask him."

You'd think, to hear my father, that he was the cagey one, the astute bargainer. All his years a loyal slavey he had worked his heart out for peanuts, protecting the boss's interest, saving him a dollar – and only the year before he had been slugged holding off two armed thugs to keep them from getting at the boss's safe. My father had been out of work, and things were so desperate in the house with no money for food or rent that he went finally (and at the cost of his pride) to Iscovitz, one of his rich Rumanian connections who owned a tobacco factory. Iscovitz had nothing to offer my father except a job as night watchman.

"I've got a man already, an old *cukker* half blind, half deaf. I'll let him go, Avrom Mendl, and give you the job."

My father refused; he wouldn't take another man's job; but

Iscovitz argued he needed a younger man, would have to let the old man go eventually – so my father came in as second night watchman. The old man ducked for cover when the heist took place, but not my father. Unarmed, he stood up to the thugs, and was cracked over the head for it.

He lay in bed three weeks with a bandaged head and fractured shoulder.

A few days after the foiled stickup a basket of fruit came to the house with a card from Iscovitz, and one night the millionaire Iscovitz himself came to visit. It was a hot night and the millionaire sat by my father's bed a few minutes fanning himself with a folded newspaper. "Take your time, Avrom Mendl, and don't worry. I don't want to see you in my place till you're better," he admonished my father, then came to the kitchen seeking my mother.

"He's a wonderful man," he said in Yiddish, and slipped her an envelope with a month's pay in it.

When I came to work, Myer Layevsky was out front loading his car. He blinked an eye at me, and I passed through to the office. Doing my father's bidding, I stood without removing my coat or sitting down. It took him a while to complete loading, and lugging goods through the office to the car he passed me several times, never once looking at me. This made me very nervous. Finally the car was loaded, and Layevsky came back. He straightened his hat and put a match to his cigar. "So I'll go now. You didn't brought a lunch?"

"I thought I'd go home," I said. "I live only ten minutes from here."

"Next time bring something to eat. I don't like the office shall be left alone. A customer comes in to pay and they find a closed office, they have an excuse to put off. Even a good customer will take advantage. Take off your coat and come in the back; I'll show you a hanger."

He was back at the door, and I hadn't got up nerve to ask about my pay. "Mr Layevsky? I forgot to ask you yesterday. We haven't settled yet –"

"I had in my mind to pay ten," he said, "but I need a Jewish girl in my business, so you I'll give twelve."

It was late in October when I came to work for Layevsky, and during the winter months I had to keep my coat on, it was so cold in the office. There was a hot-air register behind the door at the entrance to the stockroom, with hardly any heat coming through, and I used to stand on it stamping my feet, which were icy by midday.

"I'll tell a few words to the janitor," Layevsky kept promising, and one morning before the day's peddling, he did go down to the basement. There was a great rumbling below, and in a few minutes a rush of smoke came shooting through the register. Layevsky came back and stood over the register, rubbing his hands.

"You wouldn't be so cold no more," he said. "Come up a little bit heat now, no?"

"You mean smoke," I said.

He blinked an eye at me. "So she *has* a little sense," he said in Yiddish.


There wasn't enough work to keep me busy, and in the beginning I sat banging away at the old typewriter, getting up speed against the day he'd give me dictation. But I soon got bored with that, and one morning came to work with a book.

Layevsky spotted it immediately. "No, no, no," he said, wagging his head. "Don't bring no more a book to the office. It's not nice a customer comes in and the girl sits with a book."

"But there isn't enough work here to keep me busy," I protested.

"Who said? In an office you can always find something to do. Check over the cards; it wouldn't hurt." I took my coat to the stockroom, smouldering.

"Come here, my book lady," he called.

Hunched over the desk with knees bent and arms locked behind his back, he was peering at some cards he had fanned out, his nose almost touching, ashes dropping all over the place.

"Pick out Mrs. Oxenberg's card," he said.

I pointed to it.

"Pick it up, it wouldn't bite you. Now take a look."

I knew the cards were in order, but to satisfy him I glimpsed it briefly and returned it to the desk. "There's nothing wrong with this card."

"Look again," he said, thrusting it under my nose.

I resisted an impulse to slap it out of his hand, and turned my head away instead.

"Mrs. Oxenberg," he mused, "a good customer. I only wish I had more customers like that." Suddenly he slapped the card down, and with his nicotined finger, pointed to the last entry on it. "When did she made the last payment?"

"October twelfth," I said, "but that's before I was here."

"And today is already middle November, no? You can't see from the card that up till now she came in regular every week with a payment, and now it's a whole month she didn't come in? This you didn't notice? Maybe she's sick. Maybe she died, God forbid. Pick up the phone, find out. Attend better to my business, and you wouldn't find time to read a book in the office."

The first three weeks I worked for Layevsky he used to come back from the day's peddling before five. I would vacate the swivel chair, and he would sit down to check the day's take. No matter how much the amount varied, "That's all you took in today?" he'd ask. I took it as a joke at first, a pleasantry between us, but when I got to dislike the man, I resented it. "As if I were a salesgirl," I muttered once. "Or even a thief."

"What did you said?"

"Nothing." I had a feeling as I went to the door that he was laughing at me, but I did not look back to see.

After I'd been there a month he started coming back later each day; it was seldom before six now when he returned, and I'd stand peering through the office window looking for the car.

One night he didn't get back till seven, nor had he telephoned. Cold and hungry, I was standing on the register, and through the half-open stockroom door, saw him as he came in. He took a one-eyed look around. Lights on, no one in the office. He came loping to the stockroom.

"You're still here?"

I was incensed, indignant to the point of tears. "You speak as if I'm a guest who's overstayed her welcome." I swept by him; he followed me to the office.

"I speak like a what?"

I took my handbag from the desk. He followed me to the door.

"No, earnest," he said in Yiddish. "I speak like a *what?* Tell me." His manner was concerned, solicitous even, but I felt he was mocking me.

"Never mind," I said. This time I did look back, and saw him laughing at me.

One day a month was given over to repossessing merchandise from deadbeats. "Today I am pulling," he would say grimly; "give me the deadbeats." Deadbeat – the word was anathema to him. He couldn't say it without screwing both eyes shut. He would return at day's end, and through the office window I'd see him yanking piece by piece from the car, loading his shoulders. Draped like an Eastern merchant escaped from a bazaar holocaust, he loped from office to stockroom, muttering. "Deadbeat. You can't afford? Don't buy. I don't go in with a gun to nobody. *Chutzpah.* When it comes to take advantage, everyone knows where to find Myer Layevsky."

One day he was muttering, mulling this over, the injustice of it, the grievance to himself, when the telephone rang. I took the phone. It was Mrs. Greenberg, a good customer, an honest woman. Where's that tablecloth? she wanted to know, the one she ordered three days ago.

"It's Mrs. Greenberg," I said, my hand over the mouthpiece. "About that tablecloth, style 902 with the lace border? I told you about it –" He took the receiver from me. "Hello. Who? Oh, Mrs. Greenberg, what can I do for the lady? What tablecloth, when tablecloth? Who did you gave the message? Oh, my office lady," he said, swivelling around so that his back was to me. "You'll have to excuse. She's a young girl, she thinks about boys. Next time if you need something in a hurry, better speak to me."

I want to knock his hat off, grab the cigar from his mouth, and jump on it.

Despite having been forbidden to bring books to the office, I kept sneaking them in under my coat, and one morning, caught up in *Of Human Bondage*, I didn't hear the door. I jumped as if I'd been surprised in a criminal act; I put the book out of sight as if it were a bottle. Standing before me was a blond young man, tall, thin, with a pointed nose and white eyelashes. An albino.

"Is my dad here?" he asked. "I'm Israel Layevsky, Mr. Layevsky's son."

I told him his father would not be back before five, and loping like his old man, he went to the door. "Tell my dad I was here. And also that I came first in my class."

"Your son was here." I reported to Layevsky. "He asked me to tell you he came first in his class."

A smile came over Layevsky's face, breaking it wide open. All of a sudden he jumped up, clicked his heels together, and in baggy pants began a little dance in the office, clapping his hands. For a minute I thought he was going to ask me to partner him. He left off as suddenly as he began, and sank to the swivel chair puffing, fanning himself with his hat. "Twenty years old and going through for a doctor already since seventeen. So better don't make eyes on him," he said, wagging a roguish finger at me, "because it wouldn't help you nothing. I'm looking for a rich daughter-in-law."

One Friday, the second week in July, Myer Layevsky said, "How long do you work here now, nine months, no?"

About that, I said.

He blinked an eye at me. "You feel you're entitled to a holiday?" He handed me a roll of single dollar bills. "Count over, you'll find two weeks' pay. You don't work so hard in my place you need a holiday, but I close up anyway the office a week in July to take my missus to the country."

A holiday! The idea was thrilling. Except for day excursions to Hanlan's Point or Centre Island with Lizzie Stitsky, I had never been anywhere.

"So where will you go?" my father asked when I told him about the holiday.

"I don't know, Pa. I'll look in the paper under Summer Resorts."

"Don't look in the paper because I wouldn't let you go just anyplace, a young girl, and fall in the wrong hands."

I began boo-hooing, the disappointment was so keen, and ran to the room I shared with my sister, Gertie, slamming the door shut. I heard him in the kitchen talking it over with Ma, but as to what was being said, nothing. I heard him go to the telephone in the hall, but he spoke into the mouthpiece, keeping his voice down. He then came to the door. "Come out, my prima donna, and we'll talk about the holiday."

"Don't bother," I said, "I'm not interested any more."

"So what did I spend money on a long distance call to Mrs. Rycus?"

Mrs. Rycus, another one of my father's Rumanian connections, was a widow who had a small hotel in Huntsville and took lodgers during the summer months, mostly Rumanians.

"Poor woman," Pa said anytime he spoke of her. "Lived like a duchess in Focsani; now it's all she can do to keep a head over water."

My sister Gertie came home from work. She went to the kitchen, then came to the room we shared. "Pa says you're going to Huntsville? Mrs. Rycus says she can take you, but you'll have to share a room with the cook and maybe help out in the kitchen."

"That's great," I said.

"Why, what's wrong with that?" my sister said. "At least you'll be out in the country, and that's something, isn't it?"

"Have you got a bathing suit?" my father asked me at supper. "Mrs. Rycus said you'll need one."

"You mean an apron," I said, and my father flared up.

"Don't be so smart. I can still phone Mrs. Rycus and cancel."

My mother winked at me to keep quiet and not ruin my chance of a holiday.

First thing Saturday morning I went to Eaton's, and in the bargain basement equipped myself with a few assorted summer items, including a bathing suit, and Monday morning my father put me on the train for Huntsville. He fussed about securing me a window seat, then fussed again about whether it would be best to put my case on the rack or at my feet. The conductor called *All Aboard!* and my father unexpectedly leaned down to kiss me. His kiss, embarrassing both of us, landed on my ear. Through the window I saw him on the platform.

"Don't forget what I told you," he was saying.

I was to be met by Mrs. Rycus's truck driver, Bill Thompson. "You'll wait till a man approaches you. Don't you mention the name first," my father had warned me. "If he says Bill Thompson, you'll get in the truck with him. Have a good time," my father called, and as we pulled out, he raised his hat to me!

The station emptied quickly at Huntsville. I waited ten minutes, and the only living soul to show up was a good-looking boy, about twenty, who positioned himself inside the door, giving me the once-over. Could this be Bill Thompson? I was expecting an old man. Forgetting my father's warning, I jumped from the bench. "Is your name Bill Thompson?" "That's right," he said, and I got in the truck with him. We drove four miles to the hotel, the truck driver all the while stealing flirtatious glances at me as I sat puffing away on the cigarette he had given me. My father, fearful I might fall into wrong hands under Summer Resorts, should have seen this!

Mrs. Rycus, a lot shorter and greyer than I remembered, was on the hotel veranda to greet me. "Sura Rivka." She smiled, giving me my Jewish name, and stubbing out her cigarette, came slowly forward on swollen legs to embrace me. "Come, we'll go in the garden for tea," she said in an accent as thick as my father's. "Bill, take her suitcase up to Mrs. Schwartz's room," and the truck driver, picking it up, gave me a wink.

Sitting at café tables in the garden were about a dozen ladies, all in brightly coloured dresses, some with straw hats on their heads, others with kerchiefs.

Mrs. Rycus clapped for attention. "I have a surprise for you," she said, putting her arm around my waist. "This lovely girl is Avrom Mendl's daughter."

A fluster and flurry ensued at all tables. There were cries of *No! I don't believe it! So big!*

Mrs. Rycus whispered, "Don't be shy, darling. These are all Daddy's friends." Piloted by Mrs. Rycus, I was taken from table to table, each lady in turn kissing and complimenting me. I had never been called darling or kissed so much in my life. One lady, a Mrs. Ionescu, wouldn't let go of me. "Sit by me, darling," she coaxed, as the tea trolley was wheeled in by a maid. The trolley contained such a variety of things, I couldn't take them all in at a glance. Sandwiches, small sausages, black olives, fruit, iced cakes, cream buns. I pointed to a cream bun, and the maid put it on my plate.

"Tea or coffee?" she asked.

"Tea, please."

"Milk or lemon?"

"Milk, please."

Wasn't this thrilling! I was with real quality now, classier by far than anything I had read about in books. I wondered if I should have said please to the maid. I had said it twice – maybe even once was infra dig?

"What grade are you in school?" I was asked by a Mrs. Kayserling.

"I'm not in school any more. I'm working."

"Clever girl," she said. "What kind of work?"

I had got over my initial shyness and felt at ease now, on top of everything. Incorrigible show-off, I rattled away like one o'clock. "Oh, at a sort of bookkeeping job. I work for a Myer Layevsky, a very funny man. He sells goods on time."

"Goods?" another lady asked.

"Yes. Sheets, towels, blankets, Axminster rugs, and lace panels.

He calls it goods."

"On time?" another lady asked.

"Yes. To poor people," I said, offhandedly dismissing the poor as if my only connection with them was through my job. "It's a dollar down and a dollar when you ketch me." I loped across the lawn imitating Myer Layevsky. I blinked an eye at the assembled company. "That's all the money you took in today?" And they fell about.

After tea the ladies retired for a siesta, and I went up to the cook's room to unpack. Dinner was not till eight, and it was now only six – was I expected to help? I went downstairs and located the kitchen. Mrs. Rycus was at the stove beside a fat lady in an apron, a waitress was putting hors d'oeuvres on a tray, and Bill, in a far corner of the kitchen, was emptying a garbage container.

"Mrs. Schwartz, this is Sura Rivka, the daughter of a very dear friend, and for the next week your room companion," said Mrs. Rycus, introducing me to the fat lady in an apron. She then introduced me to Leona, the waitress.

"What can I do?" I asked Mrs. Rycus. "My father said I was to give you a hand in the kitchen –"

"Certainly not," she said. "That was Daddy's suggestion, not mine." Nothing was expected of me except I come to the kitchen in the morning and get my own breakfast. "The dining-room does not open till one," she said. "The ladies don't come down to breakfast; they take a cup of hot chocolate and a biscuit or something like that in their rooms. I'm short a waitress, so if you don't mind to give Leona a hand with the trays, I would appreciate it. But only if you like, darling; otherwise, Leona can manage herself. Meantime, go for a little walk to the beach, it's very pretty there. Bill, take the garbage to the incinerator, then show her where the beach is."

It was a fifteen-minute walk to the beach, Bill flirting with me all the way, and by the time we got there I was in love with the good-looking truck driver, head over heels.

At dinner that night I was seated with Mrs. Kayserling and her husband, Aaron, who had come for a few days in the country. I came to the dining-room hungry as a bear, but when I saw the array of silver at my place I was dismayed, appalled, my appetite left me. "When I was your age I could eat an ox," Mrs. Kayserling chided me. I made out that I had a very small appetite, so small it caused my father worry sometimes. After dinner we went to the lounge for coffee, and I sat listening to nostalgic talk of Rumania. Wonderful stories, and told for my benefit, I expect, as my father was featured in most of them. Tales of escapades, derring-do. My father? Fabulous stories, fascinating to listen to – but in the end they had the effect of sending me to bed unhappy, depressed. In Focsani my father had been on easy terms with these people, on equal footing with them. What a contrast now between their way of living and ours. He, so far as I knew, was the only failure of the Focsani émigrés, the only pauper.

But I was up early next morning, happy again, restored. What was the matter with me? I was holidaying in the country, *and* in love. After breakfast I helped Leona with the trays, then went to the beach in my new bathing suit. I had not been there ten minutes when Bill Thompson arrived. "Mrs. Rycus sent me. I'm supposed to keep an eye on you," he said, ogling me. On the way back I let him kiss me, and remembering my first kiss, could not for the rest of the day fix my attention on anything.

Wednesday morning at trays Leona was not at all friendly. Was she in love with Bill too? Later in the day I went to market with Bill and the cook, and sat between them in the cab, thrilled at the truck driver's proximity. Thursday morning Bill told me he and Leona were going to town that night for a movie. "See if Mrs. Rycus will let you come too," he said.

"Go, darling," Mrs. Rycus said, "there is nothing here for you to do."

Bill sat between us, and in the dark of the cinema, held my hand all through *Catherine the Great* with Elizabeth Bergner.

What a wonderful week. The excitement of being in love, the secrecy, the preoccupation, the thralldom of it. The ruses I contrived to meet my love at the incinerator for a few minutes before dinner, and again after dinner for walks along the country road ... But the inevitable Sunday arrived. The holiday was over. I was to leave by the six o'clock train. I took my things from the cook's closet, snuffling over my open case. To go back to my dreary home, my miserable job, and never again to see Bill. He had said something about getting work in Toronto, but I knew for sure I'd lose him to Leona, who was prettier than me, and older.

Mrs. Rycus came to the room. "I shall miss you, darling. It's such a pity you have to go back to the hot city. Wait," she said, "I have an idea. Leave everything. Go down and phone your Mr. Layevsky. Ask him to let you stay another week. It won't cost him anything; you'll stay as my guest."

I was so nervous when Layevsky's voice came over the long distance wire I had to make my request a second time before he understood me.

"It won't cost you anything, Mr Layevsky. I don't expect to get paid."

"So what can I complain? Stay long as you like," he said, and hung up. That worried me, I didn't like the sound of it, but surely that was only Layevsky's way? He would have ordered me back if he didn't want me to stay.

I managed to get word to Bill. I told him at the incinerator I was staying another week, and again that night after dinner I excused myself from the lounge on the pretence of going up to bed, then sneaked down the back staircase to meet him.

Monday morning Leona handed me Mrs. Rycus's tray. "She wants you to bring it," she said.

I knocked, Mrs. Rycus called "Come," and I brought the tray to her.

"Sit down a minute, Sura Rivka," Mrs. Rycus said, and I took the chair beside her bed. She put her cigarette in a holder, smiled at me, and began. "You're a big girl, a young lady now, and I would not presume to lecture you, but as I am such a close friend to Daddy you won't take offence? Bill is a nice boy, but just a boy from the village. Common. He is not for you, darling, and I don't like for you to be so much with him. You understand what I mean?"

I wanted the floor to open up. I wanted to drop out of sight never again to be seen by Mrs. Rycus. I reached forward almost toppling the hot chocolate in her lap.

"Yes, of course I understand. You don't want me to go to the market with him any more –"

"To the market is all right, and to the pictures if Leona goes too is all right. But at night alone with him for a walk? No, darling, this worries me."

So she had known all along. I could die for shame. Talking so cleverly in front of the ladies, then sneaking down the back staircase for hugs and kisses with the truck driver.

I went to the cook's room and stayed there, ignoring the one o'clock signal for lunch. Mrs. Rycus came up to fetch me.

"I want to go home," I bawled.

"Darling," she said, embracing me. "I could bite my tongue. You must excuse an old lady. Come down to lunch. Please, for my sake."

Next morning at her usual time she came to the kitchen with instructions for the cook. "Sura Rivka," she said, handing me a list. "If you don't mind to do me a favour, go with Bill to town. I need a few things from the drugstore, and he will not be able to attend to everything."

Bill, instead of continuing on the main road, turned sharply off onto a side road. "How come you stood me up last night? Are you playing hard to get?" He made a grab for me, and tried some fancy stuff. I slapped his hand. He lit a cigarette and backed the truck onto the main road again. "You Jewish girls are all alike," he said. "There's only one thing you're after, that wedding band."

Through the corner of my eye I studied his face as he drove sullenly to town. His head had assumed peculiar contours; it looked flat on top, something I had not noticed before. I was out of love. Leona was welcome to him. I had a longing suddenly to go home.

To see my father, who had raised his hat to me in the station, to see my mother, and even my sister Gertie. After lunch I sought out Mrs. Rycus. "Please, I want to go home on the six o'clock train. Not because of anything you said yesterday, honestly. It's just that I'm homesick."

"Darling," she said, "I understand what it is to be homesick."

Oh, I was glad to be on my way. I wouldn't have to think up funny stories to amuse the ladies at tea-time. At home I didn't have to sing for my supper; I could be as glum as I pleased. My father might call me prima donna, my mother might ask if I'd got up on the wrong side of the bed.

Pa was at the station to meet me. "You had enough of the country?" he said, and we boarded a streetcar.

Next morning, apprehensive of my encounter with Layevsky, I put off going to work till nine o'clock. By nine he'd be on his way for the day's drumming, and I could let myself in with the office key. I arrived ten past nine and through the office window saw a girl sitting at the desk. She swivelled around as I entered. She was blonde, with buck-teeth and eyeglasses. Definitely not a Jewish girl. I stammered, "Are you – is this –"

"This is Supreme Housefurnishings," she said briskly. "Did you want to see some merchandise?"

"No, no," I said, collecting my wits. "I used to work here, but I've got another job now." I put the key on the desk. "I always meant to return this, but with one thing and another –"

"Thank you," she said, and turned to the cards, dismissing me.

Deposed! Supplanted! It hit me like a stone to see her swivelling about in my chair ...

My father had dozed off again. I roused him. "Pa!"

He excused himself again. "I had some pills this morning, it makes me very sleepy. We were talking about something – that man you saw downstairs."

"That's right. Myer Layevsky. He's the one that gave me a

week's holiday, and I went to Mrs. Rycus in Huntsville, remember?"

"Oh, yes," said my father. "She was a wonderful woman, Mrs. Rycus. You know we grew up together in Focsani? In Rumania she lived like a duchess, but here she had a hard time to keep a head over water."

"I'll go now, Pa, and see you tomorrow."

My father held his hand out, and as was our custom except for the time he kissed me on the train, we shook hands on leave-taking.

Myer Layevsky was still under the big tree where I had settled him. He beckoned me, and I cut across the lawn.

"Didn't I told you maybe later it will come back to my mind?"

"Then you *do* remember," I said, exhilarated beyond all reason.

"I gave you a week off, but that wasn't enough for you. You made me a long distance call, no?"

"That's right. You know why I didn't want to come back? I fell in love that summer. With a *shaygitz*," I added mischievously.

That stopped him. He cocked an eye at me. "Did you married him?"

"No, I married a nice Jewish boy."

"Better," he said, nodding his head and chewing his dead cigar. "Better."

I had, in fact, married a nice gentile boy – but there was no need for Myer Layevsky to know that.

# BARRY CALLAGHAN

# The Black Queen

Hughes and McCrae were fastidious men who took pride in their old colonial house, the clean simple lines and stucco walls and the painted pale blue picket fence. They were surrounded by houses converted into small warehouses, trucking yards where houses had been torn down, and along the street, a school filled with foreign children, but they didn't mind. It gave them an embattled sense of holding on to something important, a tattered remnant of good taste in an area of waste overrun by rootless olive-skinned children.

McCrae wore his hair a little too long now that he was going grey, and while Hughes with his clipped moustache seemed to be a serious man intent only on his work, which was costume design, McCrae wore Cuban heels and lacquered his nails. When they'd met ten years ago Hughes had said, "You keep walking around like that and you'll need a body to keep you from getting poked in the eye." McCrae did all the cooking and drove the car.

But they were not getting along these days. Hughes blamed his bursitis but they were both silently unsettled by how old they had suddenly become, how loose in the thighs, and their feet, when they were showering in the morning, seemed bonier, the toes longer, the nails yellow and hard, and what they wanted was tenderness, to be able to yield almost tearfully, full of a pity for themselves that would not be belittled or laughed at, and when they stood alone in their separate bedrooms they wanted that tenderness from each other, but when they were having their bedtime tea in the kitchen, as they had done for years using lovely green and white Limoges cups, if one touched the other's hand then suddenly they both withdrew into an unspoken, smiling aloofness, as if some line of privacy had been crossed. Neither could bear their thinning wrists and the little pouches of darkening flesh under the chin. They spoke of being with younger people and even joked slyly about bringing a young man home, but that seemed such a betrayal of everything that they had believed had set them apart from others, everything they believed had kept them together, that they sulked and nettled away at each other, and though nothing had apparently changed in their lives, they were always on edge, Hughes more than McCrae.

One of their pleasures was collecting stamps, rare and mint-perfect, with no creases or smudges on the gum. Their collection, carefully mounted in a leatherbound blue book with seven little plastic windows per page, was worth several thousand dollars. They had passed many pleasant evenings together on the Direc-toire settee arranging the old ochre- and carmine-coloured stamps. They agreed there was something almost sensual about holding a perfectly preserved piece of the past, unsullied, as if everything didn't have to change, didn't have to end up swamped by decline and decay. They disapproved of the new stamps and dismissed them as crude and wouldn't have them in their book. The pages for the recent years remained empty and they liked that; the emptiness was their statement about themselves and their values, and Hughes, holding a stamp into the light between his tweezers, would say, "None of that rough trade for us."

One afternoon they went down to the philatelic shops around Adelaide and Richmond streets and saw a stamp they had been after for a long time, a large and elegant black stamp of Queen Victoria in her widow's weeds. It was rare and expensive, a dead-letter stamp from the turn of the century. They stood side by side over the glass counter-case, admiring it, their hands spread on the glass, but when McCrae, the overhead fluorescent light catching his lacquered nails, said, "Well, I certainly would like that little black sweetheart," the owner, who had sold stamps to them for several years, looked up and smirked, and Hughes suddenly snorted, "You old queen, I mean why don't you just quit wearing those goddamn Cuban heels, eh? I mean why not?" He walked out leaving McCrae embarrassed and hurt and when the owner said, "So what was wrong?" McCrae cried, "Screw you," and strutted out.

Through the rest of the week they were deferential around the house, offering each other every consideration, trying to avoid any squabble before Mother's Day at the end of the week when they were going to hold their annual supper for friends, three other male couples. Over the years it had always been an elegant, slightly mocking evening that often ended bitter-sweetly and left them feeling close, comforting each other.

McCrae, wearing a white linen shirt with starch in the cuffs and mother-of-pearl cuff links, worked all Sunday afternoon in the kitchen and through the window he could see the crab-apple tree in bloom and he thought how in previous years he would have begun planning to put down some jelly in the old pressed glass jars they kept in the cellar, but instead, head down, he went on stuffing and tying the pork loin roast. Then in the early evening he heard Hughes at the door, and there was laughter from the front room and someone cried out, "What do you do with an elephant who has three balls on him ... you don't know, silly, well you walk him and pitch to the giraffe," and there were howls of laughter and the clinking of glasses. It had been the same every year, eight men sitting down to a fine supper with expensive wines, the table set with their best silver under the antique carved wooden candelabra.

Having prepared all the raw vegetables, the cauliflower and

carrots, the avocados and finger-sized miniature corns-on-the-cob, and placed porcelain bowls of homemade dip in the centre of a pewter tray, McCrae stared at his reflection for a moment in the window over the kitchen sink and then he took a plastic slipcase out of the knives and forks drawer. The case contained the dead-letter stamp. He licked it all over and pasted it on his forehead and then slipped on the jacket of his charcoal-brown crushed velvet suit, took hold of the tray, and stepped out into the front room.

The other men, sitting in a circle around the coffee table, looked up and one of them giggled. Hughes cried, "Oh my God." McCrae, as if nothing was the matter, said, "My dears, time for the crudités." He was in his silk stocking feet, and as he passed the tray he winked at Hughes who sat staring at the black queen.

## IRENA FRIEDMAN KARAFILLY

# The Neilson Chocolate Factory

This is a story which starts with the casual unwrapping of a Neilson *Crispy Crunch*, a name which suddenly – far away from Toronto – is as evocative as the warm fragrance of chocolate which forever lingered over the neighbourhood.

"What, a chocolate factory?" my friends would laugh. "In Toronto?"

It's true, the factory made the neighbourhood sound like the world-famous Berne or Haarlem, though in fact it was a rather undistinguished area which some called Little Italy and others Little Portugal. Well, some of *us* called it that. The Italian and Portuguese immigrants who lived there were not likely to think of it as anything resembling their homelands. But though the winters were harsh and inflation kept rising, more and more of them seemed to move into the neighbourhood, planting tomatoes and vine in their backyards and sweeping the dry autumn leaves with a fervour equal only to their longing for the warm regions they had left behind. At four or five in the morning, one could see window after window light up in the houses around the factory as the men would get up to go to work, often labouring for twelve, fifteen hours a day while their wives scrubbed and laundered and waited on tables and the children played football on the icy streets. Only on Sundays, an air of contentment would settle over the neighbourhood and the smell of chocolate would give way to that of homebaked bread or roasting lamb. Only then did those rapidly maturing faces seem to relax as uncles and aunts would arrive and, taking little Giorgio or Rafael on their knee, ask:

"What are you gonna be when you grow up, hey?" while the child, barely able to restrain his pride, would answer: "Me, I'm gonna be a doctor," or – as inevitably – "Me, I'm gonna build chocolate factories!"

Some of the men on my street were employees of the Neilson factory, but the only person I knew was Manuel de Sousa, my landlord. The funny thing was, I could never find out just what he did there. An inscrutable Portuguese immigrant, his English seemed hopelessly inadequate whenever we had a disagreement. Which, I might have known from the start, the two of us -- worlds apart – were bound to have our share of.

"Hello, I see you have a flat for rent," I said, that rainy September evening when I finally found him home. Manuel, I remember, glared at me as though I had come to expropriate him.

"How many?" he snapped after a prolonged scrutiny.

"One, only me," I said, smiling, trying not to look overly eager. But, almost at once, he started to close the door in my face.

"Too big, too expensive for you," he said and I wondered whether it would be in my favor to tell him I was a free-lance journalist and needed extra space for an office.

"Hundred and forty dollars, *too much!*"

Hundred and forty dollars, in Toronto, hardly seemed like too much. "How many rooms?" I asked.

"Three and one kitchen, no fridge, no stove."

"Oh I see." Even so, it seemed like a bargain – I could always pick these up second hand, I decided. "Can I see?" I asked. And at last, he stepped aside to let me pass.

"You no have husband?" he asked.

"No, I'm ... not married." To say I was divorced would not, I suspected, help me get the flat. And I needed no more than one glance to know that I definitely wanted the place. An entire floor really, it was surprisingly beautiful – bright and immaculate, with a sun room and stained-glass windows. I was much too excited to notice, until the very end, the absence of one obvious room.

"No bathroom?" I asked, puzzled to have missed it and wondering why in the world he was acting so indifferent.

"Downstairs," he said, flicking off the lights.

And I, again: "Can I see?"

Well, it turned out the bathroom was in the basement and that I would have to share it with him. Though it was perfectly clean, I remember thinking it could be a problem, for – he told me then – he lived right there, across the hall from the bathroom. Now, it was my turn to feign nonchalance.

"You live alone?" I asked while he, with sudden defiance, snapped: "You want the flat, yes or no?"

I didn't understand any of it but I could take care of myself. I said yes, I would take it – quickly, before he could change his mind. Above all, I was puzzled that a man in his mid-thirties would own a three-storey house and live, alone, in the musty basement.

"You sure you can pay the rent?" he asked as I wrote out the first month's cheque.

"I'm sure," I said and, ignorant as I was, added: "Don't worry, I earn as much as a man."

Monday must have been the day they mixed the chocolate at the factory, for on those days the smell was so strong, one expected those red, home-grown tomatoes to have a cocoa taste. I moved into the flat the first Monday in October and I remember wondering whether I would eventually sicken of the sweet, persistent smell which Manuel, wearing his factory clothes, seemed to have brought with him right into my flat.

"So much furniture!" he said when I and two friends came back with my possessions from Montreal. "You buy it all?" he asked, looking, I remember, baffled and awed. He hovered around us, eyeing with inexplicable intensity the velvet couch, the Persian rugs. Now and then, he would give us a hand but mostly, he just stood there, pretending to busy himself with a light fixture or cupboard door, but looking the way a man might while handing over a family heirloom to a pawnbroker. He seemed curious too about my friends, Stuart and Jean-Paul.

"That man, the tall one, he your husband, no?" he said when the two of them had gone to return the trailer.

"I'm not married," I repeated. I couldn't understand why he should look so downcast about it. Did he, I wondered, feel uneasy about having a single woman in the house? Did he mind my bringing male friends over?

Stuart and Jean-Paul drove back that night and the next few days assured me Manuel was likely to keep a perfectly respectful distance. Both he and the Melos upstairs worked day and night, coming home, it seemed, only to eat and sleep. My desk was in the sun room, overlooking the garden, and each day, I would see him arrive in his chocolate-stained overalls and bend over the crisp, leafy plants, picking a ripe tomato, a green pepper. He pretended not to know I was there, though more than once, he must have heard the typewriter. His daily vegetable picking – slow and self-absorbed – was one of several rituals I was getting to know. Twice or three times a week, he would take out the garbage bins before going to work and, when he came home, carry them back under my windows where he would linger for suspiciously long moments, whisling and rattling the lids and, from time to time, glancing furtively into the lit-up living room. Once a week, on Saturdays, he would drive down to Kensington Market and return with heavy sacks of potatoes and newspaper-wrapped fish which he fried every Saturday before going out into the driveway to wash and polish his '71 Chevy. The car stood locked up in the garage all week, but he washed it faithfully all the same: once a week, after the trip to the market.

It was an unusually mild fall and I was beginning to discover the city – looking for curtain material in cluttered textile shops or for a paper lantern in Chinatown. Toronto seemed supremely organized for shopping purposes: fabric and hardware stores on Spadina, second-hand furniture on Queen Street. Each day, the radius of familiar territory expanded and each day, the toy-like streetcars would bring me back to the more familiar streets I was beginning to think of as home. That was the fall I wore nothing but black until one day, I perceived the Italian and Portuguese widows smiling at me like unlikely but sympathetic sisters. I could see it so plainly in their eyes: Ah, so young, poor thing, and already in mourning! I didn't mind their silent solicitude. There was something comforting in that feeling of shared bereavement – shared anything, I suppose. But soon after that, my black outfit – skirt, sweater, leotards – began to seem like a parody of their loss and I went back to wearing green corduroy skirts and maroon sweaters – the clothes which, I had to admit, were more properly mine.

Manuel's place was directly under my living room and, judging from the area it occupied, must have consisted of no more than one small room where he slept and cooked his fish and his potatoes. I say *must have* because he seemed as secretive about his place as an adolescent hiding old *Playboys*. When, one evening, I knocked on his door to ask about the fuse box (which turned out to be in his room), he kept the door open a crack, so that all I could see was the pale green corner with its peeling paint. It was not until a day or two later, however, that I fully realized the extent of his shame, his pride.

That afternoon (it was Saturday and Manuel was, as usual, washing his car in the driveway), I found my telephone dead and opening the back door, asked whether I might use his. I would have preferred to ask Ava-Maria upstairs but I had seen her leave with her husband only a short while earlier, on their way to the market and laundry.

Manuel turned off the hose and said yes, he would bring it up in a minute. I noticed, while waiting, that the vine leaves had turned quite yellow and the tomatoes were beginning to rot. I thought, with some surprise, that he must have had a plug phone, but the surprise turned to pained astonishment when he came upstairs carrying an *unwired* telephone which he at once proceeded to connect to an old phone box out in the hall.

"Manuel, I am sorry ... I didn't know you were going to –"

"No trouble, no trouble," he kept repeating, crouching on the floor with two screwdrivers.

"I'm sorry, really, I'm sorry."

"Is okay, you no have stove yet?"

"No, I'll probably get one this week."

"Everything costs too much money, no?" he smiled. He told me then about the job he used to have in the Sudbury mines and how, one winter, he slipped on the ice and broke his back.

"Nine months I no work," he said, "But Workmen's Compensation, they no pay me." He told me they paid only for work accidents. "And now," he said, "I wait another year for marry." He looked at my living room wistfully, then turned to face me again.

"I read your name in newspaper last week," he said, "Raoul and Ava-Maria, they want to know why you no have husband, I tell them you write for *Toronto Star*, right?"

"And you, what do you do?" I asked, just then more out of desire to change the subject than real curiosity.

"I work at Neilson Chocolate Factory."

"Yes, I know, but what do you do, exactly?"

"Chocolate, lots and lots of chocolate, mountains of chocolate," he said with a great gesture. "You like chocolate?"

"Yes, I like." I was gradually lapsing into his kind of speech.

"In Portugal, even in holidays, we no have much chocolate and now ... I no like," he finished sadly. I was intrigued by his talk of marriage. He was always alone. He had no visitors, male or female. And he worked about fourteen hours every day.

"Do you have a fiancée?" I asked, dialing the telephone company.

"No," he said, "I no have enough money." He waited while I talked to the telephone people, watching the squirrels in the garden pluck the rose hips from his bushes and disappear quickly among the yellowing foliage of his vegetable garden. I too had no visitors that first month. I was new in Toronto and was just beginning to meet people.

Those first two weeks, while looking for a stove, I would often eat at Lydia's Roti Shop around the corner. Lydia was a big Jamaican with an enormous bust pressing against the white jersey she wore day in and day out. Her voluptuous, knowing body seemed strangely incongruous with the shy and self-effacing expression on her aging face. She looked like a woman whose adolescence had congealed below the lines and wrinkles of middle age. She was married to a man from Trinidad and her roti shop was a favorite hangout for other islanders. A mother to some and object of sexual fantasies to others, she kept the place open day and night, making excellent, the best, roti. I acquired a great taste for the spicy, cheap stuff and for the Caribbean music the customers played on the juke box. Bent over the oozing pancake, I would eavesdrop on their conversations.

"Listen to me, man, you let that woman have a finger and, I tell you, she'll soon want a hand!"

"Hey, man, you don't know what you talking about, Pearl and me, we –" The voices sharp and urgent and, whatever the subject, as inexplicably optimistic as that relentless music. They knew how to live it up, those islanders and, late at night, it was an especially good place to go to, the hot spice lingering in my mouth for a long time after. Barely five minutes away, Manuel's house – the street – was always a startling surprise after Lydia's shop. Everyone, it seemed, went to bed here by ten. Like Manuel and Raoul, they all had to get up at four or five in the morning and leave for work before it was quite light. I don't know whether Neilson's had a night shift or not, but the chocolate smell continued to hover over the neighbourhood long after the workers had gone to sleep.

Now that I think about it, my problems with Manuel seemed to start when I first hung up my curtains. At the time, I didn't give it a thought, but he seemed to take it as a personal affront that I should want to protect my privacy. Perhaps he thought it was a rebuke for his curiosity, perhaps he saw it as an assertion of immoral intentions (I say *intentions* because, living below me, he must have known my lifestyle was above reproach). In any case, he began greeting me with extreme coldness, looking at once guilty and accusing whenever we met on the stairs and muttering under his breath when I said "How are you?" It is possible, however, that his mood had nothing to do with me, for twice that week, some friend of his arrived at the house and, for a long time, banged on Manuel's door and called his name. It was sometime past nine and Manuel had just arrived from work, but he did not come to the door and I did not let the man in. If there was anything I understood, even then, it was that he would want no one to see his place.

It was the week before Hallowe'en and, every afternoon, some child would ring my bell and ask me to buy a Neilson chocolate bar.

"How much?" I would ask.

"One dollar."

"One dollar!" It seemed like a lot, even for a large bar, but – for some reason – they all pushed the same product and all, somewhat timidly, demanded one dollar. When I asked why it cost so much, they just stared at me with their dark, somber eyes, so that I was never sure whether they had understood me. Only one of them – a fat, red-cheeked boy with energetic gestures – did not lose his bearings. Perhaps someone had already prepared him for the question, for the words were hardly out of my mouth when, meeting my eyes, the boy said: "It's for the poor people, the Greek and Portuguese and Italian people." Something told me he was lying, but I bought the chocolate anyway and ate it all that same night. Only after it was finished did I start to curse the boy. The chocolate bar turned out to be full of almonds and probably worth close to a dollar, but all the same, I was by then quite certain that the boy had lied.

My search for an antique table took me to the outlying suburbs of Toronto where families renovating or selling a home would advertise in the paper, quickly disposing of their possessions for half the price an antique dealer might want. I had no car in those days and used public transit, speculating about a given area on the basis of passengers getting on and off the subway. At Rosedale, for example, there would be elderly, meticulously dressed women, or bearded men who worked as editors or radio producers; at Davisville, secretaries and hairdressers would get off; at Finch, housewives with small children and businessmen returning home. Sometimes, I would wonder whether Manuel, or the Melos, ever made it to these parts of town, to the ravines and lake, and what they might have thought of the pink faces framed by coiffed hair or fur collars. Far from the city centre, the buses had the blank serenity of people on their way to church and the further away one got, the paler and more homogeneous the faces seemed.

Heading back, on the other hand, the buses and trains would become microcosms of cosmopolitan fervour: the Greek and Jamaican and Chinese returning home from factories and fish shops, chattering in a language they would have identified as English, though no English-speaking person could hope to understand more than the occasional word. Here, a Macedonian tailor might be heard discussing the sign for his shop with an Italian barber, or a black hosiery sorter her child's tonsilitis with a blonde Ukrainian mother. The further south one got, the more weary and uncouth the faces seemed. But the eyes – most often black, but sometimes blue or green – were strangely luminous and, glancing at my sixty-dollar boots or suede coat, bright with patience and hope.

Hallowe'en night brought the children to my door once again, this time in large groups of five or six, dressed as queens and gypsies and cowboys, and repeating their "Trick or treat" over and over, as though I might otherwise fail to understand their lisping command. They came well into the night, the sons and daughters of my weary neighbours who would greet me on the street, but cautiously, making it clear that some time would have to pass before they knew how to treat me. Judging from the quantity of Neilson chocolates in the children's bags, many of them indeed were employed at the factory, but the children – with their feather crowns and painted faces – had not yet lost their enthusiasm.

"Look at all the *Burnt Almonds* I got!" they'd say, or "Pepita's mother gave you more *Rosebuds* than me!"

Ah, how sweet must have been the sleep of those dark-eyed children who lived by the factory and who, night after night, drifted into dreams of luscious, aromatic plenty.

I had meanwhile settled down to a routine of work and relaxation – going out to the theatre, meeting new friends.

"Can you imagine?" my visitors would say, "tons and tons of chocolate processed every day, *yum!*"

I was beginning to have quite a few visitors and could not help but notice that each time a car would park in front of the house, one of my neighbours would be watching from the windows across. In a way, even then, I could appreciate their point of view: why, they must have asked, does she not go to work in the morning? Why does an attractive woman live all alone? And why, yes why, do all these men come to visit – in the morning, at night?

At first, I was amused and joked about it with my visitors, most of whom were in fact professional acquaintances. Soon, however, my life in the house became incomprehensibly difficult.

In the first place, Manuel was developing personal habits which made the bathroom unusually disagreeable. The bathroom, I should point out, had been unpleasant even before that. I couldn't possibly have known this that first day, but the plumbing was so cheap that flushing the toilet brought about a kind of gurgling in the drains of both sink and bath, sometimes so violent that it seemed as though any moment, both would overflow with toilet water. Now – it was the beginning of November – I began to find the yellow sink spattered with chocolate-like stains and strewn with black hair. A week later, Manuel stopped flushing the toilet, going on to make every conceivable effort to offend me. It was an unmistakable protest, but why? What was he trying to tell me? It wasn't long before I was allowed to find out.

All through October, I had lived with no heat whatsoever.

Occasionally, at night, it would get rather cold but it had been for the most part a sunny, warm month and, knowing how hard Manuel worked for his money, I had not complained. Right after Hallowe'en, however, fall arrived, with surprisingly low temperatures and gusty winds which blew away the last leaves of vine Manuel had planted. The neighbourhood cats, which used to hide among the swiss chard, were now plainly visible in the balding garden and, every day, I would hear the hissing of their encounters intermingled with the howling of the wind. Still, the heat was not turned on and, reluctant to complain, I began to spend more and more time by the steamed-up windows of Lydia's shop. Going home, the sharp air made the chocolate seem to come from a great distance – as though heralding the approach of snow – and my warm breath would be visible in the chilly night. At last, I decided to speak to him.

"Manuel," I said, hearing him come home one night, "it's very cold now, could you please –"

He did not let me finish my sentence. "Yes," he said, "I wanting to speak to you. Today, when I come home for lunch, you have friend in your flat!"

"Yes?" I said, thrown off by his finger which pointed accusingly in my face. What did my friend have to do with the heat?

"All the time," he went on, "you have friends and friends, you make music, laughing – I can no sleep all night!"

"But Manuel," I said, "I've never had a friend later than eleven."

"You lying, you have friend after one last night!"

"Oh no, that was a long-distance call."

"No!"

"Yes!"

It went on like that for a while, Manuel claiming I had men overnight, I – truthfully – denying; Manuel repeating he couldn't get any sleep, asking when did I do any work anyway; and I, losing my patience, saying it was none of his business, I worked when I wanted to, I didn't have to keep his hours!

Well, that was just what he seemed to be waiting for.

"Yes, you must," he finally said, "From tomorrow, no friends and you go sleeping at ten, like everybody."

I could hardly believe my ears. "Look," I said, "you can't tell me what to do, the flat –"

"You no go to sleep and work, I want new tenant end of December!"

At last, I gave up. I couldn't understand his outrage, the obvious lies. I liked working at night so that, in fact, most of my friends came for lunch or tea and, as I had pointed out, no one had ever stayed past eleven, though I certainly did not want to be denied my rights.

What was I to do?

He couldn't evict me, I knew, but he could make life unbearable unless I complied with his wishes. That was clearly out of the question. I was not about to start retiring at ten. I could not possibly live without friends. And I couldn't – I had meanwhile forgotten all about it – go on without heat. It was all very well for Manuel and the Melos – they were out most of the time – but I – was he trying to freeze me out, I wondered; was there someone else he wanted to rent the place to?

I decided to talk to an acquaintance who worked for Legal Aid, making my way downtown through the first snowstorm of the season. Already, I was beginning to think I would probably have to go, but "It's out of the question," the lawyer said; my landlord could do nothing to evict me, unless – he said – unless he had relatives he wanted to rent the flat to. I don't know why, but it was only then that I remembered seeing Manuel go down the week before with two gallons of paint. I had thought nothing of it at the time but there, in the lawyer's office, I had an overwhelming intuition.

"Manuel," I confronted him that very night, "you are planning to move upstairs, aren't you?"

He looked confused as a child, then – all at once – belligerent. "How you know that?" he asked.

I just glared, looking – I hoped – confident and wilful.

"You speaking to Raoul?"

"No, no – Look," I finally said, "if you wanted the place to yourself, why didn't you tell me last month?"

He looked down at his feet. "I change my mind," he said, guiltily, but with a curious sense of pride.

"Are you getting married?"

"No – one, two years maybe."

"Then why do you suddenly want the flat, why?"

He shrugged his shoulders and would not tell me. One thing I did know: If he wanted the place for himself, there was nothing I could do. Like it or not, I would have to start looking for a new place. It was damn annoying and I wanted to insist that he owed me an explanation, at the very least. Yet, with some part of me I must have understood something because, despite it all, I could feel no hostility toward him.

"I'll be out end of the month," I said, turning to climb the stairs, but stopped by the offended look on his face.

"No!" he said, leaving his door unguarded for once, "you no have to go before end of December, I give you one month, two."

"Well, I don't want to stay any longer than I have to."

"But please," he begged, "you no understand, I ... you Canadian, I Portuguese, you can no understand."

"Maybe not," I said and went up the stairs to my flat. I could hear him pacing downstairs for a long time after, well past eleven, anyway.

The colder it got, the more powerful the chocolate smell seemed to grow. By mid-November, the factory seemed to be stepping up its production toward Christmas and I hardly saw Manuel in the next two weeks. The day after our confrontation, the heat was turned on and, for the rest of that month, the bathroom was kept as immaculate as it had been at the start. The utter desolation of the garden, however, made it difficult to believe that I had lived in that house for less than two months. I had thought, when I learned I'd have to go, that I would look for a place downtown, away from the immigrants' disapproving eyes and their stifling lifestyle. But in the following days, as I'd pass Lydia's shop or watch the children play around the factory, the thought of leaving the street, of breathing plain winter air devoid of all sweetness, became as painfully sharp as first frost. There was only one apartment building on the street and, for days, I had ignored the red sign: APARTMENT FOR RENT. I wanted to be able to come and go, to pull up my blinds at ten or eleven without feeling like the scarlet lady in some small village.

Well, it was a two-bedroom apartment and though it had nothing special to recommend it, I took it on impulse one afternoon, on my way from the Italian grocery. I felt curiously fortunate once I paid the deposit – as though, after all, I had been permitted to stay close to home.

Manuel was a changed man after our encounter. He had painted his room downstairs and found a new immigrant to move in as soon as he moved up to the first floor. Once or twice, I heard visitors' voices downstairs and he seemed to have bought himself a radio. One day, he came back from the market with crated grapes and, over the weekend made, he later told me, fifty bottles of wine, which left the basement area sticky with dark, purple stains and attracted innumerable fruit flies multiplying rapidly, though we sprayed and sprayed.

When Ava-Maria told him I had fallen and sprained my ankle, he came up to see me and, shy as a village boy, handed me a box of Neilson chocolates.

"One day you tell me you like chocolates, remember?"

"I remember," I said. "Thank you very much."

There was an awkward silence between us, then – looking up at the ceiling – he said: "I gonna help you move, OK?"

"Oh no," I protested, "really, it's not necessary."

But he looked as obstinate as he had that first day. "Yes," he said, "I gonna help you."

And that was that. He would not take no for an answer, saying he knew someone with a truck and that he and Raoul would help. I don't know why, but I could not bring myself to eat those chocolates, finally packing them with my kitchen stuff.

When the day came, they showed up as agreed, he and Raoul and Ava-Maria, the four of us carrying the bookshelves, the couch, the Tiffany lamp. We were all a little awkward, I think, but Manuel made every effort to help me forget that, all said and done, I was still getting evicted. At one point, Ava-Maria and I stood watching while Manuel and her husband manoeuvered the large secretarial desk which – Manuel insisted, laughing – could not have come through that door. Ava-Maria smiled and moved closer beside me.

"You still mad?" she asked, searching my eyes in the dark.

"I'm not ... mad," I said, more embarrassed than ever.

"Manuel," she said, "he no like to live in basement after you come here."

"But why, has he told you why?"

She shrugged her shoulders, much as Manuel himself had done – as though, the gesture seemed to say, I could not possibly hope to understand.

"You are a woman and you Canadian," she said at last, "and you make lots of money – he no like that."

"But I'm not rich," I protested, "I have no money in the bank."

She only smiled – the slight, resigned smile an adult might bestow upon a slow child. "You no work in a factory," she said. "You born here."

The men meanwhile had managed to get the desk through the door, though the collapsible typewriter stand kept springing out.

"You gonna write lots of stories for *Toronto Star*, yes?" Manuel said, grinning, and I nodded, smiling back.

As soon as I get settled, I thought, I'm going to contact Neilson's and do a story for *Weekend Magazine*. I did phone their PR man several times that year and told his secretary what I wanted. She had a polished, executive-secretary's voice, but her name was Miss Lopes. She said her boss, Mr. Amado, would call me back as soon as he was free. He never did.

## MATT COHEN

# The Sins of Tomas Benares

A narrow, three story house near College Street had been the home of the Benares family since they arrived in Toronto in 1936. Beside the front door, bolted to the brick, was a brass name-plate that was kept polished and bright: DR. TOMAS BENARES.

Benares had brought the name-plate – and little else – with him when he and his wife fled Spain just before the Civil War. For twenty years it had resided on the brick beside the doorway. And then, after various happinesses and tragedies – the tragedies being unfortunately more numerous – it had been replaced triumphantly by a new nameplate: DR. ABRAHAM BENARES. This son, Abraham, was the only child to have survived those twenty years.

Abraham had lost not only his siblings, but also his mother. The day his name-plate was proudly mounted Tomas could at last say to himself that perhaps his string of bad fortune had finally been cut, for despite everything he now had a son who was a doctor, like himself, and who was married with two children.

By 1960, the Benares household was wealthy in many ways.

True, the family had not moved to the north of the city like many other immigrants who had made money, but during the era of the DR. ABRAHAM BENARES name-plate the adjoining house was purchased to give space for an expanded office and to provide an investment for Abraham Benares' swelling income as a famous internist. The back yards of both houses were combined into one elegant lawn that was tended twice a week by a professional gardener, an old Russian Jew who Tomas Benares had met first in his office, then at the synagogue. He spent most of his time drinking tea and muttering about the injustices that had been brought upon his people, while Tomas himself, by this time retired, toothless, and bent of back, crawled through the flower beds on his knees wearing the discarded rubber dishwashing gloves of his son's extraordinarily beautiful wife.

Bella was her name. On anyone else such a name would have been a joke; but Bella's full figure and dark, Mediterranean face glowed with such animal heat that from the first day he met her Tomas felt like an old man in her presence. Of this Bella seemed entirely unaware. After moving into the house she cooked for Tomas, pressed her scorching lips to his on family occasions, even hovered over him during meals, her fruity breath like a hot caress against his neck. After her children were born she began to refer to Tomas as grandfather, and sometimes while the infants played on the living room floor she would stand beside Tomas with the full weight of her fleshy hand sinking into his arm. "Look at us," she said to Tomas once, "three generations."

A few years after the birth of his daughter, Abraham Benares was walking with her down to College Street, as he did every Saturday, to buy a newspaper and a bag of apples, when a black Ford car left the street and continued its uncontrolled progress along the sidewalk where Abraham was walking. Instinctively, Abraham scooped Margaret into his arms, but the car was upon him before he could move. Abraham Benares, forty-one years old and the former holder of the city intercollegiate record for the one hundred yard dash, had time only to throw his daughter onto the adjacent lawn while the car mowed him down.

The next year, 1961, the name-plate on the door changed again: DR. TOMAS BENARES reappeared. There had been no insurance policy and the old man, now seventy-four years of age but still a licensed physician, recommenced the practice of medicine. He got the complaining gardener to redivide the yard with a new fence, sold the house next door to pay his son's debts, and took over the task of providing for his daughter-in-law and his two grandchildren.

Before reopening his practice, Tomas Benares got new false teeth and two new suits. He spent six months reading his old medical textbooks and walked several miles every morning to sweep the cobwebs out of his brain. He also, while walking, made it a point of honour never to look over his shoulder.

On the eve of his ninety-fourth birthday Tomas Benares was sixty-two inches tall and weighed one hundred and twelve pounds. These facts he noted carefully in a small diary. Each year, sitting in his third floor bedroom-study, Tomas Benares entered his height and weight into the pages of this diary. He also summarized any medical problems he had experienced during the year past, and made his prognosis for the year to come. There had once been an essay-like annual entry in which he confessed his outstanding sins and moral omissions from the previous year and outlined how he could correct or at least repent them in the year to follow. These essays had begun when Tomas was a medical student, and had continued well past the year in which his wife died. But when he had retired the first time from practising medicine and had the time to read over the fifty years of entries, he had noticed that his sins grew progressively more boring with age. And so, after that, he simply recorded the number of times he had enjoyed sexual intercourse that year.

Now, almost ninety-four, Tomas Benares couldn't help seeing that even this simple statistic had been absent for almost a decade. His diary was getting shorter while his life was getting longer. His last statistic had been when he was eighty-six – one time; the year before – none at all. But in his eighty-fourth year there had been a

dozen transgressions. Transgressions! They should have been
marked as victories. Tomas brushed back at the wisps of white hair
that still adorned his skull. He couldn't remember feeling guilty or
triumphant, couldn't remember any detail at all of the supposed
events. Perhaps he had been lying. According to the entry, his
height during that erotic year had been sixty-four inches, and his
weight exactly twice that – one hundred and twenty-eight pounds.
In 1956, when he had begun compiling the statistics, there had been
only one admission of intercourse, but his height had been sixty-
five inches and his weight one hundred and forty.

Suddenly, Tomas had a vision of himself as an old-fashioned
movie. In each frame he was a different size, lived a different life.
Only accelerating the reel could make the crowd into one person.

He was sitting in an old blue armchair that had been in the living
room when Marguerita was still alive. There he used to read aloud
in English to her, trying to get his accent right, while in the adjacent
kitchen she washed up the dinner dishes and called out his mistakes. Now he imagined pulling himself out of the armchair,
walking to the window to see if his grandson Joseph's car was
parked on the street below. He hooked his fingers, permanently
curved, into the arms of his chair. And then he pulled. But the chair
was a vacuum sucking him down with the gravity of age. Beside
him was a glass of raspberry wine. He brought it to his lips, wet the
tip of his tongue. He was on that daily two-hour voyage between
the departure of his day nurse and the arrival of Joseph. Eventually,
perhaps soon, before his weight and height had entirely shrunk
away and there were no statistics at all to enter into his diary, he
would die. He wanted to die with the house empty. That was the last
wish of Tomas Benares.

But even while his ninety-fourth birthday approached, Tomas
Benares was not worrying about dying. To be sure he had become
smaller with each year, and the prospect of worthwhile sin had
almost disappeared; but despite the day nurse and the iron gravity
of his chair, Tomas Benares was no invalid. Every morning this

whole summer – save the week he had the flu – his nurse, whose name was Elizabeth Rankin, had helped him down the stairs and into the yard where, on his knees, he tended his gardens. While the front of the house had been let go by his careless grandson, Joseph, the back was preserved in the splendour it had known for almost fifty years. Bordering the carefully painted picket fence that surrounded the small yard were banks of flowers, the old straw-berry patch, and in one corner a small stand of raspberry canes that were covered by netting to keep away the plague of thieving sparrows.

This morning, too, the morning of his birthday, Elizabeth Rankin helped him down the stairs. Elizabeth Rankin had strong arms, but although he could hardly walk down the three flights of stairs by himself – let alone climb back up – he could think of his own father, who had lived to be one hundred and twenty-three and of his grandfather Benares, who had lived to the same age. There was in fact no doubt that this enormous number was fate's stamp on the brow of the Benares men, though even fate could not *always* cope with automobiles.

But, as his own father had told Tomas, the Benares were to consider themselves blessed because fate seemed to pick them out more frequently than other people. For example, Tomas' father, who was born in 1820, had waited through two wives to have children, and when one was finally born, a boy, he had died of an unknown disease that winter brought to the Jewish quarter of Kiev. So frightened had he been by this show of God's spite that Tomas' father had sold the family lumbering business and rushed his wife back to Spain, the cradle of his ancestors, where she bore Tomas in 1884. Tomas' grandfather had, of course, been hale and hearty at the time: one hundred and four years old, he had lived on the top floor of the house just as Tomas now lived on the top floor of his own grandson's house.

That old man, Tomas' grandfather, had been a round, brown apple baked dry by the sun and surrounded by a creamy white fringe of beard. He had been born in 1780 and Tomas, bemoaning the emptiness of his diary on the occasion of his oncoming ninety-fourth, realized suddenly that he was holding two hundred years in his mind. His father had warned him: the Benares men were long-lived relics whose minds sent arrows back into the swamp of the past, so deep into the swamp that the lives they recalled were clamped together in a formless gasping mass, waiting to be shaped by those who remembered. The women were more peripheral: stately and beautiful they were easily extinguished; perhaps they were bored to death by the small, round-headed stubborn men who made up the Benares tribe.

"We were always Spaniards," the old man told Tomas, "stubborn as donkeys." *Stubborn as a donkey*, the child Tomas had whispered. Had his mother not already screamed this at him? And he imagined ancient Spain: a vast, sandy expanse where the Jews had been persecuted and in revenge had hidden their religion under prayer shawls and been stubborn as donkeys.

And they hadn't changed, Tomas thought gleefully, they hadn't changed at all: filled with sudden enthusiasm and the image of himself as a white-haired, virile donkey, he pulled himself easily out of his chair and crossed the room to the window where he looked down for Joseph's car. The room was huge: the whole third floor of the house save for an alcove walled off as a bathroom. Yet even in the afternoon the room was dark as a cave, shadowed by its clutter of objects that included everything from his marriage bed to the stand-up scale with the weights and sliding rule that he used to assess himself for his yearly entry.

From the window he saw that his grandson's car had yet to arrive. On the sidewalk instead were children travelling back and forth on tricycles, shouting to each other in a fractured mixture of Portuguese and English. As always, when he saw children on the sidewalk, he had to resist opening the window and warning them to watch out for cars. It had been Margaret, only four years old, who had run back to the house to say that "Papa is sick," then had insisted on returning down the street with Tomas.

Two hundred years: would Margaret live long enough to sit

frozen in a chair and feel her mind groping from one century to the next? Last year, on his birthday, she had given him the bottle of raspberry wine he was now drinking. "Every raspberry is a blessing," she had said. She had a flowery tongue, like her brother, and when she played music Tomas could sense her passion whirling like a dark ghost through the room. What would she remember? Her mother who had run away; her grandmother whom she had never known; her father, covered by a sheet by the time she and Tomas had arrived, blood from his crushed skull seeping into the white linen.

They had come a long way, the Benares: from the new Jerusalem in Toledo to two centuries in Kiev, only to be frightened back to Spain before fleeing again, this time to a prosperous city in the New World. But nothing had changed, Tomas thought, even the bitterness over his son's death still knifed through him exactly as it had when he saw Margaret's eyes at the door, when Joseph, at the funeral, broke into a long, keening howl.

Stubborn as a donkey. Tomas straightened his back and walked easily from the window towards his chair. He would soon be ninety-four years old; and if fate was to be trusted, which it wasn't, there were to be thirty more years of anniversaries. During the next year, he thought, he had better put some effort into improving his statistics.

He picked up his diary again, flipped the pages backward, fell into a doze before he could start reading.

On his ninety-fourth birthday Tomas slept in. This meant not waking until after eight o'clock; and then lying in bed and thinking about his dreams. In the extra hours of sleep Tomas dreamed that he was a young man again, that he was married, living in Madrid, and that at noon the bright sun was warm as he walked the streets from his office to the café where he took lunch with his cronies. But in this dream he was not a doctor but a philosopher; for some strange reason it had been given to him to spend his entire life thinking about oak trees, and while strolling the broad, leafy streets it was precisely this subject that held his mind. He had also the duty, of course, of supervising various graduate students, all of whom were writing learned dissertations on the wonders of the oak; and it often, in this dream, pleased him to spend the afternoon with these bright and beautiful young people, drinking wine and saying what needed to be said.

In the bathroom, Tomas shaved himself with the electric razor that had been a gift from Joseph. Even on his own birthday he no longer trusted his hand with the straight razor that still hung, with its leather strop, from a nail in the wall. This, he suddenly thought, was the kind of detail that should also be noted in his annual diary – the texture of his shrinking world. Soon everything would be forbidden to him, and he would be left with only the space his own huddled skeleton could occupy. After shaving, Tomas washed his face, noting the exertion that was necessary just to open and close the cold water tap, and then he went back to the main room where he began slowly to dress.

It was true, he was willing to admit, that these days he often thought about his own death; but such thoughts did not disturb him. In fact, during those hours when he felt weak and sat in his chair breathing slowly, as if each weak breath might be his last, he often felt Death sitting with him. A quiet friend, Death; one who was frightening at first, but now was a familiar companion, an invisible brother waiting for him to come home.

But home, for Tomas Benares, was still the world of the living. When Elizabeth Rankin came to check on him, she found Tomas dressed and brushed. And a few minutes later he was sitting in his own garden, drinking espresso coffee and listening to the birds fuss in the flowering hedges that surrounded his patio. There Tomas, at peace, let the hot sun soak into his face. Death was with him in the garden, in the seductive buzz of insects, the comforting sound of water running in the nearby kitchen. The unaccustomed long sleep only gave Tomas the taste for more. He could feel himself drifting off, noted with interest that he had no desire to resist, felt Death pull his chair closer, his breath disguised as raspberries and mimosa.

At seventy-four years of age, also on his birthday, Tomas Benares had gone out to his front steps, unscrewed his son's name-plate and reaffixed his own. In the previous weeks he had restored the house to the arrangement it had known before his original retirement.

The front hall was the waiting room. On either side were long wooden benches, the varnished oak polished by a generation of patients. This front hall opened into a small parlour that looked onto the street. In that room was a desk, more chairs for waiting, and the doctor's files. At first his wife ran that parlour; after her death, Tomas had hired a nurse.

Behind the parlour was the smallest room of all. It had space for an examination table, a glass cabinet with a few books and several drawers of instruments, and a single uncomfortable chair. On the ceiling was a fluorescent light, and the window was protected by venetian blinds made of heavy plastic.

After Abraham's death his widow, Bella, and the children had stayed on in the Benares household and so on the morning of the reopening Tomas had gone into the kitchen to find Bella making coffee and feeding breakfast to Joseph and Margaret. He sat down wordlessly at the kitchen table while Bella brought him coffee and toast, and he was still reading the front section of the morning paper when the doorbell rang. Joseph leapt from the table and ran down the hall. Tomas was examining the advertisement he had placed to announce the recommencement of his practice.

"Finish your coffee," said Bella. "Let her wait. She's the one who needs the job."

But Tomas was already on his feet. Slowly he walked down the hall to the front parlour. He could hear Joseph chatting with the woman, and was conscious of trying to keep his back straight. He was wearing, for his new practice, a suit newly tailored. His old tailor had died, but his son had measured Tomas with the cloth tape, letting his glasses slide down to rest on the tip of his nose exactly like his father had. Now in his new blue suit, a matching tie, and one of the white linen shirts that Marguerita had made for him, Tomas stood in his front parlour.

"Doctor Benares, I am Elizabeth Rankin; I answered your advertisement for a nurse."

"I am pleased to meet you, Mrs. Rankin."

"Miss Rankin." Elizabeth Rankin was then a young woman entering middle age. She had brown hair parted in the middle and then pulled back in a bun behind her neck, eyes of a darker brown in which Tomas saw a mixture of fear and sympathy. She was wearing a skirt and a jacket, but had with her a small suitcase in case it was necessary for her to start work right away.

"Would you like to see my papers, Doctor Benares?"

"Yes, if you like. Please sit down."

Joseph was still in the room and Tomas let him watch as Elizabeth Rankin pulled out a diploma stating that she had graduated from McGill University in the biological sciences, and another diploma showing that she had received her RN from the same university.

"I have letters of reference, Doctor Benares."

"Joseph, please get a cup of coffee for Miss Rankin. Do you –"

"Just black, Joseph."

They sat in silence until Joseph arrived with the coffee, and then Tomas asked him to leave and closed the door behind him.

"I'm sorry," Elizabeth Rankin said. "I saw the advertisement and ..."

She trailed off. It was six months since Tomas had seen her, but he recognized her right away; she was the woman who had been driving the car that had killed his son. At the scene of the accident she had shivered in shock until the ambulance arrived. Tomas had even offered her some sleeping pills. Then she had reappeared to hover on the edge of the mourners at Abraham's funeral.

"You're a very brave woman, Miss Rankin."

"No, I ..." Her eyes clouded over. Tomas, behind the desk, watched her struggle. When he had seen her in the hall, his first reaction had been anger.

"I thought I should do something," she said. "I don't need a salary, of course, and I *am* a qualified nurse."

"I see that," Tomas said dryly.

"You must hate me," Elizabeth Rankin said.

Tomas shrugged. Joseph came back into the room and stood beside Elizabeth Rankin. She put her hand on his shoulder and the boy leaned against her.

"You mustn't bother Miss Rankin," Tomas said, but even as he spoke he could see Elizabeth's hand tightening on the boy's shoulder.

"Call Margaret," Tomas said to Joseph, and then asked himself why, indeed, he should forgive this woman. No reason came to mind, and while Joseph ran through the house, searching for his sister, Tomas sat in his reception room and looked carefully at the face of Elizabeth Rankin. The skin below her eyes was dark, perhaps she had trouble sleeping; and though her expression was maternal she had a tightly drawn quality that was just below the surface, as though the softness were a costume.

He remembered a friend, who had been beaten by a gang of Franco's men, saying he felt sorry for them. When Tomas' turn came, he had felt no pity for his assailants. And although what Elizabeth Rankin had done was an accident, not a malicious act, she was still the guilty party. Tomas wondered if she knew what he was thinking, wondered how she could not. She was sitting with one leg crossed over the other, her eyes on the door through which the sounds of the children's feet now came. And when Margaret, shy, sidled into the room, Tomas made a formal introduction. He was thinking, as he watched Margaret's face, how strange it was that the victims must always console their oppressors.

Margaret, four years old, curtsied and then held out her hand. There was no horrified scream, no flicker of recognition.

"Miss Rankin will be coming every morning," Tomas announced. "She will help me in my office."

"You are very kind, Doctor Benares."

"We will see," Tomas said. It was then that he had an extraordinary thought, or at least a thought that was extraordinary for him. It occurred to him that Elizabeth Rankin didn't simply want to atone, or to be consoled. She wanted to be taken advantage of.

Tomas waited until the children had left the room, then closed the door. He stood in front of Elizabeth Rankin until she, too, got to her feet.

"Pig," Tomas Benares hissed: and he spat at her face. The saliva missed its target and landed, instead, on the skin covering her right collarbone. There it glistened, surrounded by tiny beads, before gliding down the open V of her blouse.

The eyes of Elizabeth Rankin contracted briefly. Then their expression returned to a flat calm. Tomas, enraged, turned on his heel and walked quickly out of the room. When he came back fifteen minutes later, Elizabeth Rankin had changed into her white uniform and was sorting through the files of his son.

Bella said it wasn't right.

"That you should have *her* in the house," she said. "It's disgusting."

"She has a diploma," Tomas said.

"And how are you going to pay her? You don't have any patients."

This discussion took place in the second floor sitting room after the children were asleep. It was the room where Bella and Abraham used to go to have their privacy.

"At first I thought maybe you didn't recognize her," Bella started again, "and so I said to myself, what sort of a joke is this? Maybe she didn't get enough the first time, maybe she has to come back for more."

"It was an accident," Tomas said.

"So you forgive her?" Bella challenged. She had a strong, bell-like voice which, when she and Abraham were first married, had been a family joke, one even she would laugh at; but since his death the tone had grown rusty and sepulchral.

Tomas shrugged.

"I don't forgive her," Bella said.

"It was an accident," Tomas said. "She has to work it out of her system."

"What about me? How am I going to work it out of my system?"

At thirty, Bella was even more beautiful than when she had been married. The children had made her heavy, but grief had carved away the excess flesh. She had jet-black hair and olive skin that her children had both inherited. Now she began to cry and Tomas, as always during these nightly outbursts of tears, went to stand by the window.

"Well?" Bella insisted. "What do you expect me to do?"

When she had asked this question before, Tomas advised her to go to sleep with the aid of a pill. But now he hesitated. For how many months, for how many years could he tell her to obliterate her evenings in sleeping pills.

"You're the saint," Bella said. "You never wanted anyone after Marguerita."

"I was lucky," Tomas said. "I had a family."

"I have a family."

"I was older," Tomas said.

"So," Bella repeated dully, "you never did want anyone else."

Tomas was silent. When Abraham brought her home he had asked Tomas what he thought of her. "She's very beautiful," Tomas had said. Abraham had happily agreed. Now she was more beautiful but, Tomas thought, also more stupid.

"It is very hard," Tomas said, "for a man my age to fall in love."

"Your wife died many years ago ..."

Tomas shrugged. "I always felt old,'' he said, "ever since we came to Canada." All this time he had been standing at the window, and now he made sure his back was turned so that she wouldn't see his tears. The day Abraham had been killed he had cried with her. Since then, even at the funeral, he had refused to let her see his tears. Why? He didn't know. The sight of her, even the smell of her walking into a room, seemed to freeze his heart.

"If there was –" Bella started. She stopped. Tomas knew that he should help her, that she shouldn't have to fight Abraham's ghost and his father, but he couldn't bring himself to reach out. It was like watching an ant trying to struggle its way out of a pot of honey.

"If there was someone else," Bella said. "Even a job."

"What can you do?" Tomas asked, but the question was rhetorical: Bella had married Abraham the year after she had finished high school. She couldn't even type.

"*I* could be your receptionist, instead of that –"

"Nurse," Tomas interrupted. "I need a nurse, Bella."

"I can put a thermometer in someone's mouth," Bella said. "Are people going to die while you're next door in the office?"

"A doctor needs a nurse," Tomas said. "I didn't invent the rules."

"There's a rule?"

"It's a custom, Bella."

He turned from the window.

"And anyway," Bella said, "who's going to take care of the children?"

"That's right, the children need a mother."

"We need Bella in the kitchen making three meals a day so at night she can cry herself to sleep – while the murderer is working off her guilt so at night she can go out and play with the boys, her conscience clean."

"You don't know what she does at night –"

"You're such a saint," Bella said suddenly. "You are such a saint the whole world admires you, do you know that?"

"Bella –"

"The holy Doctor Benares. At seventy-four years of age he ends his retirement and begins work again to provide for his widowed daughter and his two orphaned grandchildren. Has the world ever seen such a man? At the *shul* they're talking about adding a sixth book to the Torah." She looked at Tomas, and Tomas, seeing her go out of control, could only stand and watch. She was like an ant, he was thinking. Now the ant was at the lip of the pot. It might fall back into the honey, in which case it would drown; or it might escape after all.

"You're such a saint," Bella said in her knife-edged voice, "you're such a saint that you think poor Bella just wants to go out and get laid."

She was teetering on the edge now, Tomas thought.

"You should see your face now," Bella said. "*Adultery*, you're thinking. *Whore*."

"It's perfectly normal for a healthy –"

"Oh, healthy *shit!*" Bella screamed. "I just want to go out. Out, out, *out!*"

She was standing in the doorway, her face beet-red, panting with her fury. Tomas, staying perfectly still, could feel his own answering blush searing the backs of his ears, surrounding his neck like a hot rope.

"Even the saint goes for a walk," Bella's voice had dropped again. "Even the saint can spend the afternoon over at Herman Levine's apartment, playing cards and drinking beer."

Tomas could feel his whole body burning and chafing inside his suit. *The saint*, she was calling him. And what had he done to her? Offered her and her family a home when they needed it. "Did I make Abraham stay here?" Tomas asked. And then realized, to his shame, that he had said the words aloud.

He saw Bella in the doorway open her mouth until it looked like the muzzle of a cannon. Her lips struggled and convulsed. The room filled with unspoken obscenities.

Tomas reached a hand to touch the veins in his neck.

They were so engorged with blood he was choking. He tore at his tie, forced his collar open.

"Oh, God," Bella moaned.

Tomas was coughing, trying to free his throat and chest. Bella was in the corner of his hazed vision, staring at him in the same detached way he had watched her only a few moments before.

*The saint*, Tomas was thinking, *she calls me the saint*. An old compartment of his mind suddenly opened, and he began to curse at her in Spanish. Then he turned his back and walked upstairs to his third floor bedroom.

In the small hours of the morning, Tomas Benares was lying in the centre of his marriage bed, looking up at the ceiling of the bedroom and tracing the shadows with his tired eyes. These shadows: cast by the streetlights they were as much a part of his furniture as was the big oak bed, or the matching dressers that presided on either side – still waiting, it seemed, for the miraculous return of Marguerita.

As always he was wearing pyjamas – sewing had been another of Marguerita's talents – and like the rest of his clothes they had been cleaned and ironed by the same Bella who had stood in the doorway of the second floor living room and bellowed and panted at him like an animal gone mad. The windows were open and while he argued with himself Tomas could feel the July night trying to cool his skin, soothe him. But he didn't want to be soothed, and every half hour or so he raised himself on one elbow and reached for a cigarette, flaring the light in the darkness and feeling for a second the distant twin of the young man who had lived in Madrid forty years ago, the young man who had taken lovers (all of them beautiful in retrospect), whispered romantic promises (all of them ridiculous), and then had the good fortune to fall in love and marry a woman so beautiful and devoted that even his dreams could never have imagined her. And yet it was true, as he had told Bella, that when he came to Canada his life had ended. Even lying with Marguerita in this bed he had often been unable to sleep, had often, with this very gesture, lit up a small space in the night in order to feel close to the young man who had been deserted in Spain.

Return? Yes, it had occurred to him after the war was finished. Of course, Franco was still in power then, but it was his country and there were others who had returned. And yet, what would have been the life of an exile returned? The life of a man keeping his lips perpetually sealed, his thoughts to himself; the life of a man who had sold his heart in order to have the sights and smells that were familiar.

Now, Tomas told himself wryly, he was an old man who had lost his heart for nothing at all. Somehow, over the years, it had simply disappeared; like a beam of wood being eaten from the inside, it had dropped away without him knowing it.

Tomas Benares, on his seventy-fourth birthday, had just put out a cigarette and lain back with his head on the white linen pillow to resume his study of the shadows, when he heard the footsteps on the stairs up to his attic. Then there was the creak of the door opening and Bella, in her nightgown and carrying a candle, tiptoed into the room.

Tomas closed his eyes.

The footsteps came closer, he felt the bed sag with her weight. He could hear her breathing in the night, it was soft and slow; and then, as he realized he was holding his own breath, he felt Bella's hand come to rest on his forehead.

He opened his eyes. In the light of the candle her face was like stone, etched and lined with grief.

"I'm sorry," Tomas said.

"I'm the sorry one. And imagine, on your birthday."

"That's all right. We've been too closed-in here, since –" Here he hesitated, because for some reason the actual event was never spoken. "Since Abraham died."

Bella now took her hand away, and Tomas was aware of how cool and soft it had been. Sometimes, decades ago, Marguerita had comforted him in this same way when he couldn't sleep. Her hand on his forehead, fingers stroking his cheeks, his eyes, soothing murmurs until finally he drifted away, a log face-down in the cool water.

"There are still lives to be lived," Bella was saying. "The children."

"The children," Tomas repeated. Not since Marguerita had there been a woman in this room at night. For many years he used to lock the door when he went to bed, and even now he would still lock it on the rare times he was sick in case someone – who? – should dare to come on a mission of mercy.

"I get tired," Bella said. Her head drooped and Tomas could see, beyond the outline of her nightdress, the curve of her breasts, the fissure between. A beautiful woman, he had thought before ... He was not as saintly as Bella imagined. On certain of the afternoons Bella thought he was at Herman Levine's, Tomas had been visiting a different apartment, that of a widow who was once his patient. She, too, knew what it was like to look at the shadows on the ceiling for one year after another, for one decade after another.

Now Tomas reached out for Bella's hand. Her skin was young and supple, not like the skin of the widow, or his own. There came a time in every person's life, Tomas thought, when the inner soul took a look at the body and said: Enough, you've lost what little beauty you had and now you're just an embarrassment – I'll keep carrying you around, but I refuse to take you seriously. Tomas, aside from some stray moments of vanity, had reached that point long ago; but Bella, he knew, was still in love with her body, still wore her own bones and skin and flesh as a proud inheritance and not an aging inconvenience.

"Happy birthday," Bella said. She lifted Tomas' hand and pressed it to her mouth. At first, what he felt was the wetness of her mouth. And then it was her tears that flowed in tiny, warm streams around his fingers.

She blew out the candle at the same time that Tomas reached for her shoulder; and then he drew her down so she was lying beside him – her on top of the covers and him beneath, her thick, jet hair folded into his neck and face, her perfume and the scent of her mourning skin wrapped around him like a garden. Chastely he cuddled her to him, her warm breath as soothing as Marguerita's had once been. He felt himself drifting into sleep, and he turned towards the perfume, the garden, turned towards Bella to hold her in his arms the way he used to hold Marguerita in that last exhausted moment of waking.

Bella shifted closer, herself breathing so slowly that Tomas thought she must be already asleep. He remembered, with relief, that his alarm was set for six o'clock; at least they would wake before the children. Then he felt his own hand, as if it had a life of its own, slide in a slow caress from Bella's shoulder to her elbow, touching, in an accidental way, her sleeping breast.

Sleep fled at once, and Tomas felt the sweat spring to his skin. Yet Bella only snuggled closer, breasts and hips flooding through the blanket like warm oceans. Tomas imagined reaching for and lighting a cigarette, the darkness parting once more. A short while ago he had been mourning his youth and now, he reflected, he was feeling as stupid as he ever had. Even with the widow there had been no hesitation. Mostly on his visits they sat in her living room and drank tea; sometimes, by a mutual consent that was arrived at without discussion, they went to her bedroom and performed sex like a warm and comfortable bath. A bath, he thought to himself, that was how he and Bella should become; chaste, warm, comforts to each other in the absence of Abraham. It wasn't right, he now decided, to have frozen his heart to this woman – his daughter-in-law, after all; surely she had a right to love, to the warmth and affection due to a member of the family. *Bella*, he was ready to proclaim, *you are the mother of my grandchildren, the chosen wife of my son. And if you couldn't help shouting, at least you were willing to comfort me.*

Tomas held Bella closer. Her lips, he became aware, were pressed against the hollow of his throat, moving slowly, kissing the skin and now sucking gently at the hairs that curled up from his chest. Tomas let his hand find the back of her neck. There was a delicate valley that led down from her skull past the thick, black hair. He would never have guessed she was built so finely.

Now Bella's weight lifted away for a moment, though her lips stayed glued to his throat, and then suddenly she was underneath the covers, her leg across his groin, her hand sliding up his chest.

Tomas felt something inside of him break. And then, as he raised himself on top of Bella the night, too, broke open; a gigantic black and dreamless mouth, it swallowed them both. He kissed her, tore at her nightgown to suck at her breast, penetrated her so deeply that she gagged; yet though he touched and kissed her every private place; though they writhed on the bed and he felt the cool sweep of her lips as they searched out his every nerve; though he even opened his eyes to see the pleasure on her face, her black hair spread like dead butterflies over Marguerita's linen pillows, her mouth open with repeated climax, the night still swallowed them, obliterated everything as it happened, took them rushing down its hot and endless gorge until Tomas felt like Jonah in the belly of the whale: felt like Jonah trapped in endless flesh and juice. And all he had to escape with was his own sex: like an old sword he brandished it in the blackness, pierced open tunnels, flailed it against the wet walls of his prison.

"Bella, Bella, Bella." He whispered her name silently. Every time he shaped his lips around her name, he was afraid the darkness of his inner eye would part, and Abraham's face would appear before him. But it didn't happen. Even as he scratched Bella's back, bit her neck, penetrated her from behind, he taunted himself with the idea that somewhere in this giant night Abraham must be waiting. His name was on Tomas' lips: Abraham his son. How many commandments was he breaking? Tomas wondered, pressing Bella's breasts to his parched cheeks.

Tomas felt his body, like a starved man at a banquet, go out of control. Kissing, screwing, holding, stroking: everything he did Bella wanted, did back, invented variations upon. For one brief second he thought that Marguerita had never been like this, then his mind turned on itself and he was convinced that this *was* Marguerita, back from the dead with God's blessing to make up, in a few hours, a quarter century of lost time.

But as he kissed and cried over his lost Marguerita, the night began to lift and the first light drew a grey mask on the window.

By this time he and Bella were lying on their stomachs, side by side, too exhausted to move.

The grey mask began to glow, and as it did Tomas felt the dread rising in him. Surely God Himself would appear to take His revenge, and with that thought Tomas realized he had forgotten his own name. He felt his tongue searching, fluttering between his teeth, tasting again his own sweat and Bella's fragrant juices. He must be, he thought, in Hell. He had died and God, to drive his wicked soul crazy, had given him this dream of his own daughter-in-law, his dead son's wife.

"Thank you, Tomas."

No parting kiss, just soft steps across the carpet and then one creak as she descended the stairs. Finally, the face of his son appeared. It was an infant's face, staring uncomprehendingly at its father.

Tomas sat up. His back was sore, his kidneys felt trampled, one arm ached, his genitals burned. He stood up to go to the bathroom and was so dizzy that for a few moments he had to cling to the bedpost with his eyes closed. Then, limping and groaning, he crossed the room. When he got back to the bed there was no sign that Bella had been there – but the sheets were soaked as they sometimes were after a restless night.

He collapsed on the covers and slept dreamlessly until the alarm went off. When he opened his eyes his first thought was of Bella, and when he swung out of bed there was a sharp sting in his groin. But as he dressed he was beginning to speculate, even to hope, that the whole episode had been a dream.

A few minutes later, downstairs at breakfast, Tomas found the children sitting alone at the table. Between them was a sealed envelope addressed to "Dr. Tomas Benares, M.D."

"Dear Tomas," the letter read, "I have decided that it is time for me to seek my own life in another city. Miss Rankin has already agreed to take care of the children for as long as necessary. I hope you will all understand me and remember that I love you. As always, Bella Benares."

On his birthday, his garden always seemed to reach that explosive point that marked the height of summer. No matter what the weather, it was this garden that made up for all other deprivations, and the fact that his ninety-fourth birthday was gloriously warm and sunny made it doubly perfect for Tomas to spend the day outside.

Despite the perfect blessing of the sky, as Tomas opened his eyes from that long doze that had carried the sun straight into the afternoon, he felt a chill in his blood, the knowledge that Death, that companion he'd grown used to, almost fond of, was starting to play his tricks. Because sitting in front of him, leaning towards him as if the worlds of waking and sleeping had been forced together, was Bella herself.

"Tomas, Tomas, it's good to see you. It's Bella."

"I know," Tomas said. His voice sounded weak and grumpy; he coughed to clear his throat.

"Happy birthday, Tomas."

He pushed his hand across his eyes to rid himself of this illusion.

"Tomas, you're looking so good."

Bella: her face was fuller now, but the lines were carved deeper, bracketing her full lips and corrugating her forehead. And yet she was still young, amazing: her movements were lithe and supple: her jet-black hair was streaked, but still fell thick and wavy to her shoulders; her eyes still burned, and when she leaned forward to take his hand between her own the smell of her, dreams and remembrances, came flooding back.

"Tomas, are you glad to see me?"

"You look so young, Bella." This in a weak voice, but Tomas' throat-clearing cough was lost in the rich burst of Bella's laughter. Tomas, seeing her head thrown back and the flash of her strong teeth, could hardly believe that he, a doddering old man, whose knees were covered by a blanket in the middle of summer, had only a few years ago actually made love to this vibrant woman. Now she was like a racehorse in voracious maturity.

"Bella, the children."

"I know, Tomas. I telephoned Margaret: she's here. And I telephoned Joseph, too. His secretary said he was at a meeting all afternoon, but that he was coming here for dinner."

"Bella, you're looking wonderful, truly wonderful." Tomas had his hand hooked into hers and, suddenly aware that he was half-lying in his chair, was using her weight to try to lever himself up.

Instantly Bella was on her feet, her arm solicitously around his back, pulling him into position. She handled his weight, Tomas thought, like the weight of a baby. He felt surrounded by her, overpowered by her smell, her vitality, her cheery goodwill. *Putan*, Tomas whispered to himself. What a revenge. Twenty years ago he had been her equal; and now, suddenly – what had happened? Death was in the garden; Tomas could feel his presence, the familiar visitor turned trickster. And then Tomas felt some of his strength returning, strength in the form of contempt for Bella, who had waited twenty years to come back to this house; contempt for Death, who waited until a man was an ancient, drooling husk to test his will.

"You're the marvel, Tomas. Elizabeth says you work every day in the garden. How do you do it?"

"I spit in Death's face," Tomas rasped. Now he was beginning to feel more himself again, and he saw that Bella was offering him a cup of coffee. All night he had slept, and then again in the daytime. What a way to spend a birthday! But coffee would heat the blood, make it run faster. He realized that he was famished.

Bella had taken out a package of cigarettes now, and offered one to Tomas. He shook his head, thinking again how he had declined in these last years. Now Joseph wouldn't let him smoke in bed, even when he couldn't sleep. He was only allowed to smoke when there was someone else in the room, or when he was outside in the garden.

"Tomas. I hope you don't mind I came back. I wanted to see you again while – while we could still talk."

Tomas nodded. So the ant had escaped the honey pot after all, and ventured into the wide world. Now it was back, wanting to tell its adventures to the ant who had stayed home. Perhaps they hadn't spent that strange night making love after all; perhaps in his bed they had been struggling on the edge of the pot, fighting to see who would fall back and who would be set free.

"So," Bella said. "It's been so long."

Tomas, watching her, refusing to speak, felt control slowly moving towards him again. He sat up straighter, brushed the blanket off his legs.

"Or maybe we should talk tomorrow," Bella said. "When you're feeling stronger."

"I feel strong." His voice surprised even himself – not the weak squawk it sometimes was now, a chicken's squeak hardly audible over the telephone, but firm and definite, booming out of his chest the way it used to. Bella: she had woken him up once, perhaps she would once more.

He could see her moving back, hurt; but then she laughed again, her rich throaty laugh that Tomas used to hear echoing through the house when his son was still alive. He looked at her left hand; Abraham's modest engagement ring was still in place, but beside it was a larger ring, a glowing bloodstone set in a fat gold band. "Tomas," Bella was saying, "you really are a marvel, I swear you're going to live to see a hundred."

"One hundred and twenty-three," Tomas said. "Almost all of the Benares men live to be one hundred and twenty-three."

For a moment, the lines deepened again in Bella's face, and Tomas wished he could someday learn to hold his tongue. A bad habit that should have long ago been entered in his diary.

"You will," Bella finally said. Her voice had the old edge. "*Two* hundred and twenty-three, you'll dance on all our graves."

"Bella ."

"I shouldn't have come."

"The children –"

"They'll be glad to see me, Tomas. They always are."

"Always?"

"Of course. Did you think I'd desert my own children?" Tomas shook his head.

"Oh, I left, Tomas, I left. But I kept in touch. I sent them letters and they wrote me back. That woman helped me."

"Elizabeth?"

"I should never have called her a murderer, Tomas. It was an accident."

"They wrote you letters without telling me?"

Bella stood up. She was a powerful woman now, full-fleshed and in her prime; even Death had slunk away in the force of her presence. "I married again, Tomas. My husband and I lived in Seattle. When Joseph went to university there, he lived in my home."

"Joseph lived with you?"

"My husband's dead now, Tomas, but I didn't come for your pity. Or your money. I just wanted you to know that I would be in Toronto again, seeing my own children, having a regular life."

"A regular life," Tomas repeated. He felt dazed, dangerously weakened. Death was in the garden again, he was standing behind Bella, peeking out from behind her shoulders and making faces. He struggled to his feet. Only Bella could save him now, and yet he could see the fear on her face as he reached for her.

"Tomas, I –"

"You couldn't kill me!" Tomas roared. His lungs filled his chest like an eagle in flight. His flowering hedges, his roses, his carefully groomed patio snapped into focus. He stepped towards Bella, his balance perfect, his arm rising. He saw her mouth open, her lips begin to flutter. Beautiful but stupid, Tomas thought; some things never change. At his full height he was still tall enough to put his arm around her and lead her to the house.

"It's my birthday." His voice boomed with the joke. "Let me offer you a drink to celebrate your happy return."

His hand slid from her shoulder to her arm: the skin was smooth as warm silk. Her face turned towards his: puzzled, almost happy, and he could feel the heat of her breath as she prepared to speak.

"Of course I forgive you," Tomas said.

# ROHINTON MISTRY

# Swimming Lessons

The old man's wheelchair is audible today as he creaks by in the hallway: on some days it's just a smooth whirr. Maybe the way he slumps in it, or the way his weight rests has something to do with it. Down to the lobby he goes, and sits there most of the time, talking to people on their way out or in. That's where he first spoke to me a few days ago. I was waiting for the elevator, back from Eaton's with my new pair of swimming trunks.

"Hullo," he said. I nodded, smiling.

"Beautiful summer day we've got."

"Yes," I said, "It's lovely outside."

He shifted the wheelchair to face me squarely. "How old do you think I am?"

I looked at him blankly, and he said, "Go on, take a guess."

I understood the game; he seemed about seventy-five although the hair was still black, so I said, "Sixty-five?" He made a sound between a chuckle and a wheeze: "I'll be seventy-seven next month." Close enough.

I've heard him ask that question several times since, and everyone plays by the rules. Their faked guesses range from sixty to seventy. They pick a lower number when he's more depressed than usual. He reminds me of Grandpa as he sits on the sofa in the lobby, staring out vacantly at the parking lot. Only difference is, he sits with the stillness of stroke victims, while Grandpa's Parkinson's disease would bounce his thighs and legs and arms all over the place. When he could no longer hold the *Bombay Samachar* steady enough to read, Grandpa took to sitting on the veranda and staring emptily at the traffic passing outside Firozsha Baag. Or waving to anyone who went by in the compound: Rustomji, Nariman Hansotia in his 1932 Mercedes-Benz, the fat ayah Jaakaylee with her shopping bag, the *kuchrawalli* with her basket and long bamboo broom.

The Portuguese woman across the hall has told me a little about the old man. She is the communicator for the apartment building. To gather and disseminate information, she takes the liberty of unabashedly throwing open her door when newsworthy events transpire. Not for Portuguese Woman the furtive peerings from thin cracks or spyholes. She reminds me of a character in a movie, *Barefoot In The Park* I think it was, who left empty beer cans by the landing for anyone passing to stumble and give her the signal. But PW does not need beer cans. The gutang-khutang of the elevator opening and closing is enough.

The old man's daughter looks after him. He was living alone till his stroke, which coincided with his youngest daughter's divorce in Vancouver. She returned to him and they moved into this low-rise in Don Mills. PW says the daughter talks to no one in the building but takes good care of her father.

Mummy used to take good care of Grandpa, too, till things became complicated and he was moved to the Parsi General Hospital. Parkinsonism and osteoporosis laid him low. The doctor explained that Grandpa's hip did not break because he fell, but he fell because the hip, gradually growing brittle, snapped on that fatal day. That's what osteoporosis does, hollows out the bones and turns effect into cause. It has an unusually high incidence in the Parsi community, he said, but did not say why. Just one of those mysterious things. We are the chosen people where osteoporosis is concerned. And divorce. The Parsi community has the highest divorce rate in India. It also claims to be the most westernized community in India. Which is the result of the other? Confusion again, of cause and effect.

The hip was put in traction. Single-handed, Mummy struggled valiantly with bedpans and dressings for bedsores which soon appeared like grim spectres on his back. *Mamaiji*, bent double with her weak back, could give no assistance. My help would be enlisted to roll him over on his side while Mummy changed the dressing. But after three months, the doctor pronounced a patch upon Grandpa's lungs, and the male ward of Parsi General swallowed him up. There was no money for a private nursing home. I went to see him once, at Mummy's insistence. She used to say that the blessings of an old person were the most valuable and potent of all, they would last my whole life long. The ward had rows and rows of beds; the din was enormous, the smells nauseating, and it was just as well that Grandpa passed most of his time in a less than conscious state.

But I should have gone to see him more often. Whenever Grandpa went out, while he still could in the days before parkinsonism, he would bring back pink and white sugar-coated almonds for Percy and me. Every time I remember Grandpa, I remember that; and then I think: I should have gone to see him more often. That's what I also thought when our telephone-owning neighbour, esteemed by all for that reason, sent his son to tell us the hospital had phoned that Grandpa died an hour ago.

*The postman rang the doorbell the way he always did, long and continuous; Mother went to open it, wanting to give him a piece of her mind but thought better of it, she did not want to risk the vengeance of postmen, it was so easy for them to destroy letters; workers nowadays thought no end of themselves, strutting around* like peacocks, ever since all this Shiv Sena agitation about Maharashtra for Maharashtrians, threatening strikes and Bombay bundh all the time, with no respect for the public; bus drivers and conductors were the worst, behaving as if they owned the buses and were doing favours to commuters, pulling the bell before you were in the bus, the driver purposely braking and moving with big jerks to make the standees lose their balance, the conductor so rude if you did not have the right change.

But when she saw the airmail envelope with a Canadian stamp her face lit up, she said wait to the postman, and went in for a fifty paisa piece, a little baksheesh for you, she told him, then shut the door and kissed the envelope, went in running, saying my son has written, my son has sent a letter, and Father looked up from the newspaper and said, don't get too excited, first read it, you know what kind of letters he writes, a few lines of empty words, I'm fine, hope you are all right, your loving son – that kind of writing I don't call letter-writing.

Then Mother opened the envelope and took out one small page and began to read silently, and the joy brought to her face by the letter's arrival began to ebb; Father saw it happening and knew he was right, he said read aloud, let me also hear what our son is writing this time, so Mother read: My dear Mummy and Daddy, Last winter was terrible, we had record-breaking low temperatures all through February and March, and the first official day of spring was colder than the first official day of winter had been, but it's getting warmer now. Looks like it will be a nice warm summer. You asked about my new apartment. It's small, but not bad at all. This is just a quick note to let you know I'm fine, so you won't worry about me. Hope everything is okay at home.

After Mother put it back in the envelope, Father said everything about his life is locked in silence and secrecy. I still don't understand why he bothered to visit us last year if he had nothing to say; every letter of his has been a quick note so we won't worry – what does he think we worry about, his health, in that country everyone eats well whether they work or not, he should be worrying

*about us with all the black market and rationing, has he forgotten
already how he used to go to the ration-shop and wait in line every
week; and what kind of apartment description is that, not bad at all;
and if it is a Canadian weather report I need from him, I can go with
Nariman Hansotia from A Block to the Cawasji Framji Memorial
Library and read all about it, there they get newspapers from all
over the world.*

The sun is hot today. Two women are sunbathing on the stretch of
patchy lawn at the periphery of the parking lot. I can see them
clearly from my kitchen. They're wearing bikinis and I'd love to
take a closer look. But I have no binoculars. Nor do I have a car to
saunter out to and pretend to look under the hood. They're both luscious and gleaming. From time to time they smear lotion over their
skin, on the bellies, on the inside of the thighs, on the shoulders.
Then one of them gets the other to undo the string of her top and
spread some there. She lies on her stomach with the straps undone.
I wait. I pray that the heat and haze make her forget, when it's time
to turn over, that the straps are undone.

But the sun is not hot enough to work this magic for me. When
it's time to come in, she flips over, deftly holding up the cups, and
reties the top. They arise, pick up towels, lotions and magazines,
and return to the building.

This is my chance to see them closer. I race down the stairs to
the lobby. The old man says hullo. "Down again?"

"My mailbox," I mumble.

"It's Saturday," he chortles. For some reason he finds it extremely funny. My eye is on the door leading in from the parking
lot.

Through the glass panel I see them approaching. I hurry to the
elevator and wait. In the dimly lit lobby I can see their eyes are
having trouble adjusting after the bright sun. They don't seem as
attractive as they did from the kitchen window. The elevator
arrives and I hold it open, inviting them in with what I think is a
gallant flourish. Under the fluorescent glare in the elevator I see

their wrinkled skin, aging hands, sagging bottoms, varicose veins. The lustrous trick of sun and lotion and distance has ended.

I step out and they continue to the third floor. I have Monday night to look forward to, my first swimming lesson. The high school behind the apartment building is offering, among its usual assortment of macramé and ceramics and pottery classes, a class for non-swimming adults.

The woman at the registration desk is quite friendly. She even gives me the opening to satisfy the compulsion I have about explaining my non-swimming status.

"Are you from India?" she asks. I nod. "I hope you don't mind my asking, but I was curious because an Indian couple, husband and wife, also registered a few minutes ago. Is swimming not encouraged in India?"

"On the contrary," I say. "Most Indians swim like fish. I'm an exception to the rule. My house was five minutes walking distance from Chaupatty beach in Bombay. It's one of the most beautiful beaches in Bombay, or was, before the filth took over. Anyway, even though we lived so close to it, I never learned to swim. It's just one of those things."

"Well," says the woman, "that happens sometimes. Take me, for instance. I never learned to ride a bicycle. It was the mounting that used to scare me, I was afraid of falling." People have lined up behind me. "It's been very nice talking to you," she says, "hope you enjoy the course."

The art of swimming had been trapped between the devil and the deep blue sea. The devil was money, always scarce, and kept the private swimming clubs out of reach; the deep blue sea of Chaupatty beach was grey and murky with garbage, too filthy to swim in. Every so often we would muster our courage and Mummy would take me there to try and teach me. But a few minutes of paddling was all we could endure. Sooner or later something would float up against our legs or thighs or waists, depending on how deep we'd gone in, and we'd be repulsed and stride out to the sand.

Water imagery in my life is recurring. Chaupatty beach, now the high-school swimming pool. The universal symbol of life and regeneration did nothing but frustrate me. Perhaps the swimming pool will overturn that failure.

When images and symbols abound in this manner, sprawling or rolling across the page without guile or artifice, one is prone to say, how obvious, how skilless; symbols, after all, should be still and gentle as dewdrops, tiny, yet shining with a world of meaning. But what happens when, on the page of life itself, one encounters the ever-moving, all-engirdling sprawl of the filthy sea? Dewdrops and oceans both have their rightful places; Nariman Hansotia certainly knew that when he told his stories to the boys of Firozsha Baag.

The sea of Chaupatty was fated to endure the finales of life's everyday functions. It seemed that the dirtier it became, the more crowds it attracted: street urchins and beggars and beachcombers, looking through the junk that washed up. (Or was it the crowds that made it dirtier? – another instance of cause and effect blurring and evading identification.)

Too many religious festivals also used the sea as repository for their finales. Its use should have been rationed, like rice and kerosene. On Ganesh Chaturthi, clay idols of the god Ganesh, adorned with garlands and all manner of finery, were carried in processions to the accompaniment of drums and a variety of wind instruments. The music got more frenzied the closer the procession got to Chaupatty and to the moment of immersion.

Then there was Coconut Day, which was never as popular as Ganesh Chaturthi. From a bystander's viewpoint, coconuts chucked into the sea do not provide as much of a spectacle. We used the sea, too, to deposit the leftovers from Parsi religious ceremonies, things such as flowers, or the ashes of the sacred sandalwood fire, which just could not be dumped with the regular garbage but had to be entrusted to the care of Avan Yazad, the guardian of the sea. And things which were of no use but which no one had the heart to destroy were also given to Avan Yazad. Such as old photographs.

After Grandpa died, some of his things were flung out to sea. It was high tide; we always checked the newspaper when going to perform these disposals; an ebb would mean a long walk in squelchy sand before finding water. Most of the things were probably washed up on shore. But we tried to throw them as far out as possible, then waited a few minutes; if they did not float back right away we would pretend they were in the permanent safekeeping of Avan Yazad, which was a comforting thought. I can't remember everything we sent out to sea, but his brush and comb were in the parcel, his *kusti*, and some Kemadrin pills, which he used to take to keep the parkinsonism under control.

Our paddling sessions stopped for lack of enthusiasm on my part. Mummy wasn't too keen either, because of the filth. But my main concern was the little guttersnipes, like naked fish with little buoyant penises, taunting me with their skills, swimming underwater and emerging unexpectedly all around me, or pretending to masturbate – I think they were too young to achieve ejaculation. It was embarrassing. When I look back, I'm surprised that Mummy and I kept going as long as we did.

I examine the swimming-trunks I bought last week. Surf King, says the label, Made in Canada/Fabriqué Au Canada. I've been learning bits and pieces of French from bilingual labels at the supermarket too. These trunks are extremely sleek and streamlined hipsters, the distance from waistband to pouch tip the barest minimum. I wonder how everything will stay in place, not that I'm boastful about my endowments. I try them on, and feel that the tip of my member lingers perilously close to the exit. Too close, in fact, to conceal the exigencies of my swimming lesson fantasy: a gorgeous woman in the class for non-swimmers, at whose sight I will be instantly aroused, and she, spying the shape of my desire, will look me straight in the eye with her intentions; she will come home with me, to taste the pleasures of my delectable Asian brown body whose strangeness has intrigued her and unleashed uncontrollable surges of passion inside her throughout the duration of the swimming lesson.

I drop the Eaton's bag and wrapper in the garbage can. The swimming-trunks cost fifteen dollars, same as the fee for the ten weekly lessons. The garbage bag is almost full. I tie it up and take it outside. There is a medicinal smell in the hallway; the old man must have just returned to his apartment.

PW opens her door and says, "Two ladies from the third floor were lying in the sun this morning. In bikinis."

"That's nice," I say, and walk to the incinerator chute. She reminds me of Najamai in Firozsha Baag, except that Najamai employed a bit more subtlety while going about her life's chosen work.

PW withdraws and shuts her door.

*Mother had to reply because Father said he did not want to write to his son till his son had something sensible to write to him, his questions had been ignored long enough, and if he wanted to keep his life a secret, fine, he would get no letters from his father.*

*But after Mother started the letter he went and looked over her shoulder, telling her what to ask him, because if they kept on writing the same questions, maybe he would understand how interested they were in knowing about things over there; Father said go on, ask him what his work is at the insurance company, tell him to take some courses at night school, that's how everyone moves ahead over there, tell him not to be discouraged if his job is just clerical right now, hard work will get him ahead, remind him he is a Zoroastrian:* manashni, gavashni, kunashni, *better write the translation also: good thoughts, good words, good deeds – he must have forgotten what it means, and tell him to say prayers and do* kusti *at least twice a day.*

*Writing it all down sadly, Mother did not believe he wore his* sudra *and* kusti *anymore, she would be very surprised if he remembered any of the prayers; when she had asked him if he needed new* sudras *he said not to take any trouble because the Zoroastrian Society of Ontario imported them from Bombay for their members, and this sounded like a story he was making up, but*

*she was leaving it in the hands of God, ten thousand miles away
there was nothing she could do but write a letter and hope for the
best.*

*Then she sealed it, and Father wrote the address on it as usual
because his writing was much neater than hers, handwriting was
important in the address and she did not want the postman in
Canada to make any mistake; she took it to the post office herself,
it was impossible to trust anyone to mail it ever since the postage
rates went up because people just tore off the stamps for their own
use and threw away the letter, the only safe way was to hand it over
the counter and make the clerk cancel the stamps before your own
eyes.*

Berthe, the building superintendent, is yelling at her son in the
parking lot. He tinkers away with his van. This happens every fine-
weathered Sunday. It must be the van that Berthe dislikes because
I've seen mother and son together in other quite amicable situ-
ations.

Berthe is a big Yugoslavian with high cheekbones. Her nationality was disclosed to me by PW. Berthe speaks a very rough-hewn
English, I've overheard her in the lobby scolding tenants for late
rents and leaving dirty lint screens in the dryers. It's exciting to
listen to her, her words fall like rocks and boulders, and one can
never tell where or how the next few will drop. But her Slavic yells
at her son are a different matter, the words fly swift and true, well-
aimed missiles that never miss. Finally, the son slams down the
hood in disgust, wipes his hands on a rag, accompanies mother
Berthe inside.

Berthe's husband has a job in a factory. But he loses several days
of work every month when he succumbs to the booze, a word
Berthe uses often in her Slavic tirades on those days, the only one
I can understand, as it clunks down heavily out of the tight-flying
formation of Yugoslavian sentences. He lolls around in the lobby,
submitting passively to his wife's tongue-lashings. The bags under
his bloodshot eyes, his stringy moustache, stubbled chin, dirty hair

are so vulnerable to the poison-laden barbs (poison works the same way in any language) emanating from deep within the powerful watermelon bosom. No one's presence can embarrass or dignify her into silence.

No one except the old man who arrives now. "Good morning," he says, and Berthe turns, stops yelling, and smiles. Her husband rises, positions the wheelchair at the favourite angle. The lobby will be peaceful as long as the old man is there.

It was hopeless. My first swimming lesson. The water terrified me. When did that happen, I wonder, I used to love splashing at Chaupatty, carried about by the waves. And this was only a swimming pool. Where did all that terror come from? I'm trying to remember.

Armed with my Surf King I enter the high school and go to the pool area. A sheet with instructions for the new class is pinned to the bulletin board. All students must shower and then assemble at eight by the shallow end. As I enter the showers three young boys, probably from a previous class, emerge. One of them holds his nose. The second begins to hum, under his breath: Paki Paki, smell like curry. The third says to the first two: pretty soon all the water's going to taste of curry. They leave.

It's a mixed class, but the gorgeous woman of my fantasy is missing. I have to settle for another, in a pink one-piece suit, with brown hair and a bit of a stomach. She must be about thirty-five. Plain looking.

The instructor is called Ron. He gives us a pep talk, sensing some nervousness in the group. We're finally all in the water, in the shallow end. He demonstrates floating on the back, then asks for a volunteer. The pink one-piece suit wades forward. He supports her, tells her to lean back and let her head drop in the water.

She does very well. And as we all regard her floating body, I see what was not visible outside the pool; her bush, curly bits of it, straying out at the pink Spandex V. Tongues of water lapping against her delta, as if caressing it teasingly, make the brown hair come alive in a most tantalizing manner. The crests and troughs of little waves, set off by the movement of our bodies in a circle around her, dutifully irrigate her; the curls alternately wave free inside the crest, then adhere to her wet thighs, beached by the inevitable trough. I could watch this forever, and I wish the floating demonstration would never end.

Next we are shown how to grasp the rail and paddle, face down in the water. Between practising floating and paddling, the hour is almost gone. I have been trying to observe the pink one-piece suit, getting glimpses of her straying pubic hair from various angles. Finally, Ron wants a volunteer for the last demonstration, and I go forward. To my horror he leads the class to the deep end. Fifteen feet of water. It is so blue, and I can see the bottom. He picks up a metal hoop attached to a long wooden stick. He wants me to grasp the hoop, jump in the water, and paddle, while he guides me by the stick. Perfectly safe, he tells me. A demonstration of how paddling propels the body.

It's too late to back out; besides, I'm so terrified I couldn't find the words to do so even if I wanted to. Everything he says I do as if in a trance. I don't remember the moment of jumping. The next thing I know is, I'm swallowing water and floundering, hanging on to the hoop for dear life. Ron draws me to the rails and helps me out. The class applauds.

We disperse and one thought is on my mind: what if I'd lost my grip? Fifteen feet of water under me. I shudder and take deep breaths. This is it. I'm not coming next week. This instructor is an irresponsible person. Or he does not value the lives of non-white immigrants. I remember the three teenagers. Maybe the swimming pool is the hangout of some racist group, bent on eliminating all non-white swimmers, to keep their waters pure and their white sisters unogled.

The elevator takes me upstairs. Then gutang-khutang. PW opens her door as I turn the corridor of medicinal smells. "Berthe was screaming loudly at her husband tonight," she tells me.

"Good for her," I say, and she frowns indignantly at me.

The old man is in the lobby. He's wearing thick wool gloves. He wants to know how the swimming was, must have seen me leaving with my towel yesterday. Not bad, I say.

"I used to swim a lot. Very good for the circulation." He wheezes. "My feet are cold all the time. Cold as ice. Hands too."

Summer is winding down, so I say stupidly, "Yes, it's not so warm any more."

The thought of the next swimming lesson sickens me. But as I comb through the memories of that terrifying Monday, I come upon the straying curls of brown pubic hair. Inexorably drawn by them, I decide to go.

It's a mistake, of course. This time I'm scared even to venture in the shallow end. When everyone has entered the water and I'm the only one outside, I feel a little foolish and slide in.

Instructor Ron says we should start by reviewing the floating technique. I'm in no hurry. I watch the pink one-piece pull the swim-suit down around her cheeks and flip back to achieve perfect floatation. And then reap disappointment. The pink Spandex triangle is perfectly streamlined today, nothing strays, not a trace of fuzz, not one filament, not even a sign of post-depilation irritation. Like the airbrushed parts of glamour magazine models. The barrenness of her impeccably packaged apex is a betrayal. Now she is shorn like the other women in the class. Why did she have to do it?

The weight of this disappointment makes the water less manageable, more lung-penetrating. With trepidation, I float and paddle my way through the remainder of the hour, jerking my head out every two seconds and breathing deeply, to continually shore up a supply of precious, precious air without, at the same time, seeming too anxious and losing my dignity.

I don't attend the remaining classes. After I've missed three, Ron the instructor telephones. I tell him I've had the flu and am still feeling poorly, but I'll try to be there the following week.

He does not call again. My Surf King is relegated to an unused drawer. Total losses: one fantasy plus thirty dollars. And no watery rebirth. The swimming pool, like Chaupatty beach, has produced a stillbirth. But there is a difference. Water means regeneration only if it is pure and cleansing. Chaupatty was filthy, the pool was not. Failure to swim through filth must mean something other than failure of rebirth – failure of symbolic death? Does that equal success of symbolic life? death of a symbolic failure? death of a symbol? What is the equation?

*The postman did not bring a letter but a parcel, he was smiling because he knew that every time something came from Canada his* baksheesh *was guaranteed, and this time because it was a parcel Mother gave him a whole rupee, she was quite excited, there were so many stickers on it besides the stamps, one for Small Parcel, another Printed Papers, a red sticker saying Insured; she showed it to Father, and opened it, then put both hands on her cheeks, not able to speak because the surprise and happiness was so great, tears came to her eyes and she could not stop smiling, till Father became impatient to know and finally got up and came to the table.*

*When he saw it he was surprised and happy too, he began to grin, then hugged Mother saying our son is a writer, and we didn't even know it, he never told us a thing, here we are thinking he is still clerking away at the insurance company, and he has written a book of stories, all these years in school and college he kept his talent hidden, making us think he was just like one of the boys in the Baag, shouting and playing the fool in the compound, and now what a surprise; then Father opened the book and began reading it, heading back to the easy chair, and Mother so excited, still holding his arm, walked with him, saying it was not fair him reading it first, she wanted to read it too, and they agreed that he would read the first story, then give it to her so she could also read it, and they would take turns in that manner.*

*Mother removed the staples from the padded envelope in which he had mailed the book, and threw them away, then straightened the folded edges of the envelope and put it away safely with the other envelopes and letters she had collected since he left.*

The leaves are beginning to fall. The only ones I can identify are maple. The days are dwindling like the leaves. I've started a habit of taking long walks every evening. The old man is in the lobby when I leave, he waves as I go by. By the time I'm back, the lobby is usually empty.

Today I was woken up by a grating sound outside that made my flesh crawl. I went to the window and saw Berthe raking the leaves in the parking lot. Not in the expanse of patchy lawn on the periphery, but in the parking lot proper. She was raking the black tarred surface. I went back to bed and dragged a pillow over my head, not releasing it till noon.

When I return from my walk in the evening, PW, summoned by the elevator's gutang-khutang, says, "Berthe filled six black garbage bags with leaves today."

"Six bags!" I say. "Wow!"

Since the weather turned cold, Berthe's son does not tinker with his van on Sundays under my window. I'm able to sleep late.

Around eleven, there's a commotion outside. I reach out and switch on the clock radio. It's a sunny day, the window curtains are bright. I get up, curious, and see a black Olds Ninety-Eight in the parking lot, by the entrance to the building. The old man is in his wheelchair, bundled up, with a scarf wound several times round his neck as though to immobilize it, like a surgical collar. His daughter and another man, the car-owner, are helping him from the wheelchair into the front seat, encouraging him with words like: that's it, easy does it, attaboy. From the open door of the lobby, Berthe is shouting encouragement too, but hers is confined to one word: yah, repeated at different levels of pitch and volume, with variations on vowel-length. The stranger could be the old man's son, he has the same jet black hair and piercing eyes.

Maybe the old man is not well, it's an emergency. But I quickly scrap that thought – this isn't Bombay, an ambulance would have arrived. They're probably taking him out for a ride. If he is his son, where has he been all this time, I wonder.

The old man finally settles in the front seat, the wheelchair goes in the trunk, and they're off. The one I think is the son looks up and catches me at the window before I can move away, so I wave, and he waves back.

In the afternoon I take down a load of clothes to the laundry room. Both machines have completed their cycles, the clothes inside are waiting to be transferred to dryers. Should I remove them and place them on top of a dryer, or wait? I decide to wait. After a few minutes, two women arrive, they are in bathrobes, and smoking. It takes me a while to realize that these are the two disappointments who were sunbathing in bikinis last summer.

"You didn't have to wait, you could have removed the clothes and carried on, dear," says one. She has a Scottish accent. It's one of the few I've learned to identify. Like maple leaves.

"Well," I say, "some people might not like strangers touching their clothes."

"You're not a stranger, dear," she says, "you live in this building, we've seen you before."

"Besides, your hands are clean," the other one pipes in. "You can touch my things any time you like."

Horny old cow. I wonder what they've got on under their bathrobes. Not much, I find, as they bend over to place their clothes in the dryers.

"See you soon," they say, and exit, leaving me behind in an erotic wake of smoke and perfume and deep images of cleavages. I start the washers and depart, and when I come back later, the dryers are empty.

PW tells me, "The old man's son took him out for a drive today. He has a big beautiful black car."

I see my chance, and shoot back: "Olds Ninety-Eight."

"What?"

"The car," I explain, "it's an Oldsmobile Ninety-Eight."

She does not like this at all, my giving her information. She is visibly nettled, and retreats with a sour face.

*Mother and Father read the first five stories, and she was very sad after reading some of them, she said he must be so unhappy there, all his stories are about Bombay, he remembers every little thing about his childhood, he is thinking about it all the time even though he is ten thousand miles away, my poor son, I think he misses his home and us and everything he left behind, because if he likes it over there why would he not write stories about that, there must be so many new ideas that his new life could give him.*

*But Father did not agree with this, he said it did not mean that he was unhappy, all writers worked in the same way, they used their memories and experiences and made stories out of them, changing some things, adding some, imagining some, all writers were very good at remembering details of their lives.*

*Mother said, how can you be sure that he is remembering because he is a writer, or whether he started to write because he is unhappy and thinks of his past, and wants to save it all by making stories of it; and Father said that is not a sensible question, anyway, it is now my turn to read the next story.*

The first snow has fallen, and the air is crisp. It's not very deep, about two inches, just right to go for a walk in. I've been told that immigrants from hot countries always enjoy the snow the first year, maybe for a couple of years more, then inevitably the dread sets in, and the approach of winter gets them fretting and moping. On the other hand, if it hadn't been for my conversation with the woman at the swimming registration desk, they might now be saying that India is a nation of non-swimmers.

Berthe is outside, shovelling the snow off the walkway in the parking lot. She has a heavy, wide pusher which she wields expertly.

The old radiators in the apartment alarm me incessantly. They continue to broadcast a series of variations on death throes, and go from hot to cold and cold to hot at will, there's no controlling their temperature. I speak to Berthe about it in the lobby. The old man is there too, his chin seems to have sunk deeper into his chest, and his face is a yellowish grey.

"Nothing, not to worry about anything," says Berthe, dropping rough-hewn chunks of language around me. "Radiator no work, you tell me. You feel cold, you come to me, I keep you warm," and she opens her arms wide, laughing. I step back, and she advances, her breasts preceding her like the gallant prows of two ice-breakers. She looks at the old man to see if he is appreciating the act: "You no feel scared, I keep you safe and warm."

But the old man is staring outside, at the flakes of falling snow. What thoughts is he thinking as he watches them? Of childhood days, perhaps, and snowmen with hats and pipes, and snowball fights, and white Christmases, and Christmas trees? What will I think of, old in this country, when I sit and watch the snow come down? For me, it is already too late for snowmen and snowball fights, and all I will have is thoughts about childhood thoughts and dreams, built around snowscapes and winter-wonderlands on the Christmas cards so popular in Bombay; my snowmen and snowball fights and Christmas trees are in the pages of Enid Blyton's books, dispersed amidst the adventures of the Famous Five, and the Five Find-Outers, and the Secret Seven. My snowflakes are even less forgettable than the old man's, for they never melt.

It finally happened. The heat went. Not the usual intermittent coming and going, but out completely. Stone cold. The radiators are like ice. And so is everything else. There's no hot water. Naturally. It's the hot water that goes through the rads and heats them. Or is it the other way around? Is there no hot water because the rads have stopped circulating it? I don't care, I'm too cold to sort out the cause and effect relationship. Maybe there is no connection at all.

I dress quickly, put on my winter jacket, and go down to the lobby. The elevator is not working because the power is out, so I take the stairs. Several people are gathered, and Berthe has announced that she has telephoned the office, they are sending a man. I go back up the stairs. It's only one floor, the elevator is just a bad habit. Back in Firozsha Baag they were broken most of the time. The stairway enters the corridor outside the old man's apartment, and I think of his cold feet and hands. Poor man, it must be horrible for him without heat.

As I walk down the long hallway, I feel there's something different but can't pin it down. I look at the carpet, the ceiling, the wallpaper: it all seems the same. Maybe it's the freezing cold that imparts a feeling of difference. PW opens her door: "The old man had another stroke yesterday. They took him to the hospital."

The medicinal smell. That's it. It's not in the hallway any more.

*In the stories that he'd read so far Father said that all the Parsi families were poor or middle-class, but that was okay; nor did he mind that the seeds for the stories were picked from the sufferings of their own lives; but there should also have been something positive about Parsis, there was so much to be proud of: the great Tatas and their contribution to the steel industry, or Sir Dinshaw Petit in the textile industry who made Bombay the Manchester of the East, or Dadabhai Naoroji in the freedom movement, where he was the first to use the word* swaraj, *and the first to be elected to the British Parliament where he carried on his campaign; he should have found some way to bring some of these wonderful facts into his stories, what would people reading these stories think, those who did not know about Parsis – that the whole community was full of cranky, bigoted people; and in reality it was the richest, most advanced and philanthropic community in India, and he did not need to tell his own son that Parsis had a reputation for being generous and family-oriented. And he could have written some- thing also about the historic background, how Parsis came to India from Persia because of Islamic persecution in the seventh century, and were the descendants of Cyrus the Great and the magnificent Persian Empire. He could have made a story of all this, couldn't he?*

*Mother said what she liked best was his remembering every-thing so well, how beautifully he wrote about it all, even the sad things, and though he changed some of it, and used his imagina-tion, there was truth in it.*

*My hope is, Father said, that there will be some story based on his Canadian experience, that way we will know something about our son's life there, if not through his letters then in his stories; so far they are all about Parsis and Bombay, and the one with a little bit about Toronto, where a man perches on top of the toilet, is shameful and disgusting, although it is funny at times and did make me laugh, I have to admit, but where does he get such an imagina-tion from, what is the point of such a fantasy; and Mother said that she would also enjoy some stories about Toronto and the people there; it puzzles me, she said, why he writes nothing about it, especially since you say that writers use their own experience to make stories out of.*

*Then Father said this is true, but he is probably not using his Toronto experience because it is too early; what do you mean, too early, asked Mother and Father explained it takes a writer about ten years time after an experience before he is able to use it in his writing, it takes that long to be absorbed internally and under-stood, thought out and thought about, over and over again, he haunts it and it haunts him if it is valuable enough, till the writer is comfortable with it to be able to use it as he wants; but this is only one theory I read somewhere, it may or may not be true.*

*That means, said Mother, that his childhood in Bombay and our home here is the most valuable thing in his life just now, because he is able to remember it all to write about it, and you were so bitterly saying he is forgetting where he came from; and that may be true, said Father, but that is not what the theory means, according to the theory he is writing of these things because they are far enough in the past for him to deal with objectively, he is able to achieve what critics call artistic distance, without emotions interfering; and what do you mean emotions, said Mother, you are saying he does not feel anything for his characters, how can he write so beautifully about so many sad things without any feelings in his heart?*

*But before Father could explain more, about beauty and emotion and inspiration and imagination, Mother took the book and said it was her turn now and too much theory she did not want to listen to, it was confusing and did not make as much sense as reading the stories, she would read them her way and Father could read them his.*

My books on the windowsill have been damaged. Ice has been forming on the inside ledge, which I did not notice, and melting when the sun shines in. I spread them in a corner of the living room to dry out.

The winter drags on. Berthe wields her snow pusher as expertly as ever, but there are signs of weariness in her performance. Neither husband nor son is ever seen outside with a shovel. Or anywhere else, for that matter. It occurs to me that the son's van is missing, too.

The medicinal smell is in the hall again, I sniff happily and look forward to seeing the old man in the lobby. I go downstairs and peer into the mailbox, see the blue and magenta of an Indian aerogramme with Don Mills, Ontario, Canada in Father's flawless hand through the slot.

I pocket the letter and enter the main lobby. The old man is there, but not in his usual place. He is not looking out through the glass door. His wheelchair is facing a bare wall where the wallpaper is torn in places. As though he is not interested in the outside world any more, having finished with all that, and now it's time to see inside. What does he see inside, I wonder? I go up to him and say hullo. He says hullo without raising his sunken chin. After a few seconds his grey continence faces me. "How old do you think I am?" His eyes are dull and glazed; he is looking even further inside than I first presumed.

"Well, let's see, you're probably close to sixty-four."

"I'll be seventy-eight next August." But he does not chuckle or wheeze. Instead, he continues softly, "I wish my feet did not feel so cold all the time. And my hands." He lets his chin fall again.

In the elevator I start opening the aerogramme, a tricky business because a crooked tear means lost words. Absorbed in this while emerging, I don't notice PW occupying the centre of the hallway, arms folded across her chest: "They had a big fight. Both of them have left."

I don't immediately understand her agitation. "What ... who?"

"Berthe. Husband and son both left her. Now she is all alone."

Her tone and stance suggest that we should not be standing here talking but do something to bring Berthe's family back. "That's very sad," I say, and go in. I picture father and son in the van, driving away, driving across the snow-covered country, in the dead of winter, away from wife and mother; away to where? how far will they go? Not son's van nor father's booze can take them far enough. And the further they go, the more they'll remember, they can take it from me.

*All the stories were read by Father and Mother, and they were sorry when the book was finished, they felt they had come to know their son better now, yet there was much more to know, they wished there were many more stories; and this is what they mean, said Father, when they say that the whole story can never be told, the whole truth can never be known; what do you mean, they say, asked Mother, who they, and Father said writers, poets, philosophers. I don't care what they say, said Mother, my son will write as much or as little as he wants to, and if I can read it I will be happy.*

*The last story they liked the best of all because it had the most in it about Canada, and now they felt they knew at least a little bit, even if it was a very little bit, about his day-to-day life in his apartment; and Father said if he continues to write about such things he will become popular because I am sure they are interested there in reading about life through the eyes of an immigrant,*

*it provides a different viewpoint; the only danger is if he changes
and becomes so much like them that he will write like one of them
and lose the important difference.*

The bathroom needs cleaning. I open a new can of Ajax and scour
the tub. Sloshing with mug from bucket was standard bathing
procedure in the bathrooms of Firozsha Baag, so my preference
now is always for a shower. I've never used the tub as yet; besides,
it would be too much like Chaupatty or the swimming pool,
wallowing in my own dirt. Still, it must be cleaned.

When I've finished, I prepare for a shower. But the clean
gleaming tub and the nearness of the vernal equinox give me the
urge to do something different today. I find the drain plug in the
bathroom cabinet, and run the bath.

I've spoken so often to the old man, but I don't know his name.
I should have asked him the last time I saw him, when his
wheelchair was facing the bare wall because he had seen all there
was to see outside and it was time to see what was inside. Well,
tomorrow. Or better yet, I can look it up in the directory in the
lobby. Why didn't I think of that before? It will only have an initial
and a last name, but then I can surprise him with: hullo Mr. Wilson,
or whatever it is.

The bath is full. Water imagery is recurring in my life: Chaupatty
beach, swimming pool, bathtub. I step in and immerse myself up
to the neck. It feels good. The hot water loses its opacity when the
chlorine, or whatever it is, has cleared. My hair is still dry. I close
my eyes, hold my breath, and dunk my head. Fighting the panic, I
stay under and count to thirty. I come out, clear my lungs and
breathe deeply.

I do it again. This time I open my eyes under water, and stare
blindly without seeing, it takes all my will to keep the lids from
closing. Then I am slowly able to discern the underwater objects.
The drain plug looks different, slightly distorted; there is a hair
trapped between the hole and the plug, it waves and dances with the

movement of the water. I come up, refresh my lungs, examine quickly the overwater world of the washroom, and go in again. I do it several times, over and over. The world outside the water I have seen a lot of, it is now time to see what is inside.

The spring session for adult non-swimmers will begin in a few days at the high school. I must not forget the registration date.

The dwindled days of winter are now all but forgotten; they have grown and attained a respectable span. I resume my evening walks, it's spring, and a vigorous thaw is on. The snowbanks are melting, the sound of water on its gushing, gurgling journey to the drains is beautiful. I plan to buy a book of trees, so I can identify more than the maple as they begin to bloom.

When I return to the building, I wipe my feet energetically on the mat because some people are entering behind me, and I want to set a good example. Then I go to the board with its little plastic letters and numbers. The old man's apartment is the one on the corner by the stairway, that makes it number 201. I run down the list, come to 201, but there are no little white plastic letters beside it. Just the empty black rectangle with holes where the letters would be squeezed in. That's strange. Well, I can introduce myself to him, then ask his name.

However, the lobby is empty. I take the elevator, exit at the second floor, wait for the gutang-khutang. It does not come: the door closes noiselessly, smoothly. Berthe has been at work, or has made sure someone else has. PW's cue has been lubricated out of existence.

But she must have the ears of a cockroach. She is waiting for me. I whistle my way down the corridor. She fixes me with an accusing look. She waits till I stop whistling, then says: "You know the old man died last night."

I cease groping for my key. She turns to go and I take a step towards her, my hand still in my trouser pocket. "Did you know his name?" I ask, but she leaves without answering.

*Then Mother said, the part I like best in the last story is about Grandpa, where he wonders if Grandpa's spirit is really watching him and blessing him, because you know I really told him that, I told him helping an old suffering person who is near death is the most blessed thing to do, because that person will ever after watch over you from heaven, I told him this when he was disgusted with Grandpa's urine-bottle and would not touch it, would not hand it to him even when I was not at home.*

*Are you sure, said Father, that you really told him this, or you believe you told him because you like the sound of it, you said yourself the other day that he changes and adds and alters things in the stories but he writes it all so beautifully that it seems true, so how can you be sure; this sounds like another theory, said Mother, but I don't care, he says I told him and I believe now I told him, so even if I did not tell him then it does not matter now.*

*Don't you see, said Father, that you are confusing fiction with facts, fiction does not create facts, fiction can come from facts, it can grow out of facts by compounding, transposing, augmenting, diminishing, or altering them in any way; but you must not confuse cause and effect, you must not confuse what really happened with what the story says happened, you must not loose your grasp on reality, that way madness lies.*

*Then Mother stopped listening because, as she told Father so often, she was not very fond of theories, and she took out her writing pad and started a letter to her son; Father looked over her shoulder, telling her to say how proud they were of him and were waiting for his next book, he also said, leave a little space for me at the end, I want to write a few lines when I put the address on the envelope.*

# THE AUTHORS

**Neil Bissoondath** was born in Trinidad in 1955 and is the nephew of V.S. Naipaul. He emigrated to Toronto in 1973 to attend York University, where he majored in French while beginning his writing career. In addition to *Digging Up the Mountains*, from which "Christmas Lunch" is reprinted, he is the author of *A Casual Brutality* and a second collection of short stories, *On the Eve of Uncertain Tomorrows*, to be published fall 1990.

**Dionne Brand** was born in the Caribbean and has lived in Toronto for the past 20 years. She has produced five books of poetry and a number of works of non-fiction. In 1990/91, she will be the University of Toronto's writer-in-residence. "At the Lisbon Plate" is from her collection of short stories, *Sans Souci and Other Stories*, which was published by Williams-Wallace Publishers in 1988.

**Barry Callaghan** is a poet, translator and writer of short shories whose work has been published in Canada, the United States and England, and translated into several languages. He founded and edits *Exile* magazine, and Exile Editions, and has won several national magazine awards for his work as a journalist. Born in Toronto in 1937, he is now a professor of contemporary literature at Atkinson College, York University, Toronto.

**Matt Cohen** was born in Kingston, Ontario in 1942. Since the publication of his first novel in 1969, Cohen has established a reputation as one of Canada's greatest literary talents. His novels include the "Salem Quartet" – *The Disinherited*, *The Colours of War*, *The Sweet Second Summer of Kitty Malone* and *Flowers of Darkness*. He is also the author of three short story collections, *Columbus and the Fat Lady*, *The Expatriate* and *Café Le Dog*. His newest novel, *Emotional Arithmetic*, will be published fall 1990.

**Shirley Faessler** was born in Toronto and grew up in the Kensington Market area, which was then almost entirely Jewish. She would later use the market as the setting for most of her stories. *A Basket of Apples and Other Stories* was published in 1988. A novel, *Everything in the Window*, was published nine years earlier.

**Timothy Findley** was born in Toronto and now lives in the country nearby. His novel, *The Wars*, was a winner of the Governor-General's Award and established him as one of Canada's leading writers. His other books include *The Last of the Crazy People*, *The Butterfly Plague*, *Famous Last Words*, *Not Wanted on the Voyage* and *The Telling of Lies*. Findley is also the author of two collections of short stories, *Dinner Along the Amazon* and *Stones*.

**Cynthia Flood's** short fiction has appeared in many Canadian literary journals, on the CBC, in six anthologies and on film. Her 1987 collection, *The Animals in their Elements*, was published by

Talonbooks of Vancouver, and she is currently writing a sequence of stories with the working title *The Small Colonial Girl*. She is the 1990 winner of McClelland & Stewart's Journey Prize for short fiction. Born in Toronto, Cynthia Flood has for many years made her home in Vancouver.

**Katherine Govier** is a native of Edmonton who has lived in Calgary, Washington, D.C. and London, England, and now lives in Toronto with her husband and two children. The most recent of her three novels, *Between Men*, was published in 1989. "Brunswick Avenue" is from *Fables of Brunswick Avenue*, Govier's first short story collection, published in 1985.

**Irena Friedman Karafilly** was born in the U.S.S.R. and has lived in various parts of the world. Her short stories have been widely published, broadcast and anthologized. Her short story collection, *Night Cries,* was recently published by Oberon Press; a first novel, *Still Life*, is currently being marketed in New York. She lives with her daughter in Montreal, and is at work on a book of stories set in post-war Poland.

**Norman Levine's** "Because of the War" is the opening story of his new collection, *Something Happened Here*, to be published by Penguin Canada and Penguin U.K. in the spring of 1991. Levine was born in 1923 and grew up in Ottawa, graduated from McGill, then went to live in England, in St. Ives, Cornwall. His books include *Canada Made Me, From a Seaside Town, I Don't Want to Know Anyone Too Well, Thin Ice* and *Champagne Barn*. He returned to Canada in 1980, and now lives in Toronto.

**Gwendolyn MacEwen** was born in Toronto in 1941 and resided in this city until her death in 1987. In addition to her twelve books of poetry, two of which won the Governor-General's Award, she wrote two novels, two collections of short fiction, a travel book, drama for radio and theatre, and children's books. She was writer-in-residence at the University of Western Ontario in 1984/85 and at the University of Toronto in 1986/87.

**Rohinton Mistry** is the author of *Tales from Firozsha Baag*, a collection of short stories. His first novel will be published in 1991 by McClelland & Stewart in Canada, Knopf in the U.S. and Faber & Faber in the U.K..

**Jay Scott** was reared in Albuquerque, New Mexico, and worked as a journalist there for a number of years. Named film critic of *The Globe and Mail,* Scott became the only journalist ever to win the National Newspaper Award for Criticism, the Canadian equivalent of the Pulitzer Prize, three times. He is the author of *Midnight Matinees, Changing Woman: The Life and Art of Helen Hardin*, and a forthcoming biography of director Norman Jewison.